"I can't affairs. *Not with you, or with anyone else,"*

Caroline said. "Because of my son."

Noah was momentarily distracted by the unpleasant vision of Caroline having an affair with someone else. "What do you mean?" he finally asked.

"I'm not going to risk letting Ethan suffer another loss. Any man who would become part of my life would become part of Ethan's, as well. And any man I'd be interested in would be someone Ethan could look up to. Someone who could become a father figure to him. Kind of a secondhand dad."

"I see." Though he tried to dodge the fact, Noah had to admit how much that role appealed to him. Ethan was a good kid. Noah would be proud to have a son like him.

If only things were different....

Dear Reader,

Winter's here, so why not curl up by the fire with the new Intimate Moments novels? (Unless you live in a warm climate, in which case you can take your books to the beach!) Start off with our WHOSE CHILD? title, another winner from Paula Detmer Riggs called *A Perfect Hero*. You've heard of the secret baby plot? How about secret *babies*? As in *three* of them! You'll love it, I promise, because Ian MacDougall really *is* just about as perfect as a hero can get.

Kathleen Creighton's *One More Knight* is a warm and wonderful sequel to last year's *One Christmas Knight*, but this fine story stands entirely on its own. Join this award-winning writer for a taste of Southern hospitality—and a whole lot of Southern loving. Lee Magner's *Owen's Touch* is a suspenseful amnesia book and wears our TRY TO REMEMBER flash. This twisty plot will keep you guessing—and the irresistible romance will keep you happy. FAMILIES ARE FOREVER, and *Secondhand Dad*, by Kayla Daniels, is just more evidence of the truth of that statement. Lauren Nichols takes us WAY OUT WEST in *Accidental Hero*, all about the allure of a bad boy. And finally, welcome new author Virginia Kantra, whose debut book, *The Reforming of Matthew Dunn*, is a MEN IN BLUE title. You'll be happy to know that her second novel is already in the works.

So pour yourself a cup of something warm, pull the afghan over yourself and enjoy each and every one of these terrific books. Then come back next month, because the excitement—and the romance—will continue, right here in Silhouette Intimate Moments.

Enjoy!

Leslie Wainger
Executive Senior Editor

Please address questions and book requests to:
Silhouette Reader Service
U.S.: 3010 Walden Ave., P.O. Box 1325, Buffalo, NY 14269
Canadian: P.O. Box 609, Fort Erie, Ont. L2A 5X3

SECONDHAND DAD

KAYLA DANIELS

Silhouette®

INTIMATE™MOMENTS®

Published by Silhouette Books

America's Publisher of Contemporary Romance

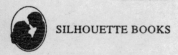

SILHOUETTE BOOKS

ISBN 0-373-07892-7

SECONDHAND DAD

Printed in U.S.A.

Books by Kayla Daniels

Silhouette Intimate Moments

Wanted: Mom and Me #760
Her First Mother #844
Secondhand Dad #892

Silhouette Special Edition

Spitting Image #474
Father Knows Best #578
Hot Prospect #654
Rebel to the Rescue #707
From Father to Son #790
Heiress Apparent #814
Miracle Child #911
Marriage Minded #1068

KAYLA DANIELS

is a former computer programmer who enjoys travel, ballroom dancing and playing with her nieces and nephews. She grew up in Southern California and has lived in Alaska, Norway, Minnesota, Alabama and Louisiana. Currently she makes her home in Grass Valley, California.

**To my parents, Neil and Lorraine Hofland,
who taught me I could be anything I wanted to be.**

Prologue

Have You Seen This Child?

The flier was old. Torn. Smudged. Like a scrap of dirty rag caught on a rusty nail beneath the abandoned railroad bridge.

He'd been looking for paper to start a fire so he could cook his dinner. Dinner was one of those dented cans of beef stew they handed out at the food bank.

He hunkered down next to his knapsack and squinted at the flier. He had a hard time reading up close these days, ever since someone'd stolen that cracked pair of eyeglasses he'd fished out of a Dumpster back in Kansas City.

It was the picture on the flier that had caught his eye. He was positive he'd seen that kid someplace, and not so long ago, either. He scratched his head. Ran his broken nails through his beard, combing out bits of debris. Then he reached for the bottle he was currently working on and took a long swig of cheap fortified wine.

Where'd he seen this kid, anyway? Leastways, a kid who looked an awful lot like this one, 'cept maybe his face was a little thinner now, his light hair longer...

For some reason, cars kept nudging into his thoughts. Something about this kid and cars...

"Ha!" His cackle of glee echoed against the steel trestlework of the old bridge. Now he remembered!

He held the flier up to the fading rays of daylight and brought his face close to it, moving his mouth while he struggled with the rest of the words.

While he read, an idea took root. Sprouted. Began to send out tentacles through the murky, wine-sodden mists of his brain.

Have You Seen This Child?

"Yep," he replied. A grin crawled over his face, revealing the gaps between his rotted teeth.

If he played his cards right, pretty soon he just might be able to *buy* himself a new pair of specs. And that would be only the beginning....

Chapter 1

Even though he'd been gone for three years, hope still leaped inside Caroline's heart whenever the phone rang. It had become as instinctive as breathing, her quick, desperate prayer that *this* time when she lifted the receiver she would finally hear Ethan's precious voice say, "Mommy?"

But tonight she was disappointed yet again. No little boy's voice greeted her ear. It was a man's voice, a rich, resonant baritone that sounded all business. "Caroline Tate?"

A stranger's voice. Hope died another quiet death inside her. She dragged her fingers through her honey-blond hair. "Yes. Who's calling, please?"

"Ma'am, my name is Noah Garrett. I'm a sheriff's investigator in Eagle River, California."

At the word *investigator,* Caroline's throat tightened. She'd spent three years' worth of profits from her gourmet soup company hiring one private investigator after another. So many raised hopes, so many false leads, so many trails that led nowhere.

She'd learned not to get too excited. "What's this about?" she asked.

"Ma'am, do you know a Jefferson Randolph Tate?"

Caroline held her voice steady. After all the fliers and TV publicity about Ethan's disappearance, any kook out there could know Jeff's name. And God knew she'd suffered more than her share of kooks during her agonizing search for her son.

"Jeff Tate is my ex-husband," she replied through gritted teeth. "He disappeared three years ago when he stole our child."

For the first time, Caroline detected hesitation at the other end of the phone line. Some quality in his silence alerted her that this could be for real, that Noah Garrett might have something important to tell her. Her heart began to pound.

"Ms. Tate," he said slowly, "I can't be certain until you come and identify him. But I think we may have found your son."

A balloon of emotion expanded and soared inside Caroline's chest, making it hard to breathe. She wouldn't allow herself to believe it yet—she *wouldn't!* She'd heard this claim too many times before, only to have her hopes cruelly dashed.

"Is he all right?" she whispered.

Pause.

Dread pierced her with a heart-stopping thrust. Dear God, the one consolation she'd clung to for three years, the only thought that had allowed her to keep a grip on sanity was her certainty that no matter what else that lousy bastard had done, Jeff would at least keep Ethan safe.

"Ethan's fine," Noah Garrett told her.

Caroline's knees dissolved with relief. She sank to the plush living-room carpet.

The investigator cleared his throat. "But Ethan's father, I'm sorry to have to tell you…passed away yesterday."

"Dead?" The word rushed from her lungs in a gasp. "Jeff's *dead?*"

"We have reason to believe the deceased is your ex-husband. He was living here under the assumed name of Jeff Tucker, but I found an expired Maryland driver's license in his possession with the name Jefferson Randolph Tate and a Baltimore address. The Baltimore police got me your phone number, and told me about your missing boy.'' Noah Garrett's professional, no-nonsense manner slipped for a second, allowing a note of compassion to enter his voice.

''But Ethan's all right?'' Caroline asked quickly.

''Yes.'' Once again, she heard that slight hesitation, that hint he was holding something back.

His phone call had left Caroline as dazed and disoriented as if a bolt of lightning had struck her. She didn't know what to believe, didn't know what to feel. But her shell-shocked mind was starting to consider the possibility that she and Ethan might be reunited very soon. She felt the rusty gears of her brain creak into motion again.

''Can I speak to him?'' she asked, flattening her hand over her heart as if to still its frantic thumping. ''Is he there with you?''

''Ethan's...not with me right now.''

''Then where—?''

''He's in good hands, don't worry.'' He sounded reluctant to say the rest of it. ''At the moment he's being kept under observation in the hospital.''

Fear propelled Caroline to her feet. ''The *hospital?* I thought you said he was—''

''He *is* fine. He's had a shock, is all, because of his father's death. The doctor thought it would be a good idea to keep a close eye on him for twenty-four hours or so.''

''Dear God.'' It hadn't even occurred to Caroline until this instant what Ethan must be going through. In spite of all Jeff's faults, Ethan had loved him.

The practical side of her nature, the one that served her so well in business, took over, shoving less important questions aside for now. ''Where did you say you're located?'' she asked, scrambling for a pen. As organized as she was, somehow there was never a writing implement within arm's reach of the telephone.

"Eagle River, California. In the northern part of the state."

"What's the nearest airport a major airline flies into?" She scribbled on the handiest sheet of paper, a sales-tax form she'd been preparing to send in to the government tomorrow.

"That would be Sacramento. It's about a two hour drive from here."

She made a note to reserve a rental car.

"Ms. Tate, I'd be happy to pick you up at the airport myself, if you'll call me back with your flight information."

Hmm. Normally Caroline didn't like depending on other people or accepting favors from them. But once she landed in Sacramento, it might take a while to complete the paperwork for the car, dig up a map, plot her route to Eagle River....

Her highest priority right now—her *only* priority—was reaching Ethan as fast as possible.

She crossed out the note about the rental car. "I'll call you back as soon as I book a flight," she told him. "What's your number?"

For the next half hour she managed to hold her emotions in suspended animation while she phoned airlines, called the sheriff's investigator back, and made arrangements with her assistant to cancel all her appointments for the rest of the week.

Once those necessary tasks were completed, she finally released her pent-up emotions. Joy and shock, relief and sorrow swept over her like water bursting through a dam. The exhilarating flood lifted her higher and higher. She wanted to laugh and cry and spin around until she collapsed on the floor in a dizzy heap. Ethan! Ethan was coming home!

Ten hours till her flight left in the morning. Already she knew that not one of them would be spent sleeping.

For the thousandth time in three years Caroline gently lifted her son's picture from the fireplace mantel. Twinkling brown eyes beamed at her from beneath an unruly shock of blond hair. His gap-toothed grin radiated such love, such innocence that it nearly broke her heart to look at him.

He was eight years old now. She couldn't begin to imagine what Ethan had gone through since the last time she'd seen him. Apprehension lapped at the shores of Caroline's happiness. What changes was she going to find in the happy, trusting, outgoing five-year-old she remembered?

Tears blurred his image. Caroline hugged the picture to her breast, ignoring the sharp corners of the frame that poked into her flesh. She drew in a long, quavering sob.

"Ethan," she moaned in a choked voice that was half prayer, half promise. "Ethan, Mommy's coming...."

Noah Garrett figured he'd recognize her, and he was right. None of the other passengers getting off the plane in Sacramento wore such an eager, desperate look or scanned the waiting crowd with such feverish intensity.

What he hadn't expected was that she'd be such a knockout. Thick blond hair cascading down to her shoulder blades, held back from her face with an expensive enameled clip. And what a face it was! Sculpted cheekbones...full, arched lips above a delicate chin...skin as smooth and pale as fresh cream.

As for her eyes...well, God help any man who fell under the spell of those luminous green eyes with their long dark lashes. Like emeralds against velvet.

Fortunately, Noah himself was immune to any such spells. To any woman at all, for that matter. Even one with long, perfectly tapered, nylon-clad legs that looked like they could wrap around a man and—

Whoa, there! He shook himself in surprise. It had been so long since he'd experienced even the faintest twinge of lust, it took him a second to recognize it when it happened.

Go back to sleep, he ordered his comatose libido. For four years, ever since the accident, his interest in sex had been zero, zip, *nada*. And that was how Noah preferred it.

Besides, Caroline Tate could turn out to be an important

player in his current investigation. And Noah *never* mixed business with pleasure.

He sidled through clusters of hugging couples, boisterous children and beaming grandparents to intercept her.

"Ms. Tate?"

She swiveled her head and veered toward him instantly, and for the first time he felt the full effect of those bewitching green eyes.

Trouble, warned a little voice inside his skull. *You could be in deep trouble if you don't watch out, Garrett.*

She stepped up to him and grasped his arm, as if afraid that this one living, breathing link to her son might decide to turn tail and run. "Sheriff Garrett?"

Her voice matched her looks perfectly, he decided. Composed and confident, even though a slight tremor betrayed her inner agitation. A pleasant touch of huskiness, like expensive aged whiskey. Too soon to tell if she always sounded this way, or if that seductive, smoky quality had been produced by a recent bout of crying.

"*Sergeant* Garrett, actually. I'm a deputy sheriff."

Her grip tightened on his arm. He could feel the imprint of each slender finger, even through the sleeve of his sport coat.

"How's Ethan?" she asked.

"He's fine. You'll be allowed to check him out of the hospital as soon as you're ready."

Noah could tell by the way the corners of her mouth crimped that she didn't like the way he said "allowed." Not that he blamed her. But she was going to hear plenty of other things this morning she didn't like, either.

She narrowed her eyes at him. Cat's eyes. "I phoned the hospital last night to check on his condition, but the nurse said they weren't allowed to give out any information."

She fell in step beside him, still clamped to his arm, while Noah steered them toward the terminal exit. "They also said they had orders not to let anyone speak to him, not even me." Her indignation and irritation struggled through. "Are you the one who gave those orders?"

"I had good reasons."

"*What* reasons? What right do you have to prevent me from speaking to my own child?" Mindful of the other people funneling onto the escalator, she lowered her voice. Her fingers dug into his arm. "Don't you understand what I've gone through ever since Ethan was stolen from me?"

Noah looked at her squarely. "Yes," he said. "As a matter of fact, I do."

He hadn't meant to reveal anything, but it seemed he had. Caroline Tate dropped his arm. But she kept studying his face in a searching way that Noah was starting to find intrusive.

He forced his jaw muscles to unclench. "There are some things we need to discuss before you talk to Ethan. Things I didn't feel were appropriate to go into last night on the phone."

The escalator deposited them near the baggage-claim area.

"What things?" she asked warily.

"Let's wait until we're in the car, all right? Do you have any luggage?"

"Just this." She touched the strap of the carry-on bag she wore slung over her shoulder. "I didn't want to waste time waiting for a suitcase."

"Good. Then we can be on our way. I'm parked in the lot across the street."

Noah ushered her through the glass doors. Warm June air embraced them, carrying the mingled smells of jet fuel and earthy agricultural scents from the surrounding farmland.

"It occurred to me after I spoke to you last night," Caroline said as they stepped off the curb. "I never even asked how Jeff died."

Noah jingled his keys in his pocket. He was good at sizing people up, but even a rookie could tell this woman didn't want or need to be handled like a hothouse flower. He could dispense with the kid-glove treatment.

"Somebody killed him," he replied.

Caroline stared at the passing sights through the window of Noah Garrett's dusty Jeep Cherokee, still trying to absorb the impact of the bombshell he'd dropped.

She'd pinpointed Eagle River on a map of California the night before, and learned from the atlas it was a town of about three thousand people, nestled in the rugged mountains at the northern end of the gold-rush country. Eventually they would ascend from the flatlands of the Central Valley into the Sierra Nevada foothills.

She tried to speak, then had to swallow before she could produce a sound. "Who killed Jeff?" she asked.

Noah took his eyes off the freeway for a second. "That's what I intend to find out."

"You're not very forthcoming with details," she remarked tartly, drumming her nails against the armrest.

"Sorry." Caroline thought she might have glimpsed a smile, but it was gone before she could be sure. "Occupational hazard," he said by way of explanation. He flicked on his turn indicator and glanced over his shoulder, taking a moment to jockey for position while he changed lanes.

Caroline took the opportunity to survey his profile. It could have been carved from the same mountains that were looming in the distance. Craggy features, a jaw like a shelf of granite, a deep cleft bisecting his square chin. She also had a feeling that once Noah Garrett set his mind on something, he would be as impossible to budge as those mountains.

She guessed his age to be mid-to-late thirties, a few years older than her own thirty-three. His close-cropped hair was a very dark brown, edging into black, like the color of burnt coffee. His eyes were a strikingly deep blue. If that smile she might or might not have imagined was any clue, the man would be drop-dead gorgeous if a full-fledged grin ever broke out. Caroline suspected that didn't happen too often, and wondered why.

Forget it, she scolded herself. *It doesn't matter.*

But it was hard to break the habit she'd developed during her search for Ethan, this need to assess strangers immediately so she could weed out the kooks and charlatans from people who were genuinely trying to help. She winced, recalling one time when desperation had driven her to consult a psychic.

She'd become an expert at reading people's eyes. Their mouths might lie, or their hands, or their voices. But their eyes never did.

Noah Garrett intrigued her because she couldn't read *his* eyes at all.

Caroline hastily assured herself that that was the only reason she found herself so fascinated by his profile. He was a puzzle, that was all. A mystery.

Caroline *hated* mysteries.

"Tell me what happened to Jeff," she said, dragging herself back to brutal reality.

Noah briefly stretched out his fingers, then curled his hands securely around the steering wheel again. "It appears he was killed during a robbery."

Caroline fought to wrap her mind around this startling piece of information. It was hard to comprehend that they were discussing the death of the man she'd once loved, the man she'd married, with whom she'd brought a child into the world. Her feelings for Jeff were such a complex mix of regret, hatred and nostalgia, she couldn't begin to sort them out.

Time enough for that later.

Despite her inner turmoil, she hadn't missed the slight emphasis in Noah's statement. "What do you mean, 'appears'?"

He sent her an appraising glance, as if impressed she'd picked up on that. "He was found in the office of the gas station where he worked. Both the safe and the cash register were empty."

"Jeff worked in a gas station?" she asked, surprised.

"Managed it. He was working there alone when it happened. It looks like the robber may have forced him to open the safe first, then hit him on the head with some kind of heavy pointed object."

Caroline's stomach lurched. "And killed him."

"Not right away. He lived long enough for...someone to

call an ambulance, but he never regained consciousness. He died at the hospital.''

"Dear God." Caroline pressed shaky fingertips to her temples. They felt like icicles.

"I'm sorry," Noah said. He raised a hand from the wheel as if instinct prompted him to offer a comforting touch. But his hand circled in midair and landed back on the wheel again. "I know it can't be easy to hear this, no matter what…bitterness you hold against Jeff."

"Funny," Caroline said, only half-aware she was speaking out loud. "All this time I've hated Jeff for what he did, for what he did to me, and to Ethan. I thought I'd rejoice if I ever found out he was dead. I used to imagine killing him myself if I ever got the chance." Suddenly, she remembered to whom she was speaking. She gave Noah a tight-lipped grimace. "Guess I shouldn't be making that particular confession right now."

"Don't worry. You're not on my list of suspects."

"The weird thing is, I'm *not* glad he's dead. I doubt I'll ever be able to forgive Jeff, but the only thing I feel for him right now is…pity."

The highway was climbing through gently rolling hills, past stands of oak and pine. The slopes wore a vibrant green carpet, though the summer heat was turning the grass a camel color along the edge of the road. Up above, the sun crept toward its zenith across a cloudless blue sky.

It was a glorious day to be alive. And in an hour or so, Caroline would finally hold her darling little boy in her arms again. After three years of searching, a thousand nights of anguish, her long, terrible quest had finally come to an end. Molten joy poured through her, radiant and pure.

"I can't thank you enough," she said, impulsively dropping her hand to Noah Garrett's thigh. "For giving me back my son."

His muscles tensed instantly. Beneath her fingers she felt hard sinew turn to steel. He shifted uneasily. "I can't take much credit for that," he said. "Jeff and Ethan moved to

Eagle River quite a while ago. I had a kidnapper living right under my nose and never would have known it if he hadn't gone and gotten himself killed.''

Obviously it was nothing but politeness that kept him from brushing her hand off his leg as if it were a tarantula. Caroline saved him the trouble and removed it herself, trying not to feel a teensy bit rejected. What difference did it make if Noah Garrett found her touch repulsive? It wasn't as if she had any *designs* on him, just because he was good-looking and seemed like a decent guy and had given her the most precious gift she'd ever received.

Caroline had sworn off men forever. Even though common sense told her that not every single member of the male species was a treacherous snake like her ex-husband, her one disastrous mistake had cost her so much that she'd vowed never, *ever* to risk making the same mistake again.

It wasn't that she distrusted all men. What she didn't trust were her own instincts where men were concerned.

Easier just to keep her distance from all of them.

So what if Noah Garrett didn't find her attractive? Now that Ethan was finally coming home, Caroline intended to devote all her emotional energies to her child. She had neither the time nor the inclination to nurse hurt feelings just because this tantalizing, unexpected spark of attraction she felt toward the handsome sheriff's deputy wasn't mutual.

It was better like this, anyway. Safer.

She shifted her gaze from the scenery and looked over at Noah. "I get the impression from the way you talk that you have some doubts Jeff was really killed by a robber."

"Not *doubts,* exactly." He dusted the ridge of his knuckles along his jaw. "But sometimes it's a mistake to latch on to the most obvious conclusion. It can blind you to other possibilities."

"What other possibilities?"

"I'm not sure yet." He adjusted his position, as if the bucket seat had suddenly become uncomfortable. "I'm hoping your son might be able to help me with that."

"Ethan? How on earth could he—oh, you mean he might know if someone had a grudge against his father." Caroline gave a bitter laugh. "Someone besides me."

Noah massaged the nape of his neck, rumpling his shirt collar in the process. "There's that, but I'm also hoping maybe he saw something."

An ominous prickle tiptoed up Caroline's spine. "*Saw* something? What do you mean?"

Noah aimed a long, measuring glance in her direction, as if trying to assess how she might handle what he had to tell her. "Ethan was the person who found Jeff and called the ambulance," he said finally. "There's reason to believe he may have seen whoever attacked his father."

Tears stung Caroline's eyes. "No," she said. "Oh, no." Her voice broke.

"There's something else I didn't want to tell you over the phone last night." He hooked a finger behind the loosened knot in his tie, as if it were still too tight. "Ethan...doesn't remember what happened. He doesn't remember finding his father, or calling for help, or seeing anyone who might have been the killer."

Horrified, Caroline twisted in her seat to stare at him. "You mean my son has *amnesia?*"

Noah shook his head. "More like a blank spot in his memory. He can't remember anything that happened between riding his bike to the gas station after school that day, and waking up in the hospital."

Caroline's fingernails gouged her palms. "You said he wasn't injured."

"He wasn't, physically. The missing part of his memory wasn't caused by a blow to the head or anything like that."

"Then—?"

"The doc says it's fairly common in traumatic events like this. The mind kind of seals off part of the memory for self-protection. Later, when the person is stronger and able to deal with the trauma, the missing memories sometimes return."

"Or sometimes they don't."

"That chunk of Ethan's memory could come back today. Or a month from now." Noah lifted one broad shoulder. "Or maybe never."

Caroline drew a deep breath. "Does he know his father's dead?"

"Yes. The doctor told him."

A sharp pain throbbed behind her breastbone as she pictured the terror Ethan must have gone through, and the grief he would be suffering now. "My poor baby." She dabbed at her eyes with her fingertips. "I hope he never has to remember." Her lower lip trembled.

Noah surprised her by bringing his hand to rest on her shoulder. His touch was warm, reassuring, oddly comforting. "I'm sorry things turned out like this," he said gruffly. "Not quite the happy ending you've dreamed about all these years."

Caroline returned a damp, wobbly smile. "All that matters is that I'm going to get Ethan back. I'll help him get through this awful experience. Together we can make it."

Noah squeezed her shoulder. "He's lucky to have you." In his eyes Caroline glimpsed a shadow of sadness. What secret sorrow did Noah have in his past? Had his own mother died when he was young, so that he'd had to grow up without one?

He cleared his throat and the shadow vanished, leaving his eyes as unreadable as they'd been before. He lifted his hand from Caroline's shoulder and replaced it on the steering wheel.

Beneath her dress and linen blazer, her skin still tingled where he'd touched her. She couldn't understand where it was coming from, this desire to know more about him. To know *all* about him.

Maybe it was a natural result of the artificial intimacy imposed on them by the close confines of the truck. Or maybe her feelings toward him sprang from gratitude. At an unconscious level she was probably attaching all kinds of special qualities to Noah Garrett simply because he was the person who was going to reunite her with her son.

Caroline had her *own* life crisis to deal with right now. She didn't have time to worry about Noah's.

Yet some impulse made her blurt out, "What did you mean back at the airport, when you said you understood what I've gone through since Jeff kidnapped Ethan?"

If she hadn't been watching Noah so carefully, she wouldn't have noticed him flinch. He took the next curve a bit too sharply, driving a wedge of space between them as Caroline tilted toward the passenger door. Just above his shirt collar a tiny vein pulsed in his neck.

He took a long time replying. "I lost a child myself," he said at last. "She died."

Caroline's hand flew to her mouth. "Oh, Noah." She slowly lowered her arm. "I'm so sorry."

He kept his eyes firmly fixed on the road. "My wife died, too. A car accident. Four years ago."

"Oh, God. I'm sorry. So very, very sorry." Caroline's mouth felt bruised with shock. If only she'd kept it shut in the first place.

Noah gave a curt nod, lips clamped into a stoic line.

Caroline had to resist the urge to reach out and convey her sympathy by physical contact. He'd already made it plain her touch was unwelcome.

"I shouldn't have pried into your personal life," Caroline said. "I had no right to, and I apologize."

"Forget it."

"I'm not a nosy person, really. But ever since Ethan disappeared…" She spread her hands helplessly. "The thing is, when your child's life is at stake it strips away all your inhibitions. I've had to grovel for help to anyone who would listen, to pester the police day after day, year after year. I've bared my soul on those tabloid TV shows so I could beg viewers—total *strangers!*—to help me find my son."

Caroline shuddered. "Every juicy detail of my life has been plastered all over the newspapers for the whole world to see." She relaxed the fist that had bunched her dress into a knot, smoothing the wrinkled fabric over her thigh. "I had to give up my privacy to get my son back," she said, "and it was a price I'd pay a million times over. But sometimes I forget that other people are still entitled to theirs.''

She peered sideways at Noah, uncertain whether he would accept her long-winded apology. He hadn't moved a muscle while she'd been rattling on and on.

To Caroline's amazement, he actually smiled. Not a full smile, just a partial one. And it was kind of crooked, as if he were out of practice. But it was a real, live smile, nonetheless.

''Boy,'' he said, ''when you apologize, you don't do it half-way, do you?''

As the tension shattered, warmth seeped through her. ''Oh, I don't do anything by halves,'' she replied with an airy wave of her hand.

''I'll bet you don't.'' If anything, the wattage of his smile increased a degree or two.

I was right, Caroline thought. He *is* drop-dead gorgeous when he smiles.

''Does that mean you accept my apology?'' she asked.

Gleaming white teeth…sexy crinkles gathered at the corners of his eyes…mouth hitched upward in an irresistible slant…

''No apology necessary. But if it makes you feel better, I'll accept it anyway.'' He winked.

A different kind of warmth trickled through Caroline, pooling in the pit of her abdomen.

She realized she was staring dreamily at Noah's mouth. Quickly, she snatched her gaze away.

Stop this! she scolded herself. Once upon a time she'd mooned over Jeff's smile, too, and look where it had gotten her.

But mile after mile, the disturbing heat lingered inside her.

Caroline stood outside the door to her son's hospital room, her heart hammering so loudly she could barely hear Noah's murmured question above the thunder in her ears.

''Do you want me to go in with you?'' he asked.

Caroline had never envisioned her reunion with Ethan as a

private affair. Somehow she'd always assumed there would be TV cameras, flashbulbs popping, reporters shouting questions.

At least she was going to be spared that. But something else she hadn't foreseen was how terrified she was going to feel when she was finally on the verge of facing her son again. What if Ethan wasn't glad to see her? What if Jeff had poisoned his mind against her?

Even worse was her sudden fear that this all might be a terrible mistake. Maybe the murder victim wasn't Jeff at all, but someone who'd stolen Jeff's driver's license.

Maybe the boy on the other side of this door *wasn't* Ethan.

Caroline didn't think she could bear it if it turned out her search wasn't over. After letting her hopes soar so high, she was afraid she would collapse into a weeping, broken heap if the boy in there turned out not to be Ethan.

"Yes," she said, swallowing to moisten her parched throat. "Please, I—I'd appreciate it if you came in with me."

"Sure." Noah hesitated, then gently tipped up her chin with the crook of his finger. "You can get through this," he said. "Everything's going to work out just fine." His eyes were fixed on hers like cobalt laser beams.

Somehow Caroline was able to draw a measure of strength from them. "I—I just can't believe this moment I've prayed and hoped for for so long has finally arrived." She emitted a shaky laugh that sounded borderline hysterical. "God, I never thought I'd be so scared to see my own son again!"

Noah looked at her steadily. "You're the bravest woman I've ever met," he said. "Just remember, you've already survived the hardest part of your ordeal."

The admiration in his voice both surprised and touched her. It meant a lot coming from a man like Noah Garrett, who'd survived such unspeakable tragedy himself, whose job forced him to confront danger and fear time and time again.

He dropped his hand and reached for the door. "Ready?"

Caroline took a deep breath. Apprehension fluttered like nausea in her stomach. Her shaky knees felt as if they were about to buckle.

"Ready," she said.

Noah opened the door. Holding her head high, Caroline stepped into the room.

There were two beds, but only the farther one was occupied. Caroline's footsteps echoed unnaturally loudly above the rushing in her ears. Dimly she was aware that Noah was following at a discreet distance.

The boy in the bed was asleep. The nurse had explained they were keeping him sedated because he was so upset about Jeff's death. He looked so small against the snowy-white hospital sheets! But as Caroline approached his bedside, a powerful wave of love and joy and triumph welled up inside her.

She saw at once it was Ethan.

Tears sprang to her eyes and a lump rose in her throat. Her own darling sweet boy! Her beloved Ethan, right here, close to her at last...

Caroline pressed a fist to her mouth to muffle a sob.

She longed to seize her child in her arms, bundle him against her breast, smother his face and hair with kisses. She fairly ached to hold the warm, alive weight of his body against hers for the first time in three years.

But poor Ethan had suffered enough shocks during the past couple of days. The last thing he needed was to be grabbed awake and assaulted with kisses by a blubbering woman.

As if in a dream, Caroline lowered her hand and allowed herself to finger one stray wisp of blond hair that fell across his forehead.

Ethan opened his eyes.

Caroline froze like a startled deer. Those huge, innocent, chocolate-brown eyes she'd been so afraid she would never gaze into again...

Ethan blinked up at her. His sleepy face registered confusion, fear, grief.

"Ethan," Caroline crooned softly. "Ethan, honey, it's Mommy."

The drowsiness fled from his face. "You can't be my mom," he said with a puzzled frown. "My mom's dead."

Chapter 2

Caroline recoiled as if Ethan had struck her. Noah clenched his fists. This wasn't the first parental kidnapping case he'd been involved with, and after hearing Ethan's words he knew immediately what Jeff Tate had done.

That bastard.

Caroline rallied valiantly. She perched on the side of her son's hospital bed, backbone ruler-straight, smile pinned to her lips. "Ethan, sweetheart, look at me. Don't you recognize me?" She stroked his cheek. "I'm not dead, honey. I've been looking for you for a long, long time, and now that I've finally found you, I'm going to take you home with me."

Ethan's chin came up a notch. "My dad said you were dead," he insisted.

Caroline's hand stopped moving. After a heartbeat or two, she resumed stroking his cheek. But fine blond hairs vibrated near her temple. A crimson stain crawled up the back of her neck like an extension of her burgundy blazer.

Usually Noah was able to keep himself emotionally detached from all the human suffering he saw in his line of work. But something about this case was starting to get to him.

He felt bad for Caroline. She deserved better than this, after all she'd been through.

"Your daddy was wrong, Ethan. Here." Caroline clasped her son's hand and brought it to the side of her face. "I'm alive, see? And I'm so happy I found you."

His fingers tentatively explored her features. His forehead was pleated with uncertainty. Then recognition filtered into his eyes, followed by confusion.

"Mommy?" he said in a tiny voice.

"Yes!" Caroline's glad cry was half laughter, half sob. She swept the boy into her arms and clutched him as if she would never let him go.

Noah Garrett, cynic and hardened investigator, felt his own eyes mist up. Caroline rocked her son, her body curved above his in a protective arch, their faces shielded by the gold curtain of her hair.

Pain crashed through Noah, catching him off guard.

He would sell his soul for one more chance to hold his own child in his arms again.

He listened to the soft murmur of whispered endearments, and all at once felt like an intruder. Like an outsider. It was a feeling he was accustomed to.

He tiptoed backward toward the door, intending to let the rest of this reunion play out in private.

Ethan raised his head from the comforting shelter of his mother's arms. His tear-filled eyes brimmed with sorrow. "My dad died," he said, chin quivering. His pale face was blotched with grief. "Did you know that?"

"Yes, honey." Caroline smoothed his tangled hair off his forehead. "I'm so sorry about that."

"He hadda accident." Ethan sniffled. "Sergeant Garrett said he was gonna find out what happened."

"I'm sure he will," Caroline said soothingly.

As Ethan rubbed his nose on the sleeve of his pajamas, he

caught sight of Noah reaching for the door. "Didja find out what happened to my dad yet?" he called.

Caroline jerked around as if she'd completely forgotten Noah's presence. No doubt she had.

He came back across the room, self-consciously aware of her gaze following him like a searchlight. "Not yet, son," he said in reply to Ethan's hopeful question. "But I'm counting on you to help me figure it out."

"Me?" Ethan hiccuped. A scared look crossed his face. "But I—I can't remember anything."

Noah hadn't been well acquainted with Jeff Tate and his son, but he'd known them enough to say hello to. That was pretty inevitable in a town this size. He'd noted the resemblance between father and son, and now that he observed Ethan with Caroline, he detected the boy's strong resemblance to his mother, too.

They shared the same delicate bone structure, the same blond hair, the same long, curly lashes, though Ethan's eyes were brown and his mother's that amazing shade of green.

Mother and son both watched while Noah pulled up a chair and sat down beside the bed.

"I know you couldn't remember much last time we talked," he said to Ethan. "But I was hoping we could talk some more, and maybe together we can figure out what happened to your dad."

He felt like the world's biggest spoilsport, interrupting Caroline's long-awaited reunion with her son. Judging by the tight seam of her mouth, she wasn't too pleased about it, either. But Noah had a murder case to solve. And he knew from experience that the trail a killer left behind grew cold quickly. Very quickly.

He needed to extract whatever information Ethan had buried in his subconscious as soon as possible.

"Let's start with school the day before yesterday. When school was out, you got on your bike...."

They'd already been over this ground before, so Ethan didn't require much prompting.

"An' I rode to my dad's gas station like I do most days after school." Ethan's chest puffed up a little. "He lets me help him pump gas and make change and stuff." At that moment it obviously hit home that he would never again help out his father. His whole body deflated, so that he suddenly looked vulnerable and forlorn.

Caroline hugged him with the protective arm she'd kept wrapped around his shoulders. The shifting expressions that played across her pretty face conveyed her inner conflict. Plainly she was sympathetic and sad for her son's sake, yet she also must resent hearing details about the new life her ex-husband had built with the child he'd stolen from her.

Noah felt sorry for both her and the boy, but he had a job to do. "So you rode to the gas station..."

"I didn't see my dad working out front, so I figured he was in the office. I parked my bike out back, just like always. I 'member thinking I was thirsty, and wondering if my dad would let me have some money to put in the Coke machine."

Ethan's eyes darted from side to side, riveted on something far, far away. "Then...and then..." He scrunched his eyelids shut and clamped his hands to his head, as if to capture the elusive memories.

When his eyes flew open he gasped, as if exhausted by the effort. "Then I—I can't 'member any more."

He looked so miserable, so frustrated and unhappy that Caroline intervened. "Sergeant, can't this wait until another time?"

He met her gaze head-on. "No," he said. "It can't."

She flushed, her eyes narrowing. Before she could protest further Noah said, "I promise not to push him. But time is critical if I'm ever going to catch—if I'm ever going to figure out what happened to his father."

"All right."

Noah sensed Caroline had only given in because she didn't want to upset Ethan further by making a scene. Not because she cared very much whether Jeff's killer was ever caught.

Which might make it tough to get her to agree with what Noah intended to request later.

"Do you remember going into the office after you parked your bike at the gas station?" he asked Ethan.

The boy shook his head unhappily.

"What's the next thing you *do* remember after that?" Noah prodded gently.

"When I woke up here," Ethan said, twisting the edge of the hospital blanket into a rope. "When the doctor told me my dad was dead." His face crumpled.

But Noah knew from official reports that Ethan was the one who'd dialed 911 for help. When the deputy and ambulance crew got there, they'd found him curled up in a fetal position on the floor beside his bleeding, unconscious father. In response to their questions, Ethan could only whimper incoherently.

The doctor had sedated him at the hospital. And when Ethan had awakened hours later, he'd lost not only his father, but all memory of whatever he'd witnessed at the gas station.

Noah tried a different tack. "Ethan, was there anybody your dad was mad at? Anybody who might have been mad at him?"

He hunched his shoulders. "No."

"Did you ever hear anyone yelling at your dad?"

"No. Well..." He rubbed his freckled nose.

"Who did you hear yelling at your dad, Ethan?"

The boy glanced at Caroline for reassurance. She nodded, offering him an encouraging smile. Her entire face radiated pure, uncomplicated, boundless love.

An unwelcome flash of curiosity escaped from the dark forbidden corners of Noah's brain. What would it feel like to have Caroline Tate gaze at *him* with such naked adoration?

For God's sake, Garrett, what's the matter with you? Get a grip.

Impatiently he slammed the door shut on his foolish mental detour. He didn't want or need such pointless, distracting thoughts, not in the middle of an investigation.

Not ever.

He channeled his attention back to the boy and away from his distracting mother. "Who was yelling at your dad?" he asked Ethan again.

Ethan looked into his lap. "It was my *dad* yelling," he mumbled.

Noah leaned closer and folded his hands between his knees. His father-confessor pose. "Who was he yelling at, son?"

"Some guy." Ethan shrugged. "I don't know who he was. I saw him hanging around the gas station a couple times."

"What did he look like?"

"He was old and dirty and had raggedy clothes on." Ethan wrinkled his nose. "He smelled bad, too."

"Where was he when your dad was yelling at him?" Noah asked.

"In the office. At the gas station."

"When was this?"

"Mmm...a few days ago."

Noah felt the faint stirring of excitement in his gut that occasionally alerted him he was onto something. Of course, sometimes what he was onto was a false lead. "What was your dad yelling at him?"

Ethan chewed his lip while he tried to remember. "Umm...he kept yelling, 'You can't do this.'"

"What else?"

"Something...about money."

"What exactly did he say about money?"

Ethan squinted at the ceiling, the floor, the bed. "I can't remember," he said finally.

"Okay." Noah patted the boy's knee. "You did great, Ethan." He snapped his fingers. "Say, do you like drawing pictures?"

Ethan fidgeted with uncertainty. "I guess."

"If I called a police sketch artist and asked him to come here, do you think you could help him draw a picture of that guy your dad was yelling at? By telling him what the man looked like?"

"Will that help you figure out what happened to my dad?"

"I don't know for sure. But it might."

"Then, okay." A pale lock of hair fell across Ethan's forehead when he nodded.

"Great." Noah flashed the boy a thumbs-up sign. "Maybe while you're helping the sketch artist, your mom and I can go get a cup of coffee." He hoisted his brows at Caroline.

She was shaking her head before he'd even finished. "I'd prefer to stay here with Ethan, thanks."

"You mean you'd pass up a chance to sample some of our world-famous Eagle River Hospital coffee?" As a rule Noah found it easier to josh people into cooperating, rather than bully them with the official weight of his badge. "Why, people have been known to break their own legs just so they can be patients here and get to drink some of our hospital's delicious coffee." He winked at Ethan.

Ethan actually giggled. His grin exposed the new adult-size incisors he had yet to grow into, so that he resembled a puffy-eyed chipmunk. He was a darn cute kid, no question about it.

Noah was glad he'd been able to make the little guy laugh.

Now, if only he could get his charm to work as effectively on the boy's mother.

"Gee, that coffee sounds fabulous," she said, rolling her lovely eyes with mock enthusiasm. "But just the same, I'd rather stay here with Ethan." An edge of steel had crept into her voice.

Noah rubbed his jaw. "Actually, there are one or two things I need to discuss with you. Alone." He hoped he wouldn't have to go into an exaggerated Groucho Marx routine, wiggling his eyebrows in Ethan's direction till his mother got the hint.

He didn't have to.

With a worried, reluctant glance at her son, Caroline said slowly, "All right. I guess I could use some coffee." As if to prove she wasn't about to cave in completely, she added, "A very *quick* cup of coffee."

She leveled her gaze at Noah over the top of her son's

tousled head, acknowledging his minor victory with a cool look that was a far cry from adoration.

Thus ended his first skirmish with the mother of his star witness. But Noah suspected it wouldn't be his last.

The entire roll call of Eagle River law enforcement, Caroline learned, consisted of Noah and three uniformed sheriff's deputies who reported to him. The sheriff himself, along with the only police artist in Tamarack County, were headquartered forty miles away in the county seat of Carleton.

By the time the sketch artist showed up it was well past noon. Ethan had already picked over the lunch delivered by a cheery hospital aide pushing a metal cart. No room service for non-patients, though.

That was the *only* reason Caroline had agreed to have lunch with Noah in the hospital cafeteria while Ethan worked with the sketch artist.

After all, she could hardly deprive the man of a meal.

"So you think this scruffy character Jeff was yelling at might have come back later and killed him?" she asked as they sat down together at an empty table.

"Possibly." Noah methodically unloaded the contents of his tray—a sandwich, a carton of milk, a slice of pie. "Worth looking into, at any rate."

Caroline clicked her tongue in exasperation. She knew the man was perfectly capable of complete sentences when it suited his purpose. But when it came to prying details about Jeff's death from him, he turned into Clint Eastwood.

She tasted her coffee, made a face. "You're not exactly a font of information," she complained, pushing the coffee away.

One corner of his mouth kicked upward. He transferred a napkin, fork and drinking straw to the table and set the tray aside.

Then he proceeded to unwrap his sandwich.

Caroline ignored her own food and glared at him. "I thought you wanted to discuss your investigation," she said.

"Isn't that why you dragged me away from the son I haven't seen in three years?"

He chewed the first bite of his sandwich before replying. "Sorry about that." He coaxed open his milk carton and took a swallow, ignoring the straw the cashier had placed on his tray. "I know all you care about is being with your son right now. But my job is to find your ex-husband's killer."

"Fine." Irritation flared into anger. Not at Noah, but at Jeff. "When you do, be sure and give me his address so I can send him a thank-you note."

Instantly Caroline felt ashamed. Good heavens, what kind of awful person would Noah think she was? But she was so damned mad at Jeff for what he'd done....

"That bastard." She slammed her unopened yogurt container back onto the table. "It wasn't cruel enough to steal our child. He had to go and tell Ethan I was dead."

Noah pushed his lunch aside. "Jeff Tate was a first-class weasel, all right." He folded his hands and tapped his thumbs together. "But I'm still obligated to do everything in my power to bring his killer to justice."

"I know." Caroline propped an elbow on the table and buried her face in her hand. "I don't really want to see anyone get away with murder. But I just can't believe Jeff would do such a horrible thing to me...."

To her dismay, she felt tears spring to her eyes. She squeezed them back. She absolutely, positively would not humiliate herself by letting Noah Garrett see her cry.

He startled her by reaching over to cover her other hand with his. Startled her with the strange electric heat that immediately raced along her nerve endings, spreading across her skin like wildfire.

Caroline fought to ignore it. Noah was just trying to be nice, that was all. Trying to calm her down, the way he might try to talk someone off a ledge. Just doing his job. Nothing personal.

Then why did this bridge of physical contact between them feel so...so intimate? Caroline wanted to curl her fingers through his, to draw him closer so that she could savor not only the heat of his hand but the heat and strength of his entire body.

She'd had no one to lean on for a long, long time. How nice it would be to drop her head onto Noah's broad, capable shoulder and snuggle against him while his strong arms came around her. He would stroke her hair with his big masculine hand, whisper tender words in her ear...

Caroline shuddered. Dear God, what was happening to her? This emotional roller coaster she'd been riding for three years was taking some dangerous swoops and turns. One moment she was overcome with joy to have Ethan back, the next moment she was shaking with rage over Jeff's treachery.

Then came moments like this, when the roller coaster careened around a blind curve and she found herself abruptly plummeting into this crazy, reckless attraction to Noah Garrett.

She had to slam the brakes on it now, before she embarrassed them both. Noah sent out all the signals of a man who was as eager to steer clear of involvement as Caroline was.

Quick, think of something intelligent to say!

She forced herself to meet his eyes. Maybe not the best way to deflect the undercurrent of sexual awareness that was setting her teeth on edge, along with other parts of her body.

"Thank you for being so considerate of Ethan's feelings," she said. "I mean, for not revealing the fact his father was murdered." She wondered how she could extract her hand from Noah's without seeming rude.

She wondered whether she wanted to.

"I figured there was no point in upsetting him further." Noah's eyes concealed their depths as effectively as the deep blue sea. "Time enough to explain it to him, once we actually know what happened."

Mesmerized, Caroline felt herself caught by his captivating gaze. She concentrated on his chin instead. Hmm. You couldn't exactly call the depression there a dimple. Definitely not a dimple. A dimple was soft and cute, and there was nothing soft and cute about this hard-edged, handsome man.

No, you'd have to call that a *cleft* slashing his rugged chin. Angled a bit off center, just enough to give him a rakish asymmetry. A carved signpost pointing the way to his...mouth.

Oh, Lord. Maybe she'd been better off looking at his eyes.

"The reason I wanted to talk to you alone," Noah said, "was to discuss your plans."

"Plans?" she echoed stupidly.

"Regarding Ethan."

"Oh." *Pull yourself together, Caroline.* "Well, as soon as I can book a flight I'm going to take him back home to Baltimore, of course." *And put an entire continent between you and me as quickly as possible.*

Noah's thumb lazily stroked her wrist, though in an absentminded rather than seductive way. Still, Caroline was having trouble focusing on their conversation.

"I'd like you to stay here for a while," he said.

For one insane second she thought he meant...never mind.

"Why?" she asked warily.

"Well, for one thing, if this police drawing helps us locate the guy who argued with Jeff, Ethan is the only person who can positively identify him."

Caroline's brows feathered upward. "You don't even know if that guy has anything to do with Jeff's murder," she pointed out.

Noah recognized the exact instant she began to resist him. A brittle note entered her voice and the pliant muscles of her hand tensed, as if she was preparing to form a fist.

Then it dawned on him that they were sitting here holding hands like two kids in a malt shop. Hell's bells, what was the matter with him, anyway? All he'd intended was to convey his sympathy for the rotten way her ex-husband had treated her. But somehow, while he wasn't paying attention, his gesture had turned into something more.

Something Noah wanted no part of.

He didn't like the way Caroline Tate made him feel, damn it! Didn't like that she made him *feel*, period.

Since the day of Beth and Molly's funeral, Noah had

crammed his emotions into a box and stuffed them away in a back closet of his soul. All he'd let himself care about was his work. It was the only way he'd survived the pain and guilt for four years.

He wasn't going to let Caroline Tate crack open that box and screw things up for him.

He reached for the dessert he no longer wanted, just to give himself an excuse to use both hands elsewhere.

"Another reason I'd like you to stick around for a while is to give Ethan's memory a chance to come back." Noah broke off a piece of pie with his fork, but didn't bother raising it to his mouth. He didn't have much appetite right now. A different kind of hunger had driven off his desire for food.

"Ethan's memory can come back just as easily in Baltimore," Caroline insisted.

Noah's attention wandered to the curved neckline of her dress. Just above it was the delicate hollow where her swanlike throat encountered the two wings of her collarbone. The dress hardly fit the commonly accepted definition of sexy. It was sort of a Pilgrim gray. Somber. Prim. Maternal. Without the barest tease of cleavage.

Yet Noah's glance kept drifting back to that enticing hollow at the base of her throat. His mouth would fit there perfectly. He bet he'd be able to taste her excited pulse beat beneath his lips if he—

All at once he desperately craved a tall, chilling glass of ice water to dump over his own head. Or into his lap.

Cripes, will you forget about her neck and her mouth and all the other delicious parts of her anatomy for a while? You've got to stop her from whisking the kid away before he has a chance to recall something that could lead to the killer.

"There's a better chance of Ethan regaining his memory here in familiar surroundings," Noah said. He didn't know whether or not that was true, but it sounded reasonable. "In Eagle River the odds are higher he'll see or hear something that jogs his memory."

Caroline was tearing off little bits of napkin, the expression on her face suggesting the napkin might be a substitute for something else. Or some*one* else. Her fingernails were clipped short, smoothly filed, painted with clear polish. Tiny half-moons peeped above her cuticles. "Did it ever occur to you that it might be better if Ethan *never* remembers what happened?"

"No. I don't believe that." His fork clinked as he dropped it next to his uneaten pie. "It's always better to know than to wonder."

Caroline gave him a skeptical glance. "You'd say that, of course. Since it would suit your own purposes to have access to the missing piece of Ethan's memory."

"True," Noah acknowledged. For some reason it bugged him to have her think that was all he cared about. "But it would be better for Ethan's sake, too."

She lowered her lashes and peered through them. "What do you mean, exactly?"

Noah leaned forward, narrowing the distance between them. Maybe the only way he was going to gain Caroline's full co-operation was to scare some sense into her.

"Let me spell it out for you." He checked over his shoulder for potential eavesdroppers. Then he brought his head close to hers, close enough to identify what shampoo she used if he'd been capable of distinguishing one brand's fragrance from another. This one was pleasantly floral, probably expensive.

He aimed his attention straight at her gorgeous green eyes. "Fact number one. There's a killer out there whom your son may eventually be able to name. Fact number two. Said killer might very well decide it's in his best interest to eliminate the one witness who can send him—or her—to the electric chair."

Color drained from Caroline's face. "What—what makes you think the killer even *knows* that Ethan might pose a threat to him?"

"You probably grew up in the big city, right?"

Puzzled, she nodded.

"Let me explain how it works in small towns. Fact number three." Noah waved his arm in the direction of downtown

Eagle River. "I guarantee you that right now, every single customer eating lunch over at the Forty-Niner Diner is also busy chewing over every tasty tidbit about this case. Small towns have a grapevine that makes the Internet look like the Pony Express."

He stretched his mouth into a grim line. "Believe me, unless the killer immediately hightailed it out of town, he knows all about Ethan's temporary amnesia and the fact that he may have seen his father's killer."

Still ashen, Caroline sank back against the molded plastic of her chair. Though she was retreating physically from him, she was not quite ready to concede defeat. "Maybe the killer *did* leave town, though. He could have been some drifter passing through." Her knuckles were white on the edge of the Formica tabletop. If she was making an effort to keep her hand from trembling, she was failing. "The killer could be long gone. He could have no idea that Ethan might incriminate him."

"It's possible." Noah fixed her with a stern look. "But are you willing to take that chance?"

The set of her chin hardened. "All the more reason for me to take Ethan back to Baltimore as soon as possible."

"The killer could buy a plane ticket, too."

Caroline flailed an arm through the air. "Then we'll move somewhere else. Someplace Ethan will be safe."

Noah moved in for the kill. "You really want to live in fear from now on? Looking back over your shoulder, knowing there's a murderer out there who may be after your son? Are you willing to take even the slightest risk that Jeff's killer might cross paths with Ethan by *accident* someday?"

He saw by the panic on Caroline's face that she wasn't. Her eyes shone with a wild gleam like a cornered animal's.

Noah felt guilty for pressing so hard, but what choice did he have? The best way Caroline could help her son was by allowing him to give Noah whatever assistance he could.

He spread his hands. "Look, I realize that seeing your ex-husband's killer brought to justice isn't high on your priority list right now. But think of Ethan. He's got a rocky road ahead of him, emotionally. Don't you agree it can only help him recover from all he's been through, to know he helped put his dad's killer behind bars?'' Reload. Aim. Fire. ''How's Ethan going to feel toward you someday, when he realizes he could have done something to help catch his father's killer, if only you hadn't removed him from where he could do the most good?''

Caroline's eyes glittered narrowly. ''That's a low blow, Sergeant.''

''Maybe so.'' Noah leveled a warning finger at her. ''But it's also the truth.''

She clung to one last thread of alternative. ''Look, I promise I'll contact you if Ethan's memory returns. I'll even bring him back here if you need him to pick someone out of a lineup.''

Noah knew that once Caroline left his jurisdiction, whatever small measure of control he had over her would vanish. Maybe she would cooperate with his investigation and maybe she wouldn't. But he wasn't about to let his star witness fly the coop without doing everything in his power to prevent it.

He might be able to convince a judge to legally prevent her from taking Ethan out of the county. But that would *really* put her back up.

Noah didn't truly believe Caroline would deliberately hinder his investigation by encouraging Ethan to keep his mouth shut. But it certainly wouldn't help his case to alienate her, either.

Which was the reason Noah was so determined to persuade Caroline Tate to stay here of her own free will.

The *only* reason.

''Just for a week,'' he said, knowing full well a week might not be enough. ''Look at it this way. It'll give Ethan some time to adjust to all the traumatic changes in his life before you have to uproot him again.''

He should have known an appeal to Caroline's maternal concern would turn the trick. With a heavy sigh of resignation, she pressed her fingertips to her mouth. ''You win,'' she said from behind her hand. Then she straightened her spine and held up an adamant finger at Noah. "But on *one* condition."

"That being?"

"I insist that Ethan have round-the-clock police protection. Sheriff's protection." She waved her hand. "Whatever you call it around here." She banged her fist on the table. "If the killer *is* still in town, I don't want him getting anywhere near my son."

Noah could hardly argue with the reasonableness of her request. "I'll talk to the sheriff."

He'd gotten more or less what he wanted. His star witness would be staying put for the time being. Noah ought to be pleased.

Why was it, then, that the prospect of continuing contact with Caroline Tate for the next week or so didn't exactly make his day?

"No. Uh-uh. Absolutely out of the question."

Sheriff Grady Reeves hoisted his bushy gray eyebrows, along with the belt beneath his middle-aged paunch. "I thought you wanted the kid protected," he said to Noah.

"I do. By a round-the-clock guard. Someone who can drive Ethan and his mother around, keep watch outside their hotel room…"

"Sorry, Noah. No can do." The sheriff settled one ample haunch against the corner of his cluttered desk and spread his beefy hands. "I don't have the budget to spare a deputy for full-time bodyguard duty."

Noah's frustration level had been climbing toward the hair-yanking stage all afternoon. Grady was an okay guy and had even been a decent cop in his day. But the sheriff's position was an elected office in Tamarack County, and above all else Grady was a politician.

It was aggravating enough that he'd insisted Noah drive all the way over here to Carleton to brief him in person on the Tate murder investigation. *Then* he'd sprung a press conference on Noah, something Noah detested. In his view it was a criminal waste of time to pose behind some damn microphone to answer questions for reporters, when he could have been out there working to dig up some *real* answers that would help him nab the killer.

As far as Noah could see, the only purpose served by the press conference had been to give the sheriff a chance to grandstand for the media. Who knows? Maybe the next time elections rolled around, the voters might actually remember that Grady Reeves had had something to do with catching that awful Tate killer, hadn't he?

That is, if Noah ever succeeded in catching him.

The odds were turning against him the longer he had to fool around arguing with the sheriff. But this most recent of Grady's demands was the most outrageous yet.

"It won't work," Noah told him. "It'll steal time from my investigation."

The sheriff's six-pointed badge, freshly polished for the press conference, winked at him. "I don't see why," Grady said, cracking his knuckles. "You won't have to personally keep your eye on them every second."

"There must be someone else who could—"

"Ah, but *you've* already established a rapport with the boy." He passed Noah a sly leer like a dirty note in school. "And from what I hear, the mother's quite a looker. I presume you don't have any problems getting along with her, eh?" Wink, wink.

Problems? Oh, man. Noah didn't even want to *think* about the kind of problems Grady's proposed arrangement would cause him.

"I agree with you, the boy needs protecting." Grady pushed himself off the edge of his desk and lumbered around behind it. "Matter of fact, I *insist* on it, now that you've brought it to my attention." He started to shuffle papers. Noah recognized the signs that he was about to be dismissed. "Fact is, this case is getting a lot of media attention, what with the reunited-mother-and-son angle and all." Grady's forehead was creased with concern. Probably for his reelection chances.

"Wouldn't look too good, would it, if someone offed the kid?"

Just the suggestion of Ethan coming to harm twisted in Noah's gut like a switchblade. The boy's safety was his ultimate priority, of course, but there had to be some other way....

With a groan of relief, Grady loosened the belt he'd cinched tight under the mistaken impression it would hold up his sagging gut in front of all those media cameras. "I'm making *you* personally responsible for the kid's protection," he told Noah. "And I can't think of a more secure hiding place to stash him and his mother than under the same roof with my best deputy."

He jabbed on the bifocals he was too vain to wear in public and dismissed his best deputy with an impatient flip of his hand. "Take 'em home with you, Noah. That's an order."

Chapter 3

Caroline sternly told herself the only reason her pulse quickened when she recognized Noah's vehicle pulling up in front of the hospital was that she was so anxious to get Ethan and herself settled in their hotel room.

She watched Noah climb out, stride around the Jeep and head swiftly for the glass doors at the hospital entrance. Even in a coat and tie, he moved with the inborn grace and easy assurance of a star quarterback. Come to think of it, he was built like a football player, too. Solid, powerful thighs propelled him forward while his broad shoulders seemed to push the air molecules aside.

He didn't look terribly happy at the moment. Caroline wondered why, then tried to shrug off her concern. Never mind, she thought. It's got nothing to do with you. Noah Garrett's state of mind is none of your business.

His stormy expression cleared the moment he caught sight of her and Ethan waiting on the sofa just inside the entrance. He changed course and veered in their direction. "Sorry I'm late," he said. "I got tied up with the sheriff longer than I thought I would."

"That's all right," Caroline replied, instantly dismissing the fifty or sixty times she'd checked her watch in the last half hour. All afternoon she'd been impatient to escape the depressing atmosphere of the hospital, with its ghostly white walls, the cloying smell of antiseptic, the muted tread of rubber-soled shoes.

Noah Garrett somehow made this pale, subdued place come alive. He had a certain restless energy that made Caroline's skin prickle like the electric air right before a thunderstorm. Though outwardly he appeared to keep his emotions carefully banked, Caroline sensed an inner fire she suspected might roar into life under the proper circumstances.

She refused to speculate about what those circumstances might be. It was bad enough that Noah made her feel like a dewy-eyed adolescent whenever he got within ten feet of her.

He shifted his sights to Ethan, who sat next to Caroline with his head bowed, feet swinging listlessly back and forth. "Well, are you all officially checked out?" Noah directed his question to her son.

"Yes, sir." Ethan directed his answer to the floor.

Caroline worried her lower lip. She realized Ethan's brooding withdrawal was only to be expected after the horrible shock he'd suffered. Two shocks, actually. Learning his father was dead, and learning his mother was alive.

She hoped the second shock wasn't horrible for him, too.

All the years her little boy had been missing, Caroline had believed that once she found him, the paralyzing sense of helplessness that gripped her would go away. Instead, it had merely changed form. She still felt helpless. Helpless to comfort her son. To make everything all better for him. To make sense out of the last three senseless years.

Even if Ethan's pain were multiplied a thousandfold, she would have borne it all herself, if she could have. But she couldn't.

She curved her arm around her son's slumped shoulders,

still rejoicing at the miracle that had finally made it possible for her to touch him again. "Ready to go, sweetheart?"

He nodded silently and slid off the couch. Over the top of his drooping head Caroline intercepted a commiserating glance from Noah. He, too, knew what it was like to feel helpless to rescue your child from life's tragedies. No doubt that was the reason she'd felt this eerie sense of...connection to him from the moment they'd met. Although Noah certainly sent off all the signals of not wanting any sympathy in return.

"I'm parked right out front." He stood aside and swept out his arm with a flourish. "Our chariot awaits." He shot a quick glance at Ethan as if checking for any trace of a smile.

There was none. But Caroline appreciated his effort and offered Noah a weak smile of her own instead. She took Ethan's hand in hers and instantly felt his resistance. With a pang of sorrow, she released him. She kept forgetting he was eight years old now, not five. And eight-year-old boys were too big to hold their mothers' hands.

Maybe staying in Eagle River for a week would turn out to be a good thing after all. If *she* was having this much trouble adjusting to her son's presence, she could only imagine the emotional struggle Ethan must be having adjusting to *hers*. Surely it would be easier for him to get used to having a mother again within the familiar surroundings of the place he considered home.

Caroline only wanted what was best for her child. He was the one person on earth who mattered to her, and she intended to devote herself to him completely from now on. Not that she hadn't been a devoted mother before Ethan had disappeared. But once her marriage to Jeff had broken up, Caroline had harbored the illusion that eventually she would find another man to love again, to share her life with.

That was before Jeff had committed the monstrous betrayal of stealing their child. By doing so, he'd completely destroyed not only Caroline's trust but also her faith in her own ability to judge men. She didn't dare make the mistake of marrying someone like Jeff again. Especially now that she had her son to consider.

No matter how flawed a father Jeff had been, his death had shattered Ethan's universe. How could Caroline risk letting Ethan get hurt again by bringing another man into their lives to be a father to her son? A man who could turn out to be as unreliable and unfaithful as Jeff and end up walking out on them both someday...

She stole a glance at Noah, with his big, reliable-looking shoulders...his steady, quiet strength...his rugged, stalwart features that reflected an iron determination to hold true to whatever course he'd chosen to follow.

Do *not* take even one more step down *that* dead-end road, Caroline warned herself. Hadn't she already proved herself to be a terrible judge of character? Besides, it wasn't as if Noah had displayed even one iota of interest in her. Envisioning him as her own personal knight in shining armor wasn't just dangerous, it was a complete waste of time.

They reached his truck, where an awkward dilemma made Caroline forget her ridiculous musings. Who was going to sit where? She could hardly sit in the back seat with Ethan while Noah drove them around like a chauffeur. Yet she didn't want to banish Ethan to the back by himself, either.

Noah solved the problem. "How 'bout riding shotgun up front with me?" he suggested to Ethan.

"'Kay." Ethan obediently crawled into the Jeep when Noah opened the passenger-side door. Caroline tried not to take it personally that he acted indifferent about whether or not he sat next to her. No matter how much it killed her to admit it, she was practically a stranger to her son right now. A ghost returned from the grave.

All thanks to the man she'd been stupid enough to marry.

When she climbed into the back seat of the Jeep she noticed several sacks of groceries stored behind it. With a jab of annoyance, she realized Noah must have stopped off to do his shopping while she and Ethan were cooling their heels in the hospital reception area, waiting for him.

See? she scolded herself. You didn't peg him as the inconsiderate type, did you? But here was the proof. He'd claimed he was late because he was tied up with the sheriff.

"All buckled in?" She detected a false ring of cheerfulness to Noah's voice as he started the engine. No doubt he would be relieved to dump Ethan and her at the hotel and turn guard duty over to some underling. He seemed awfully tense about something, the way he kept fiddling with his tie, the way his gaze kept sliding away from hers. Probably had a hot date he was late for, Caroline thought pettishly.

She squashed a twinge of what almost felt like jealousy. "How long have you lived in Eagle River?" she asked, leaning forward to talk to the back of his head. What she really wanted to ask was whether he'd learned anything new about Jeff's death. But she didn't want to talk about it in front of Ethan.

"I moved up here right after I finished my law-enforcement training and got hired on as a deputy," Noah replied over his shoulder. "Almost fifteen years ago."

The conversational ball rolled to a stop. After a few moments of silence, Caroline dutifully kicked it back. "Where are you from originally?"

"Southern California."

With her head so close to the back of his neck, she could smell a trace of his aftershave. Something sexy yet vaguely old-fashioned. Bay rum? "Do you still have family there?" she asked.

"My folks and my sister live in L.A. My sister's married, with a couple of kids. How about you?" His abrupt U-turn in the conversation seemed to Caroline less a genuine interest than a skillful attempt to parry her personal questions.

"It's just Ethan and me," she said, reaching forward to ruffle her son's hair. He didn't pull away. But he didn't turn around and give her an affectionate grin in return, either. "I was an only child, and my parents died while I was in college."

"Sorry to hear that."

"Thanks." She clicked her tongue. "I never know what you're supposed to say when people express sympathy. 'Thank you' doesn't really seem appropriate."

"Yeah." After a thoughtful pause, he added, "I know what you mean."

Caroline's heart went out to him. Even though it bumped straight into one of those No Trespassing signs he had posted around his grief.

They'd already driven by a couple of motels and appeared to be passing through the outskirts of town now. Caroline frowned, mystified. She hadn't thought to inquire about their lodging arrangements, assuming the sheriff's department must have a standard procedure for this kind of thing. Maybe since keeping Ethan out of sight would keep him safer, they were going to stay at some secluded bed-and-breakfast inn out in the country.

She'd opened her mouth to ask when Ethan blurted out, "What about my stuff?"

Noah glanced over at him. "What stuff are you talking about, honey?" Caroline asked.

He twisted around in his seat. "My clothes and stuff! My baseball mitt! My bike!" His voice teetered on the edge of panic. "I need my *stuff!*"

Noah met Caroline's eyes in the rearview mirror. She wished she hadn't instinctively searched out his reflection. It had to be just a trick of light, but his eyes seemed to burn an even intenser blue than usual.

She covered Ethan's hand with hers. "Honey, don't worry about your stuff. We'll buy you new clothes, and a new baseball mitt and bike, too, once we get home."

"No! I want *my* stuff! Please! Can't we go get it now?"

Instantly Caroline realized how badly she'd blundered. Of course Ethan would cling to the comfort of his own familiar possessions! They were all he had left of his life with his father. No wonder he was in such a panic about losing them.

Caroline would just as soon have made a big pile of everything Jeff had ever bought their son and set a match to it. But she would never, ever do that to Ethan. She tapped Noah on the shoulder. "Do you suppose we could stop by Jeff's house before we go to the hotel?"

He shifted uneasily. Whether from her touch or because of this potential delay in his schedule, she couldn't tell. "Tell you what," he said, aiming his answer at Ethan. "What if we stop by there tomorrow? I'll drive us over and we'll load all your stuff into the back of the Jeep. That sound okay to you?"

Ethan picked at a frayed hole in his jeans. "I guess that'd be all right." But he didn't look too happy.

"You don't have to make a special trip," Caroline said. "Whoever is assigned to protect Ethan can drive us over there."

"Uh…" Noah cleared his throat. "That'd be me."

"You?" Caroline blinked in surprise. Uh-oh. She hadn't counted on having to cope with Noah's disturbingly handsome presence day in and day out. She had enough emotional upheaval to deal with without constantly having to fight her own attraction to him. "But surely someone else could—I mean, I thought you'd be busy investigating Jeff's death."

"I will be," he said, turning off the pavement onto a narrow gravel road. The Jeep bounced along the washboard surface like a bucking bronco. "Don't worry. You'll be perfectly safe where we're going."

Caroline clamped her back teeth together to keep them from rattling. "And where exactly *are* we going?" A chill of suspicion began to creep up her spine. Even the most rustic bed-and-breakfast wouldn't be located on a road *this* bad. Besides, she hadn't seen any sign.

Noah swerved sharply around a pothole so that Caroline lurched sideways. "Actually, you two are going to be staying at my place," he announced, sounding both nonchalant and grim at the same time.

"What?" Caroline shrieked.

Ethan whipped his head around to stare at her. For the first time all day his brown eyes held a spark of interest.

It was the one positive aspect to this disastrous turn of events.

"Look, I'm not any happier about this than you are." Personally, Noah figured *he* was the one with the most cause to get bent out of shape about this whole setup. After all, he was the one whose privacy was being invaded. He was the one whose peace of mind was going to be under constant attack, living under the same roof with this woman and her uncanny knack for stirring up feelings he'd worked long and hard to bury.

Just the thought of her prancing around in the morning wearing only a bath towel was enough to make him—

"Call the sheriff. Talk to him again," Caroline insisted. "Tell him these arrangements are completely unacceptable."

They were standing in his kitchen, having an argument that had started out in hushed tones but had rapidly crescendoed into yelling range. Ethan was in the living room, watching TV. Noah hoped he had the volume turned up high.

"It won't do any good talking to the sheriff," he repeated for maybe the tenth time. "Facts are facts. And the fact is the department doesn't have the extra personnel for round-the-clock guard duty, and it doesn't have the extra money to pay someone even if it did."

"*I'll* pay for a hotel," she said. "*And* a bodyguard."

Noah massaged the base of his neck, trying to ward off a headache. "Well, see, there's what you might call a scarcity of professional bodyguards here in Tamarack County. And I'm not about to let some amateur who thinks he's Wyatt Earp start waving a gun around and blasting away every time he hears a twig snap."

"Fine. I'll pay for *your* hotel room, too." She folded her arms and glared at him, chin locked in a stubborn position. Noah could tell she was used to giving orders and getting her way. He supposed that was a handy quality for a successful businesswoman to have, but it wasn't going to be of much use as long as she was within Noah's jurisdiction. *He* could be stubborn, too.

Once again, he calculated that the only surefire way to gain her cooperation was through an appeal to her protective, maternal instincts. "Ethan will be much safer here than in a hotel," he pointed out. "For one thing, no one ever comes out here. Because this house is so isolated, he'll be completely out of sight. No one will even know he's still in town."

Something shifted in those gorgeous green eyes of hers. The first foreshadowing of surrender?

Noah pressed his case. "Until this investigation is over, I'm going to be busy working on it all day, and most likely all evening, too. I won't have time to keep watch over Ethan." He waved his hand, directing her eye toward the window over the sink. Through it they could both see the thick pine forest outside, birds flitting between the trees, a glimpse of the next mountain ridge through a gap in the woods. "Out here your boy will be safe because no one will know he's here. You won't have to keep him cooped up in a hotel room all day long with the curtains drawn shut."

She nibbled her lower lip in a signal of uncertainty Noah was coming to recognize. An unconscious habit that was also sexy as all get-out. That made him think about nibbling that soft, moist lip himself.

Damn it! It was a good thing he was going to be completely wrapped up in work while she was here. With luck, by the end of the day he would be much too exhausted to waste energy on such unsettling fantasies.

Noah knew why *he* wasn't thrilled about their setting up housekeeping together. But Caroline's reaction to the idea was even more vehement than he'd anticipated. It made sense that she would much prefer having time to become reacquainted with her son without the intrusive presence of a third wheel.

But Noah had already explained he wouldn't be around much. Maybe Caroline's strong objection came from the fact that she was used to being in control, to running the show by herself. Stuck here under Noah's roof, stranded more than a mile from town without a car, she would be forced into a position of dependence on him. And a woman as strong-minded and independent as Caroline Tate was bound to chafe under such circumstances.

Man, oh man, but he hoped he could solve this case quickly!

"I know this will be awkward for both of us," he said. And wasn't *that* the understatement of the year! "But it's not as if we're on different sides. After all, we both want what's best for Ethan."

Noah felt kind of guilty, playing that same trump card over and over. But he knew a parent's love for a child was the most powerful persuasion on earth. He remembered the first time he'd held his little Molly in his arms, how he'd instantly been struck by the dazzling, white-hot revelation that his highest priority for the rest of his life was going to be keeping this precious child happy and safe.

He'd failed tragically.

A knife blade of pain sliced through Noah's gut. Though he tried to fend off his memories, they taunted him with Molly's mischievous blue eyes, her dancing gold ringlets, the way her chubby cheeks dimpled when she giggled.

Noah had finally stopped wishing he'd died with Beth and Molly in the accident. But he would never stop wishing he could somehow have traded his life for theirs.

Though he fought to prevent his face from conveying his inner turmoil, Caroline's expression grew gentler while she watched him. Her stubborn resistance appeared to melt away, softening the exquisite contours of her features. Her pupils dilated like dark moons, as if for a moment she could actually see the invisible scars that marked him.

Noah didn't care one bit for this disquieting sensation of having his soul stripped naked before her. He didn't know whether to be relieved or alarmed when she dropped her hand onto the crook of his arm and said, "You're right, of course. It *is* safer for Ethan here. We'll stay."

Noah's home was a two-story log house with four bedrooms, three bathrooms, a large redwood deck and an extra

room downstairs that would have made a great family room.
Noah used it for an office.

Caroline went exploring after Noah shooed her out of the
kitchen while he fixed dinner. "Sure you don't want to come
with me, honey?" she asked Ethan again.

He shook his head slightly, his gaze glued on the television
screen. "No, thank you. I'd rather stay here."

Since their arrival at Noah's house, Ethan had sunk back
into a silent quicksand of apathy. Though anxious to coax him
out of his subdued mood, Caroline knew she would only make
matters worse by hovering over him.

So she left him in the living room while she snooped
through the rest of Noah's house on her own.

She wondered if this was where he'd lived with his wife
and daughter, or if he'd moved here since the accident that
had claimed their lives. The house seemed awfully big for one
person to live in alone. And it felt even emptier because there
really wasn't enough furniture to fill it. Though Noah kept the
place perfectly neat, Caroline could tell that creating a pleasant
home environment was down near the bottom of his priority
list.

The only bedroom that showed signs of occupancy was the
small one downstairs. Caroline ducked her head inside, then
couldn't resist tiptoeing into the room. The bed looked as if
it had been made in a hurry. A freshly ironed shirt was draped
over the back of a chair. There was a handful of scattered
change and a light patina of dust on the dresser top. Nothing
to give any clue about the personality of the man who slept
here.

The nightstand next to the bed held a lamp, a radio alarm
clock and an open book positioned face down to hold its place.
Aha! Finally some insight into Noah's character. Caroline
reached for the book. Noah struck her as the detective novel
type. No, maybe one of the classics. John Steinbeck?

She read the cover. *Advanced Techniques of Forensic Investigation*. Yawn. Well, it was certainly suitable reading for

someone who couldn't fall asleep at night. She wondered whether Noah suffered from that problem a lot. She wouldn't be a bit surprised, considering the personal tragedy he'd suffered as well as the awful things he saw every day in his work.

A sudden bang made her jump and whirl around. Wouldn't *that* be the ultimate in humiliation, to have Noah find her snooping around his bedroom? Luckily, the noise had come from elsewhere in the house. Caroline hastily replaced the book and got out of there.

She followed her nose toward the kitchen, where more banging of pots and pans and cupboard doors apparently heralded the final countdown toward dinner. Something smelled delicious.

When she detoured into the living room to fetch Ethan, it suddenly dawned on Caroline what was wrong with this house. During her entire self-guided tour, she hadn't seen any photographs, any feminine knickknacks, any child's fingerpainting—not one single memento of the years Noah had shared with his family.

How terribly sad, she thought. Here was further evidence that Noah had chosen to submerge his grief by stuffing all his memories away into some dark emotional attic.

But until he could face his grief head-on and work through it so that he wasn't afraid to be reminded of his lost loved ones, Noah would never be able to find love again.

That bothered Caroline more than it should have.

Noah had never got around to buying a dining-room table for this place, so they sat around the table in the kitchen.

"I can't claim to be the world's greatest chef, but I'm pretty sure this beats hospital food," he told Ethan with a wink as he ladled meatballs and tomato sauce over the spaghetti on the boy's plate.

"I'm sure it's delicious," Caroline said with a too-bright smile. "It certainly *smells* wonderful, anyway."

Noah had nearly had a panic attack in the supermarket earlier, while dredging his memory for what kids liked to eat. It had been a long time since he'd bought anything but microwave dinners. Thinking back to the days when knowing Molly's favorite foods had been second nature to him had caused such a severe ache in Noah's chest that he'd nearly abandoned his shopping cart and walked straight out of the supermarket.

He was pleased to see Ethan eating the spaghetti without objection, if not exactly with gusto.

"Mmm." Caroline was more than making up for Ethan's lack of enthusiasm. "This sauce is scrumptious. What's your secret recipe?"

Noah settled a napkin across his lap. Okay, so it was really a paper towel. Considering the distracted state he'd been in, it was no wonder he hadn't remembered *everything* he'd needed to buy.

He reached for a slice of garlic bread from the platter in the center of the table. "The recipe? Well, I'm not sure I should tell you, since it's a closely guarded secret that's been handed down in my family for generations." He curved the back of his hand to the side of his mouth and whispered, "The key ingredient is a can opener."

Caroline's eyes widened. She sipped the tail end of a spaghetti strand through her lips with a dainty slurp that aroused something beneath Noah's napkin. "This sauce comes out of a can?" she exclaimed. "My goodness, you'll have to tell me the brand so I can buy it after we get home."

Ethan dropped his fork with a clink.

"Won't that be nice, honey?"

Noah detected an overly eager note in her voice.

"We can make this delicious spaghetti ourselves when we go home to Baltimore," she continued.

Ethan propped his chin on his hand, picked up his fork and used it to push a meatball around his plate. "I don't wanna go to Baltimore," he mumbled.

Caroline bit her lip. "But Ethan, it's our home! It's where you were born, where you lived until—until—"

"I live *here*," he said, jabbing the meatball mercilessly. "In Eagle River. With my dad."

"Honey..." Caroline glanced helplessly at Noah. She looked about ready to cry.

"May I please be excused?" Ethan asked his plate.

Caroline crumpled her napkin and pressed it to her mouth. Hoping he wasn't overstepping his bounds, Noah said, "Sure, son."

Ethan scraped back his chair and disappeared in the direction of the living room. Caroline hesitated, then shoved back her chair, too.

"Wait." Noah laid his hand on her wrist. Her pulse fluttered in agitation beneath his fingers. "It's not my place, but I'm going to offer some free advice, anyway."

For a second or two he felt her delicate tendons stiffen with resistance. Then she sighed and scooted her chair back to the table. "Please, offer away," she said, dropping her wadded napkin beside her plate. "Obviously I need all the advice I can get, free or otherwise."

"Okay." He squeezed her wrist. "I think you've got to let Ethan take the lead here. Let him feel like he's at least partially in control of what happens to him. Right now he feels completely *out* of control. He's just lost his dad, he's lost part of his memory, and now he's found out his dad has been lying to him all along about you being dead."

Caroline drew in a shaky breath. "I could never understand why Ethan didn't call me once during all those years. He had our phone number memorized, and our address, too." Bitterness crept into her tone. "I should have figured out what Jeff must have told him, but it—it just never occurred to me that even a no-good skunk like Jeff was capable of such a monstrous lie."

Noah nodded. "If *you* feel this disillusioned, think how Ethan feels."

"Oh, God." She clenched her fist to her mouth. "He must feel torn in two."

"That's why you need to give him a measure of control.

Let him go get all his stuff tomorrow. Maybe the sight of familiar possessions will jog his memory, so that he remembers something that will lead to his father's killer.'' Noah stroked her arm reassuringly. ''That's another thing that'll make Ethan feel like he has some control.''

Caroline lowered her gaze to his hand. ''I guess the worst thing I could have done would be to whisk him back to Baltimore the second he got out of the hospital.''

''Ethan needs to feel he's got some control over his life. That he's not just a helpless victim of events.''

''You tried to tell me that from the first, but I didn't want to hear you.'' Caroline's mouth curved wistfully. She lifted her hand to the side of his face, catching Noah off guard. ''I'll bet you were a wonderful father.''

It took every last atom of his self-control not to leap away from her touch and recoil from the poignant images her words aroused. Frankly, he'd tried to steer clear of children ever since Beth and Molly died. That was one reason he'd been so opposed to taking Ethan and his mother under his wing.

At least Ethan was a boy, and twice as old as Molly had been when she died. Comparisons between the two weren't automatic. Still, it had been rough for Noah, getting back into the habit of seeing the world from a child's perspective.

The expression in Caroline's eyes made the touch of her hand feel even more intimate. ''How old was your little girl when she died?'' she asked softly.

''Four.'' Noah's voice sounded rusty. He cleared his throat and tried again. ''Four years, five months and twelve days old.'' At that moment it dawned on Noah that Molly would have been the same age as Ethan if she'd lived.

Suddenly he couldn't bear Caroline's tender touch, or the sympathy glistening in her eyes. They were too vivid reminders of what he'd lost, of what he could never get back again.

Noah's fingers still rested on the underside of her wrist, where her skin was as velvety-soft as rose petals. He removed his hand from her arm and pushed his chair back from the table. But even after he'd severed all physical contact between them, he could still feel the lingering caress of each one of her fingers branding his cheek.

He began to clear dishes with the speed of a busboy who had a long line of customers waiting for this table. "Guess I ought to show you to your room, so you can get some shut-eye. You must be completely worn out after today."

Caroline covered a yawn behind her hand and stood up. "Let me help you with these dishes first."

"No! I mean—" What *did* he mean? That he didn't want her helping him because it would only remind him of sharing chores with Beth? That he couldn't stand to be alone in the kitchen with her one minute longer than necessary, because what he really wanted was to sweep all the dishes to the floor with a crash so he could make wild crazy love to her on top of the table till it was reduced to a broken pile of kindling?

Noah whipped open the freezer door and pretended to search for something inside, just to give himself an excuse for a cold blast of air in his face.

He closed the freezer and turned to find Caroline studying him with a wary expression. He didn't blame her. He wasn't just acting like a candidate for the psychiatric ward, he felt like one.

"I'll do cleanup tonight, you do it tomorrow," he said. That sounded like a reasonable compromise, and one that would keep them in separate parts of the house for a while. By tomorrow night, he intended to uncover some new line of investigation that would keep him away from home until bedtime, at least.

"I should do cleanup tonight," Caroline protested. "After all, you did the cooking."

Noah felt like the walls were closing in on him. He'd known this whole arrangement was going to be a disaster! His privacy was his most cherished possession, along with the ability to channel all his emotions into work. Now he was trapped under the same roof with a kid who kept tugging at his heartstrings and a gorgeous mom whose compassionate green eyes and sleek, sexy curves kept tugging at...other parts of his anatomy.

She was beautiful, blond...and bad news. And for the time being she was Noah's responsibility.

"How about if I wash and you dry?" he suggested. No use fighting the inevitable.

"Just hand me a dish towel," she replied with enthusiasm.

Maybe Noah couldn't fight the inevitable. But he damn well intended to fight the feelings Caroline Tate and her son had dragged out of cold storage.

If only she wouldn't stand so close while they were doing the dishes.

Chapter 4

It was probably the silence that woke her. Back home in the Baltimore suburbs, Caroline was used to hearing the distant whoosh of traffic all night long, as well as the occasional wailing siren. Neighbors got home late or left for work early, slamming their doors, revving their car engines.

Lying in the master bedroom in Noah Garrett's house, deep in the northern California woods, Caroline couldn't hear a sound. Well, correction. If she strained her ears she could hear a couple of birds waking up outside the half-open window.

The whisper of a breeze carried the scent of pine through the curtains along with the first pearl gray light of dawn. Caroline groped for her watch on the nightstand. The master bedroom wasn't equipped with a clock. She pressed a button and squinted blearily at the illuminated watch face. Not even six yet. Obviously her internal alarm clock was still set on East Coast time.

She fluffed up her pillow and settled back to review yesterday's incredible events. A tide of joy and amazement welled up inside her till she could barely contain it without weeping.

She finally had Ethan back! Her sweet darling boy, safe and sound despite some emotional damage.

I can fix that, Caroline vowed fiercely. Ethan would get over Jeff's death, he would put those three lost years behind him and return to loving her as his mother again. Then it would be just the two of them, happy and complete in their own little family from now on.

It's not going to be that easy, cautioned a voice inside her head. For some reason the voice sounded like Noah Garrett's.

Caroline rolled onto her stomach and pulled the pillow over her head. Noah Garrett. What did *he* know, anyway? Holding himself aloof from life, hiding away out here in the wilderness...all he knew about the workings of the human heart was what he'd read in a police manual.

Instantly Caroline felt ashamed. The man was struggling to survive the kind of unspeakable tragedy most people could only imagine. Except they *couldn't* imagine it, not unless they'd been through it themselves. Who was Caroline to sit in judgment of Noah? He was dealing with his loss the best way he knew how. If that meant refusing to put his heart at risk again, why should it bother her?

"It doesn't," she said, her voice muffled by the pillow. He was only going to be part of her life for a few more days, a week at most. It would be a waste of time to make Noah Garrett's salvation her own personal project.

So why couldn't she stop thinking about him and go back to sleep?

Caroline threw back the covers in frustration. A minute later she leaped out of bed and hurried across the room, possessed by a sudden urgent need to check on Ethan. What if yesterday had all been a dream? What if Jeff wasn't really dead, if he'd come back and stolen Ethan during the night? What if Jeff's killer had somehow found Ethan, and—

Caroline gasped. Just down the hall, a tall figure loomed in the shadows outside the door to Ethan's bedroom, watching him sleep.

As she rushed forward, the figure turned in response to her

startled sound. In the murky light she recognized Noah. "Oh," she whispered, pulling up short. "My gosh, you scared me!" She splayed a hand over her thudding heart.

Noah stepped away from the door before replying. "Sorry about that." The clean smell of soap mingled with the tantalizing fragrance of bay rum. Up close Caroline could see his hair was damp from the shower. He was wearing the white shirt she'd seen hanging in his room last night, the collar unbuttoned. "I didn't expect you to be up so early." Noah's low voice rumbled along her nerve endings, doing strange things to her skin temperature. She'd been shivering ever since she'd got out of bed, but all of a sudden she felt flushed. Feverish. As if she wanted to peel off her nightgown and let the darkness cool her skin.

She wondered what Noah's reaction would be if she did. He'd probably arrest her for indecent exposure.

"I've got coffee going downstairs," he said. "Want some?"

"I'd *love* some," Caroline replied. "Just let me go back and put on my—oops, that's right. I didn't have room to pack a robe in my carry-on bag."

Noah guessed this was where he was supposed to offer her Beth's robe, or maybe his own. Except that he'd given away Beth's robe along with the rest of her and Molly's clothes. And he wasn't about to let Caroline permeate *his* robe with her warm fragrance, so that whenever he wore it he would be aroused by the memory of her sexy bare limbs enveloped by the same fabric that was touching him.

"It's kind of cool in the mornings," he said, hoping she would take the hint and put on a sweater or something.

"I'm not cold at all," she said. "Lead me to that coffee."

As he led the way down to the kitchen, Noah kicked himself for coming upstairs at all. He rarely did. After the accident he'd been in such a rush to move to a place without memories that he'd bought the first house that met his requirement of privacy, even though it was much too large for one person.

He found it convenient to confine his living space to the first floor.

The only people who ever stayed upstairs were his parents. They were the ones who'd insisted on buying a few furnishings for the master bedroom, so that Noah didn't have to give up his bed and sleep on the couch during their once-a-year visits.

In the devastating wake of the accident, Noah had given away virtually all the contents of the house he'd shared with his wife and child. At the very last second, however, he couldn't bring himself to part with Molly's bed. Once he'd moved here, though, he'd stored it in an upstairs bedroom, behind a closed door where he wouldn't have to see it.

Then last night, Ethan had dug in his heels at Caroline's suggestion they share the same room.

"But I have my own room at my *dad's* house," he'd told her indignantly.

Perhaps heeding Noah's warning to allow Ethan some control, Caroline had caved in immediately. Or maybe she just couldn't stand to be compared unfavorably to Jeff.

So Ethan had spent the night in Molly's bed. And this morning, some mysterious impulse Noah hadn't been able either to understand or resist had dragged him upstairs to watch another child sleep where his little girl used to.

Once again he cursed the circumstances that had lodged Caroline Tate and her son under his roof to torment him with all these unwelcome feelings.

And no feeling was more unwelcome than the bolt of desire that leaped through Noah when he got a good look at Caroline under the bright kitchen light. Without the enamel clip holding back her hair, her blond mane spilled over her shoulders like waves of silk, framing her face in wisps of gold. With her skin scrubbed free of makeup, she looked young enough to be Ethan's big sister instead of his mom.

But old enough to know how to drive a man wild in bed. With her feet bare, her hair all disheveled, her luscious green eyes still sultry-lidded with sleep, she looked like she'd just awakened from a night of long, slow, satisfying passion.

Not that Noah was ever going to find out whether this speculation was accurate. He shoved a mug of coffee into her hand, averting his eyes from her flimsy nightgown and trying to avoid scorching his fingers on hers.

"Mmm." She leaned back against the counter and sniffed the strong, aromatic steam. "Dark roast. My favorite." She took a sip without waiting for it to cool, then closed her eyes briefly as if to savor it. "I would have figured you for an instant-coffee kind of guy."

"Nope. Gourmet coffee, ground fresh from the beans. My one vice."

A mysterious smile touched her mouth. "I'll bet." She took another sip, smacking her lips in assessment. "French Roast?" She picked up the bag of coffee beans that sat on the counter next to the grinder.

"Not bad." As she checked the label, Noah hoisted his mug in salute. "You must be a coffee aficionado yourself."

She lifted one bare shoulder in a modest shrug. "In my business you get pretty good at telling different flavors apart."

Noah tried not to notice how the outline of her breast moved beneath the thin cotton fabric. Hell, *she* was the one who'd insisted on coming down here half naked, wasn't she? The nights must be pretty warm in Baltimore for her to wear such a skimpy nightgown. Not that it was some kind of lacy peek-aboo negligee or anything. Noah couldn't actually see anything he shouldn't.

No, it was what he *couldn't* see that was driving him crazy.

He forced himself to concentrate on the conversation instead of her tantalizing body. "You, uh, own some kind of food company, is that right?" He'd heard mention of it at some point during his investigation, but couldn't recall the details. Other than she was quite successful.

"Gourmet soup mixes." A spark of animation lit up her face. Clearly she enjoyed her work. "All-natural ingredients, all in one convenient package. Just add water."

"Would I have heard of them?" Noah's idea of convenience was an entire *meal* in one package. Still, anything you just had to add water to might have caught his attention.

"Probably not. They're mainly marketed on the East Coast." She crossed her fingers. "So far, anyway. They're called Souper Naturals. Souper, like in soup?"

"Gotcha." Noah nodded. Clever.

She mimed an advertising banner in the air. "'For the taste that's out of this world,'" she intoned in an exaggerated radio announcer's voice. Then she laughed sheepishly. "Pretty corny, huh?"

"But effective, I'll bet." She had the most incredible smile he'd ever seen.

"I do pretty well." A shadow momentarily dimmed her enthusiasm. "Maybe a little *too* well at one time." She swirled her coffee around, studying its depths.

"What do you mean?"

"Oh, nothing." She glanced up at Noah with a dismissive flip of her hand. "For a long time I blamed my success for breaking up my marriage. But eventually I realized it was only one small part of the problem." She made a moue of distaste. "No need to go into all that."

Except now she'd roused Noah's curiosity. "Actually, if you wouldn't mind talking about it, some background on your ex-husband might prove useful."

Doubt flickered in her eyes. "I don't see how. It's all ancient history. Besides, if Jeff was killed by a robber..."

"We don't know that for sure. Someone might have tried to make it *look* like a robbery." Why would a robber, for example, bother locking the safe again after forcing Jeff to open it? It couldn't have been to hide evidence of his crime, not when he'd left his mortally injured victim lying there in plain sight. Then there was that scruffy-looking stranger Ethan had seen arguing with his father...

"If you can give me some insight into Jeff's character and his past," Noah told Caroline, "it might shed some light on who might have wanted him dead." In truth, Noah considered it highly unlikely that Jeff Tate's death had anything to do with his life back in Baltimore or his marriage to Caroline. Noah might claim he was just being thorough, but he was too honest to pretend to himself that his motives were quite that noble.

Not that he was jealous or anything. Just…curious. How had a class act like Caroline Tate ever hooked up with a louse like her ex-husband?

Noah pulled out a chair for her, allowing his fingertips to brush her shoulder as she sat down. "More coffee?"

"All right."

Noah poured them both another cup and sat down across the pine table from her. "I take it your business put some kind of strain on your marriage?"

"You could say that." She blew a stream of air through her lips, stirring fine wisps of hair at her temples. "Although the business wasn't a problem until it grew profitable. As long as it stayed merely a hobby, Jeff didn't object to it."

Noah's opinion of Jeff Tate, already at basement level, sank even lower. "He resented your success."

"Resented…and feared, maybe. Jeff…" She tunneled her fingers distractedly through her hair. "Jeff was terribly insecure. He'd grown up trying to please a highly successful father who was impossible to please."

"And his mother?"

"She died when Jeff was a child. I see now that her death left him with a terrible fear of abandonment." Caroline took a sip of coffee, then twisted her mouth as if it had suddenly gone bitter. "I can't believe I'm making excuses for him, but after years of struggling to understand, I'm convinced that Jeff's deep-rooted fear of losing people he loved explains why he stole Ethan."

Did that mean Caroline had balked at allowing her ex-husband visitation with their son? Somehow Noah couldn't believe that.

As if Caroline had read his mind she said, "Even after Jeff and I split up, I never, ever tried to stand in the way of his relationship with Ethan. Ethan loved Jeff.'' She spread her hands, palms up. ''How could I deny my son contact with his own father?''

Which only made Jeff's actions even more inexcusable, as far as Noah was concerned. ''Why'd he take Ethan, then?''

Caroline crossed one shapely leg over the other, jiggling her bare foot in agitation. Though it was hardly relevant to his investigation, Noah took note that her toenails were painted a creamy pale pink, like the inside of a seashell. ''There was…an unfortunate confluence of events,'' she said. Her breasts rose and fell with a weary sigh. ''First, I need to explain about Jeff's father.''

''Go ahead.''

She used her thumbnail to trace the circumference of a pine knot in the surface of the table. ''Randolph Tate is a self-made millionaire. As a young man he started a small furniture business and over the years built it up into the largest manufacturer of hotel furniture east of the Mississippi.'' She dug her nail into the wood. ''My former father-in-law is also a cold, ruthless, self-centered bastard who was never satisfied with anything his son ever did.'' She pursed her lips. ''I'll admit that Jeff wasn't exactly an A student in school, and he definitely didn't inherit his father's head for business. But even his best efforts never earned more than a scornful lecture from Randolph Tate.''

She folded one hand atop the other as if forcing both of them to keep still. ''Jeff started working for his father right out of college, but Randolph never gave him any real authority or responsibility. Then, not long before our marriage broke up, Randolph had a heart attack. During his recovery he was forced to turn the day-to-day management of the company over to Jeff.'' Caroline shook her head sadly. ''Jeff was completely out of his league. Finally he had a chance to earn his father's respect, but all he succeeded in doing was practically running the business into the ground.''

Her face contained an unmistakable glimmer of sympathy.

Noah doubted he would have been so charitable in her position.

"When Randolph discovered Jeff had driven his company to the verge of bankruptcy, he hit the roof. It's amazing he didn't have another heart attack. Instead he cursed and screamed at Jeff, fired him, then disowned him completely." Caroline drummed her fingers on the tabletop. "Randolph was only too happy to tell me all this the day Ethan disappeared. When I rushed over there to find out if he knew why Jeff hadn't brought Ethan home from his visit."

Noah rubbed his jaw. "So you think being disowned by his father is what prompted Jeff to make off with Ethan?"

Caroline looked unhappy. "Maybe that wouldn't have been sufficient all by itself. But the day Randolph disowned Jeff was coincidentally the same day our divorce became final."

"Ah." Now it all made a terrible kind of sense. "So, in effect," Noah said slowly, "Jeff lost both his father and his wife on the same day."

Caroline sighed. "Ethan was the one person who still loved him. I suppose Jeff was panic-stricken about losing his son as well, even though that never would have happened."

Panic-stricken? That was a pretty calm state of mind compared to what Caroline must have felt, as the terrible truth of what Jeff had done had gradually dawned on her. Noah was all too well acquainted with what it felt like, that soul-searing terror that you were never going to see your child again.

Molly, he thought.

He shoved back his chair with more force than he'd intended. He could feel Caroline's startled gaze tracking him across the kitchen.

He carefully set his empty coffee mug in the sink. "Make yourself at home while I'm gone," he said, looking out the window so he didn't have to look at her. "I'll probably be working till pretty late, so—"

He was interrupted by a bone-chilling wail from somewhere overhead. Caroline's chair crashed into the cabinets as she catapulted out of it and bolted from the kitchen.

Noah followed two steps behind.

"What was your bad dream about, sweetie?" Caroline framed Ethan's face tenderly between her hands, using her thumbs to gently swipe the tears from his cheeks.

His wet lashes sparkled. "I can't...remember." He rubbed his freckled nose with his pajama sleeve. "Something... scary."

Scary, indeed. What could be more frightening than what Ethan had been through the last couple of days? Caroline hugged him to her breast again, meeting Noah's eyes over the top of her son's tousled blond head. Noah hovered in the door to the hall, allowing them a measure of privacy, yet standing by in case he was needed.

Caroline didn't want to admit to herself how glad she was he was there.

"Can I get you a drink of water, son?" he asked.

Ethan shook his head and mumbled something into the front of Caroline's nightgown. She smoothed down the small haystack of his hair. Her heartbeat was finally returning to normal after her mad dash up the stairs, propelled by a rush of terror that she would find Jeff's killer bent over Ethan's bed.

Ethan mumbled something else.

"What, honey?" She bracketed her hands on his shoulders to position him where she could see him.

Ethan sniffled. He spoke in a tiny voice, sounding as if he were about to cry again. "Mommy, how come Dad said you were dead?"

Caroline forced herself not to flinch. All at once she felt like crying herself. She exchanged another look with Noah. *What am I supposed to say?* she telegraphed him silently.

If he sent a return message, Caroline didn't receive it. But what she knew unmistakably was that he sympathized with her.

She took a deep breath. Though her own illusions about Jeff had been shattered years ago, she intended to preserve Ethan's if she could.

But she wasn't going to lie to him, either.

"I think your dad…wanted to have you all to himself. Because he loved you so much." Inside her head Caroline cursed her ex-husband for putting her in the ludicrous position of defending the indefensible thing he'd done. "I guess he told you I was dead so you wouldn't try to call me or send me a letter, because he was afraid I'd come and get you and then he might never see you again."

Ethan blinked. Confusion filled his big brown eyes. "How come he might never see me again?"

Caroline met his gaze without wavering. "Ethan, your dad shouldn't have taken you away from me. He was afraid if I found you, he might go to jail, or a judge might tell him he couldn't see you anymore."

Ethan turned even paler. "Dad might have gone to *jail?*"

"Well…probably not." Jeff must have known damn well she wouldn't press charges for Ethan's sake. "But he was afraid to take the chance of being separated from you."

Caroline's facial muscles felt stiff and unnatural, and there was a bad taste on her tongue. She felt as if she'd just told a huge lie to her son. But if hiding her resentment of Jeff was a deception, it was one she would just have to commit. When Ethan grew up he could judge his father's actions for himself.

She watched him closely while he processed this information. Clearly he was struggling. "It made me awful sad," he said finally. "When Dad told me you died and that's why I was going to live with him from now on."

Caroline fought to keep the anger and the anguish from her face.

"I guess Dad didn't know it would make me so sad," Ethan said, plucking at the sheet. "Otherwise he wouldn't have told me that."

"Your father would never do anything to hurt you," Caroline said. To her own ears her voice sounded strained and false. Luckily Ethan seemed to accept her assurance at face value.

"What about my stuff?" he asked. "Can we go get it right now?"

Caroline shot a glance at Noah. She'd forgotten his promise to drive them to Jeff's house to retrieve Ethan's belongings. Judging by the expression on his face, Noah had forgotten, too.

"Honey, Sergeant Garrett has lots of important things to do today," she explained. "We might have to wait till—"

"Sure, we can go get your stuff." Noah pushed himself away from the door frame. "I've got one or two bad guys to capture today, but I can drive you over there this evening. How's that?"

"Bad guys?" Ethan perked up. "You mean robbers and murderers and stuff?"

"Oh, I'm after some real mean desperados," Noah told him. "But I plan to have 'em all behind bars by sundown, so after dinner we can go pick up your stuff. That okay with you?"

"Sure." Ethan studied Noah with new respect. Caroline couldn't help making a wistful comparison between the man she'd married and this one. She wished she could have given her son a hero for a father, instead of a weasel. How differently all their lives would have turned out.

But Noah had his own destiny. She had hers. Their two lives were only intersecting briefly before they headed off in entirely different directions.

Useless to imagine how things might have turned out if their paths had crossed years earlier. Now Caroline no longer wanted a man in her life. And Noah's heart was too filled with sorrow to make room for anyone else.

It was too late now. For both of them.

"There goes Harland Crockett," Noah's secretary called back to him. "Didn't you say you wanted to talk to him again?"

From her desk next to the front window of the small brick sheriff's substation, Ruby Salazar had a panoramic view of

Main Street. Not much happened in downtown Eagle River that escaped Ruby's notice while she was on the job.

Noah grabbed his sport coat from the back of his chair, even though the thermometer outside must be pushing eighty. It was important to keep up appearances, after all. He scooped his notepad off his desk and headed out of his office.

"Thanks, Ruby." Harland Crockett owned the gas station Jeff Tate had managed. Noah had talked to him right after the murder, when Harland had verified that the contents of both the safe and cash register were missing. But Noah had since thought up a few more questions for Jeff Tate's employer. "Which way'd he go?"

Ruby pointed one crimson-lacquered nail across the street without taking her eyes off the computer screen in front of her. "Just walked into the diner." Noah had long ago decided his secretary must have some kind of superhuman peripheral vision, the way she could keep tabs on the outside world while focused so intently on her work. He'd never once caught her staring out the window.

"Did you send out those sketch-artist drawings in the Tate case?" he asked.

"First thing this morning, just like you asked." The sketch of the man Ethan had seen arguing with his father would now be in the hands of all law-enforcement agencies in the northern part of the state. Noah had already had one of his deputies post a bunch of them around town yesterday.

He didn't miss the mild reproof in Ruby's tone. He should have known she would carry out his instructions as promptly and efficiently as always. But something about this current case was making him edgier than usual.

"I'll be over at the diner," he said. "Guess I might as well grab a bite to eat, long as I'm there." He paused with his hand on the door. "Can I bring something back for you?" he offered, hoping to smooth her ruffled feathers.

Ruby peered at him over the gaudy red frames of the bifocals that were always either perched on the end of her nose or dangling from her neck on a gold chain. Ruby's personal

style philosophy was to make sure everything about her lives
up to her name. Hair, nails, clothing…all red. "Tuna salad,"
she said finally, deciding to let Noah make it up to her. "On
toasted whole wheat. Lettuce, no onion. With an extra pickle."

"Got it," Noah said, hoping he did. "Back in a flash."

He waited for old Mrs. Quimby's huge gas-guzzling sedan
to lumber past at approximately seven miles an hour, then
crossed the street to the Forty-Niner Diner. Eagle River's mining heyday had actually taken place a quarter of a century
after the forty-niners had arrived farther south for California's
more famous gold rush. But some enterprising predecessor of
Irene Johnson, the diner's current owner, had chosen to cap-
italize on the romantic lure of that earlier historical period.

From behind the lunch counter Irene greeted him with the
kind of embarrassed, too-bright smile you give someone
you've just been discussing behind his back. "Hey, Noah,"
she called out as the screen door banged shut behind him.

Instantly, every head in the crowded café swiveled in his
direction. The last murder in Eagle River had taken place a
good thirty years ago. Jeff Tate's killing was the biggest thing
to happen in these parts since the accident that had taken
Beth's and Molly's lives.

Well, at least now people would have something else to talk
about. Curiosity about Noah's current case was running high.
Just look how everyone in the diner was gawking at him as if
they expected him to yell "Aha!" and point out the murderer
any second.

"How 'bout a burger and fries, Irene?" Noah spied Harland
Crockett sitting in a booth near the back and started in his
direction. "Maybe a lemonade, too."

"Coming right up." Irene whipped a pencil from her tightly
permed gray curls and flipped to a blank page on her order
pad.

Noah pulled up short with a snap of his fingers. "Oh, and
Ruby wants a tuna sandwich."

"Whole wheat toast, no onion, lettuce and extra pickle?"

"Uh…" He had to think for a minute. "Yeah."

Irene ripped off the order and impaled it on the revolving metal rack that hung in front of the kitchen. By the time Noah reached Harland's booth, Irene was hot on his heels with a fresh pot of coffee. "Refill, Harland?"

The gas station owner glanced up in surprise. "I'm drinking iced tea, Irene."

"Hmm? Oh!" She smacked her forehead. "Silly me. How 'bout you, Noah? You want some coffee?" Clearly she was dying to hang around and see what kind of crumbs she could pick up pertaining to his investigation.

"Just the lemonade, thanks." Noah had had enough trouble sleeping last night. For the rest of today he was swearing off caffeine. Even though that hadn't been the cause of his insomnia.

He shoved aside the stimulating thought of Caroline Tate and waited for Irene to scurry off, disappointed, before he spoke to Harland. "Mind if I join you?"

"Sit down." Harland gestured at the empty seat across from him. "You figure out yet who stole my money?" He shoveled some meat loaf and mashed potatoes into his mouth.

Clearly the loss of his employee's life weighed less heavily on Harland's mind than the loss of his cold, hard cash. Harland owned a chain of gas stations dotted throughout Tamarack County as well as the surrounding ones. He was locally renowned in equal measure for his shrewd business dealings, his terrible toupee, and his hotheadedness. During Harland's younger days Grady Reeves had had to haul him in on more than one occasion for public brawling.

It occurred to Noah there was an outside chance Harland Crockett might know more about Jeff Tate's death than he'd claimed.

He pulled his notepad from his jacket pocket. "You ever hear Jeff Tate arguing with anyone?"

"Jeff *who?*" Harland answered with his mouth full. "Oh, you mean Tucker." The alias Jeff and Ethan had lived under. Noah wondered how Tate had explained *that* to his son.

"Arguing?" Harland repeated. "You mean like with a customer? Nah. I'd've canned his sorry butt if he had."

"What about with anyone else? Somebody who might have come around the station panhandling, for instance."

Harland snorted. "I might have given him that raise he wanted, if I'd ever heard of him shooing off panhandlers."

Noah looked up from his notes. "Jeff asked for a raise?"

"If you can believe that." Harland burped. "I mean, the guy was competent enough to pump gas, but I had to constantly get on his case to keep his paperwork up to date. Even then he'd screw up the numbers half the time."

"When did he ask for a raise?"

Harland pried a thumbnail between his teeth, chasing after a particle of food he'd missed. "Coupla days before he got killed."

Noah tapped his pencil thoughtfully. "He say why he wanted a raise?"

Harland shrugged. "He gave me some song and dance about 'unexpected expenses.' Didn't make any difference. I coulda hired any high-school kid to replace him, and he knew it."

"He get mad? Try to argue about it?"

Harland peered at Noah with sudden alertness. "Oho, wait just a second now! You accusing *me* of something?"

"Not at all," Noah replied blandly. "Just routine inquiries, that's all."

"Huh." Harland continued to regard him suspiciously as he slid out of the booth. "Well then, you can just write down in your notebook there that I did *not* whack Tucker on the head and then rob my own gas station." He dug into his pocket and flung just enough coins on the table to leave a stingy tip for Irene. "Maybe you oughtta concentrate on finding out who *did*, instead of harassing innocent citizens." He stormed out of the diner in a huff, leaving a sea of turning heads in his wake.

Noah swallowed a sigh just as Irene arrived and plopped a plate of food down in front of him. "Say, you hear anything more about that sweet little boy?'' she asked. ''Ethan? He get his memory back yet?''

''I, uh, I'm not up-to-date on his condition,'' Noah replied vaguely. For one worried second he'd thought Irene—and by extension everyone else in town—knew that Ethan and his mother were staying out at his place. Then he realized Irene was probably just pumping him for info because she hadn't been able to wheedle gossip out of anyone who worked at the hospital.

Still, her question stirred uneasiness in the pit of Noah's stomach. He'd assured Caroline that she and Ethan would be safe at his place. But would they?

''Sorry to trouble you, Irene,'' he said, sliding out of the booth, ''but I just remembered something I've gotta do. Can I get this food to go?''

Irene rolled her eyes with a put-upon expression. Whether it was because of the extra work he was creating for her or because he was so closemouthed about the case, Noah couldn't tell.

Either way, Irene seemed to move with uncharacteristic slowness while she wrapped up his food. Or maybe it just felt that way to Noah because he was in such a hurry. He wasn't sure why, but all at once an urgent need was prodding him to check on Caroline and her son, to make sure they were safe.

What if the wrong person *did* know where they were staying?

Noah was halfway home before he remembered he'd forgotten to bring Ruby her sandwich. Swell. It was barely noon, and already he had half the town mad at him.

Chapter 5

Caroline's pulse slammed into high gear at the sound of crunching gravel. Who could be coming up Noah's driveway? She stepped quickly from the stove to the sink and peeked cautiously through the checked curtains.

Her knees went weak at the reassuring sight of Noah's Jeep. She hadn't expected him till dinner. Had he come to tell her he'd caught Jeff's killer already, that she and Ethan could go home?

The possibility should have thrilled her. But for some reason, the prospect of going back to Baltimore right away didn't excite Caroline as much as she would have expected. No doubt because she'd accepted the idea that Ethan needed a few days to adjust to her again before she whisked him away from Eagle River.

As she watched Noah get out of his car, she told herself the fluttery feeling in her chest was due to relief, that was all. Relief it was him, and not someone coming after her son.

Noah strode briskly toward the back door, moving with an intentness of purpose that brought to mind the barely restrained eagerness of a man on his way to meet his lover. For a second Caroline pictured herself in that role—how her heart would leap with gladness to see him, how she would throw her arms around his neck in joyful welcome....

Stop it, she warned herself. Even if Noah were interested in her, she'd vowed never to get tangled up in that kind of reckless, romantic nonsense again. Her child was the only person on earth who mattered to her. She wasn't going to allow anyone else to distract her from the main focus of her life.

It troubled her, though, how easy it was to imagine Noah and herself as lovers.

The brooding lines of tension bracketing Noah's mouth were swept away by a lopsided smile when he came through the back door and caught sight of Caroline. "Hello."

Amazing how the sound of his voice slipped past her defenses, igniting a faint glow of warmth near her heart. His out-of-practice smile touched some primitive yearning inside her.

But what had he been looking so worried about just now?

All at once Caroline didn't quite know what to do with her arms. She crossed them, uncrossed them, linked her hands behind her back. For Pete's sake, he's not here to pick you up for the prom, she scolded herself. Quit feeling so jittery.

"I wasn't expecting you home so soon." Good heavens, that came out sounding like she was his wife or something! "I mean, I thought you wouldn't be back until dinnertime," she said quickly. "Is anything wrong?"

Noah wasn't sure how to answer her. *Just happened to be in the neighborhood and thought I'd stop by to check on you?* Hardly. This house wasn't on the way to anywhere, which was what Noah liked about it.

But he wasn't about to tell her the truth, either. *I got this weird feeling all of a sudden that you might be in danger, so I drove out here as fast as I could to make sure you were safe.*

Now that he saw his fears were unfounded, Noah was irritated with himself for overreacting. Not to mention irritated by how much the thought of something happening to her had bothered him. Caroline Tate and her son were a murder case to him, nothing more.

At least, that's what he kept trying to tell himself.

"I...just wanted to make sure you were getting settled in okay, to see if there was anything you wanted me to pick up for you in town."

She glanced at the wall-mounted phone next to the refrigerator. Lame, Garrett. Truly lame. "Gee, I can't think of anything we need," she said, "except that Ethan keeps asking about getting his things from Jeff's house."

"We'll go tonight." Noah moved farther into the kitchen, enticed by a delicious aroma. "I figure it's best to go over there after dark, so there's less chance of anyone spotting the two of you." He lifted the lid from the pot on the stove. "Soup? Mmm, smells good."

"Would you like some? Ethan and I were just about to eat, but I'm sure there's enough for three." She reached into the cupboard and brought out another bowl.

Noah thought of his congealing burger and fries still out in the car. "Sure," he said. "Sounds great."

"I made sandwiches, too." A plate of them sat on the counter, neatly cut into quarters. All that was missing were those toothpicks with the cellophane frills on the ends. Although Noah's mismatched collection of dishes and utensils was all Caroline had had to work with, she'd managed to set the table so it looked like something out of a magazine. For a centerpiece she'd stuck a cheerful bouquet of wildflowers into a glass jar.

Even though Noah knew she hadn't gone to all this trouble for him, he felt oddly touched, anyway.

"Ethan," she called. "Time to wash up for lunch."

Noah guessed that included him, too. He shed his jacket and draped it over the back of a chair. "How's he doing?" he asked.

"About as well as can be expected, I suppose." The worried look marring Caroline's smooth features obviously wasn't directed at the pot of soup she was stirring. "Though I don't really know what to expect. That's part of the problem."

"It's a tough situation, that's for sure." Noah picked up the plastic bottle of dish soap next to the sink and squirted some onto his hands.

"Ethan spent most of the morning moping in front of the TV." Caroline began to ladle soup into bowls. She was dressed more casually today than yesterday, wearing a mint green cotton blouse over tan slacks. Her long golden hair was woven into some kind of fancy braid down her back. "I did persuade him to go outside and pick some flowers for me, but he's awfully uncommunicative. I can hardly get three words in a row out of him."

Noah sudsed his hands beneath the running water. "Give him time, Caroline. He'll be all right."

Caroline. As soon as he said it, Noah was pretty sure he'd never directly addressed her by her first name before. At least he couldn't recall the melodic lilt of it in his ears, or the seductive taste of it on his tongue.

Caroline.

He shut off the faucet with an abrupt jerk. If only he could shut off his unnerving attraction for her the same way.

"Have you learned anything more about Jeff's..." She hesitated. No doubt she'd been about to say something like "killer." But with Ethan nearby, she tactfully reworded her question so he wouldn't accidentally overhear that his father had been brutally murdered. "About how Jeff died?" she finished.

Professional ethics and personal inclination cautioned Noah against revealing too much. The only person outside law enforcement whom he'd ever discussed his cases with had been Beth. On top of that, Caroline was actually involved in the investigation as the mother of an important witness.

Still, talking about the case would at least keep his mind off more dangerous subjects. Like what might happen if he backed Caroline up against the counter, teased her braid loose with his fingers and buried his lips in those soft ribbons of shimmering gold.

Noah cleared his throat. "Seems like Jeff might have been hard up for money," he said, wrestling his attention back to the investigation.

Caroline emitted a laugh devoid of humor. "Well, that would have been par for the course." She set the sandwiches on the table. "I doubt it has any bearing on his death, though. If financial hot water was going to be Jeff's undoing, he would have drowned in it long ago." She went to the door and called Ethan again.

"You could be right." Noah helped her carry soup bowls to the table. "He told his boss shortly before he died that he'd encountered some unexpected expenses. Asked for a raise."

Caroline arched her brows. "Did he get it?"

"No." Picturing Harland Crockett's response, Noah could almost feel sorry for the guy.

"Maybe he was just making up some hard-luck story so his boss would be more sympathetic."

"Maybe."

"But you don't think so."

Noah himself couldn't quite put a finger on why he suspected there was more to Jeff's death than the simple robbery it appeared to be on the surface. "Call it instinct, I guess. But people generally get killed for one of two reasons. Love or money." He recalled all those avid, curious eyes in the diner, tracking him like radar. "And believe me, if your ex-husband had had a secret girlfriend, a dozen people would have told me about her by now."

Caroline tapped her fingers on her chin. "Well, being killed by a robber is being killed for money, isn't it?"

"Probably that's exactly what happened." It was hard to explain how years of investigative experience gave you a feeling about certain cases. Call it a hunch. But Jeff Tate had been a man with a big secret. A fugitive from the law. And he'd apparently needed money all of a sudden. Was it mere coincidence that he'd fallen victim to a violent crime?

There were a number of aspects to this case that got under
Noah's collar and made him itch. Not all of them were related
to the beautiful blond mom who'd magically made his bleak
bachelor's kitchen feel homey.

"There's something else I wanted to discuss with you," he
said cautiously. "Have you given any thought to...funeral arrangements?"

Caroline's lips parted in surprise. "You mean for Jeff?"

Noah nodded. Clearly the idea hadn't even occurred to her.

"Frankly, no." She rubbed her temples. "What with finding Ethan again and then having to worry about his safety, I
can't say I've given much thought to any...um...arrange-
ments."

"Someone needs to give instructions to the funeral home."

"But I'm not his wife anymore!" Then remorse filtered
over her expression. She sighed. "But I guess I'm still the
logical person to make decisions, aren't I?"

"What about Jeff's father?"

"Oh, God. I haven't even told Randolph about Jeff yet."
Two bright spots of color flamed in her cheeks. "I haven't
spoken to him in years, not since he flat-out refused to help
me look for Ethan." Caroline twisted her hands together.
"Randolph never showed one ounce of affection for Jeff, but
still, Jeff was his son. I imagine the news of his death will
come as an awful blow."

Although he'd seen similar screwed-up relationships time
and again in his job, Noah still couldn't comprehend how such
an unbridgeable chasm could grow between a parent and child.
Randolph Tate had obviously never appreciated how blessed
he'd been. Though his son's early death was tragic, at least
Randolph Tate had seen his child reach adulthood. That was
something Noah would never experience.

*But Randolph Tate never knew what it was to love a child
and be loved in return. So which one of us is luckier?*

The question struck Noah with the stunning force of a lightning bolt. Lucky? *Him?* It was the first time since the accident
he'd ever applied that adjective to himself. The unexpected

adjustment in perspective set his head spinning, as if the foundations of the universe had shifted.

But he *had* been lucky, hadn't he, to have had Beth and Molly in his life? Even though their time together had been far too short.

"I'll call Randolph today," Caroline said, not looking too happy about it. "He'll probably agree to have Jeff brought back to Baltimore and buried next to his mother."

She whisked away her troubled expression the moment Ethan finally shuffled into the kitchen. "I was about to send out a search party," she told him, ruffling his hair. "Look, Sergeant Garrett's here to have lunch with us."

Ethan's defeated posture straightened a little. "Hey, Sergeant."

Noah pulled out a chair for Caroline. "How're you doing, Ethan?"

"Okay, I guess." Ethan climbed into a chair. "Didja catch that guy that was arguing with my dad?" There was no mistaking the hopeful eagerness in his voice.

Noah's fingers somehow brushed against Caroline's shoulders as she sat down. He felt her stiffen—not in response to his touch, he was sure, but to the implications of Ethan's question. If Ethan understood that they were looking for someone in connection with Jeff's death, then he also understood that his father's death hadn't been some kind of accident.

Of course, a much clearer vision of what had actually occurred might still be buried in Ethan's subconscious.

"That picture you helped us draw was very important," Noah said. "But it might take a while for someone to recognize him." Caroline remained tense, staring at her son in dismay. Obviously it upset her to realize Ethan understood that someone had killed his father. Noah eased his hands from the back of her chair and sat down. "Have you remembered anything more about the day your dad died?" he asked the boy. "Anything you might have seen at the gas station?"

"No, sir." Ethan dragged his spoon through his soup, gazing into the bowl as if he hoped to find some clues floating among the noodles and vegetables. "But I've tried really hard to remember. Honest."

Noah clapped a hand on the boy's shoulder. "I know you have, son. You've been a big help so far."

Ethan flushed pink to the tips of his ears, clearly pleased by Noah's praise. He reached for a sandwich and started to eat. Noah glanced across the table at Caroline.

She was still watching her son as if trying to read his mind. She lifted her spoon to her mouth with the automatic motions of a robot. Noah was willing to bet she couldn't even taste what she was eating.

Too bad. The soup was delicious. No wonder her business was such a success. Noah helped himself to a sandwich and wolfed it down in three bites.

It occurred to him that a person spying on them through the kitchen window would conclude they were your basic happy family, sitting down to share a pleasant lunch together.

Which just went to prove how deceptive appearances could be.

The neighborhood where Jeff had rented a house had certainly seen better days. Even though the streets they drove down were dark, Caroline could make out overgrown yards, sagging front porches, dilapidated roofs. Most of the homes could have used a coat of paint.

"These houses were built back in the twenties for the miners to live in," Noah explained. "Once the last mine shut down thirty years ago or so, most of them fell into disrepair."

Yet this was where Jeff had brought their son to live.

Caroline could hardly wait to get this errand over with.

After dinner tonight she'd tried to find some excuse not to go. "What if someone sees us going inside? Word will get out that Ethan's still in town."

"I've already figured out a plan," Noah had replied, setting the last clean plate back into the cupboard. "There's an attached garage with an inner door leading directly into the house. You and Ethan can duck down until we drive inside the garage, then I'll close the garage door behind us. We can slip into the house unseen.''

So that's just what they did.

Noah went around pulling down all the shades before turning on the lights. ''If any of the neighbors come to investigate, I'll answer the door and tell them I'm checking for additional evidence.'' He switched on the overhead living-room light. ''Okay, Ethan, we need to hurry. You want some help gathering up your stuff?''

Ethan had been even quieter than usual since the three of them had left Noah's place. He shook his head, looking as if he were about to cry.

''Come on, honey. Why don't you show me your room?'' Caroline curved her arm around his fragile shoulders, shoulders that had been forced to bear a much heavier burden than a child's ever should. It required some effort not to burst into tears herself.

Ethan led them to his bedroom. The house was as sparsely furnished as Noah's, but the furniture was in shabbier condition and everything was coated with a layer of dust. Caroline felt a disorienting sense of unreality, as if she were moving through a dream. Or a nightmare. Here was where Ethan had been all those years she'd been searching for him...the roof he'd slept under, the table where he'd eaten his meals, the sink where he'd brushed his teeth every night.

All that time believing his mother was dead.

Damn you, Jeff. Caroline clenched her fists. But already the raging blaze of her anger was subsiding into a pile of smoldering coals. How could she hate someone who was so pathetic? The one thing Jeff had ever succeeded at was stealing Ethan from her. And in the end Caroline had gotten her son back anyway.

She shuddered at the irony that such a joyful reunion had only been made possible by a terrible act of violence. Now that Jeff was dead, it was getting harder to maintain her anger at him for very long.

''This is it,'' Ethan mumbled.

Caroline reached around him and fumbled on the light switch. Baseball posters taped to the walls, an unmade bed, toys and clothes scattered everywhere. A typical boy's room.

"I think I saw some empty boxes in the garage," Noah said. He went to get them.

"Ethan, honey, are you sure you want to do this now?" Caroline crouched down so they were eye-to-eye. "I know it must be awful sad for you to be here. Maybe it would be easier if we came back later." She smoothed a drooping lock of hair from his forehead. "I could even come back by myself to pack up your things, if you'd like."

Ethan's chin quivered. His mouth pinched into a white seam. Then his whole face collapsed.

Caroline put her arms around him and hugged him tight. His entire small body shook with sobs. Somewhere inside her she found the strength to control her own.

"I'm so sorry, Ethan," she murmured in his ear. "So sorry about your dad…"

Had Jeff once held their son like this, too, after telling five-year-old Ethan his mommy was dead?

She heard Noah's footsteps coming down the hall. Heard them pause, then retreat.

She stroked Ethan's trembling back, cherishing every precious vertebra, every hard knob and tender angle. A fierce upwelling of protectiveness surged through her. She would never allow anyone else to put her little boy through this kind of pain again. Never. No matter what it cost her.

After a while Ethan drew back. He pulled up the hem of his T-shirt to wipe sticky tears from his cheeks. He sniffed. "I'm glad you're not dead, too, Mom," he said in a tiny quaver.

Well, it wasn't exactly "I love you," but it was sweet music to Caroline's ears, nevertheless. It was also the first time Ethan had called her "Mom." Not "Mommy" anymore. But, as she'd already discovered with mixed emotions, her son was growing up.

Noah peered around the bedroom door. "I found some boxes," he said. "Anything else I can do?"

Caroline smiled up at him gratefully. After years of relying on no one but herself, she had to admit it was nice to have a shoulder to lean on. Especially when it belonged to someone as strong and sensitive as Noah.

She levered herself to her feet and reached for one of the cardboard boxes he'd produced. "Do you want any help, sweetheart?" she asked gently.

Ethan rubbed the last trace of tears from his eyes. "No thanks, Mom." He stood a little taller. "I can do it."

She handed him the box, understanding that it was important to Ethan to take care of this sad chore himself. "Sergeant Garrett and I will be in the living room if you need us."

"Okay."

Back in the hallway, Caroline hesitated. "Do you think I should go through Jeff's bedroom?" she asked Noah in hushed, reluctant tones. "Maybe there's something of value in there. Or some keepsake Ethan might want later on."

She was relieved at Noah's answer. "I checked over his room pretty thoroughly the day he died. There's nothing in there of any financial value, and not much that might have sentimental value, either, I don't think." He nodded toward Jeff's bedroom door. "You're certainly welcome to check for yourself."

"No, that's all right," Caroline said quickly. "I'll take your word for it." Prowling through her ex-husband's personal effects was a task she was only too happy to avoid.

Out in the living room, she couldn't even bring herself to sit on Jeff's sofa. She roamed in aimless circles over the worn carpet, rubbing her hands up and down her arms even though the stale air still retained some of the day's heat. The place felt filled with ghosts.

Noah took a position near the front door. Caroline sensed his gaze following her restless movements like a shadow. His quiet air of self-possession reminded her of a fox posed motionless at the entrance to a rabbit hole. Waiting for something to happen. The technique probably worked wonders on nervous suspects who felt compelled to fill the silence with incriminating chatter.

"Do I need to notify Jeff's landlord about what happened?" Caroline finally asked. Noah's technique was effective on her, too, it seemed.

"No. The landlord's a local, so he's already aware he'll need to find a new tenant."

"Oh." Caroline absently reached out to adjust a picture hanging crookedly on the wall, then rubbed dust off her fingertips.

"Matter of fact, I spoke to Jeff's landlord this afternoon," Noah said. "I checked around town with anyone Jeff might have owed money to. They all claimed he'd been paying his bills. A little late sometimes, but he never actually skipped a rent check or anything."

Noah wasn't quite sure why he was telling all this to Caroline. Maybe just to distract her from the discomfort she was clearly suffering in her ex-husband's house. Or maybe his motives were more selfish. He'd found with Beth that talking about what he'd learned during an investigation sometimes helped him see the facts in a new light.

Caroline stopped pacing to focus her attention on him. "So if Jeff truly did need money all of a sudden, like he told his boss, it wasn't because he'd fallen behind on his bills."

"Doesn't seem so."

She tugged thoughtfully on her earlobe. "What else could he have needed money for? Was he sick?"

"Not according to Doc Morton." At Caroline's raised eyebrows, he clarified, "Jeff and Ethan's doctor."

"Some get-rich-quick scheme, maybe. Jeff was always big on those." Her lips crimped with scorn, but immediately softened in grudging remorse. "Sorry. I shouldn't speak ill of the dead."

Noah was developing a theory of his own about why Jeff Tate might have needed money all of a sudden, but right now he found his curiosity piqued by an entirely different question.

"This is none of my business, but how did the two of you end up together, anyway?"

"You mean, how on earth could I have been so blind as to marry a man with so little conscience he could steal our child?" The bitterness in Caroline's voice cut through the musty atmosphere. "Believe me, I've asked myself that question a thousand times over. Every single day Ethan was missing."

"Doesn't seem like the two of you would have been exactly...compatible." Noah phrased his observation as a deliberate understatement, hoping it would provoke a flood of indignant revelations.

It did.

"When I first met Jeff, I thought he was everything I wanted in a man. Successful, smart, considerate..." Caroline shook her head as if she couldn't believe how naive she'd been. "I had a brand-new English degree and was working at a dead-end job for an advertising agency. Jeff was a guest speaker at a night class I took on how to start your own business."

She drew the rope of her braid over her shoulder and frowned at it as if it displeased her. "From the way Jeff talked, he was running his father's furniture company singlehandedly. I was...impressed." She lowered her lashes. "Jeff was handsome and charming, and I was incredibly flattered when he took an interest in me." Her cheeks turned pink. "You see, I was kind of shy and studious when I was in school. I'd never had a real boyfriend before. Jeff simply...swept me off my feet."

Noah found it unbelievable that Caroline hadn't had to beat boyfriends off with a stick. But he couldn't think of a way to say so without sounding like he was coming on to her.

She flipped her braid back over her shoulder. "Jeff wasn't very good at selling hotel furniture, but he was a genius at selling himself. It wasn't till after we were married that I discovered all his big talk was just a facade, a way of hiding his failures and insecurities." She glanced toward the hall as if worried Ethan might overhear their conversation. "By the time I found out Jeff wasn't who I thought he was, I was already pregnant with Ethan. So I stayed with Jeff, even after he started having affairs."

Noah's disgust must have shown on his face despite his effort to maintain a neutral expression. Caroline sighed. "Like I told you before, Jeff felt threatened by my success. After Ethan was born we needed more money. I tried selling some soup mixes I'd created, because I could work out of the house and still take care of Ethan. I never dreamed the business would take off the way it did."

"So your husband felt justified in sleeping with other women." Noah didn't bother to hide his sarcasm at this point.

A reflection of the pain and humiliation she once must have felt was evident in Caroline's eyes. "Jeff was trying to get back at me for making him feel like less of a man, I suppose. He wanted a woman who would boost his ego by hanging on his every word. By being totally dependent on him."

Noah thought if ever there was a woman who didn't fit that bill, it was Caroline. Yet in Noah's case, it was her independence and strength of character that attracted him as much as her physical beauty.

"Jeff always made sure I found out about each affair, and then he'd apologize and promise never to do it again. I kept taking him back because I wanted my son to have a father, but by the time Ethan started school the atmosphere at our house was so poisoned that I finally accepted Ethan would be better off if his parents lived apart. So I kicked Jeff out and got a divorce."

"For which he repaid you by kidnapping your son." Anger upped the volume of Noah's voice a notch or two.

Caroline shot another anxious look toward the hallway. "As I told you, it was a combination of factors," she said quietly. "Being divorced by me and disowned by his father, both at the same time."

Noah thought she was being extremely understanding. Then

again, that's exactly the kind of woman Caroline was. A little *too* understanding at times, for Noah's peace of mind.

He changed the subject. "Did you contact Jeff's father today?"

Caroline nodded. Judging by the unhappy slant of her mouth, it hadn't been a pleasant phone call. "He took the news in his usual gruff, stoic manner. But I could tell he was shocked."

Noah massaged the base of his skull. "No matter how estranged Jeff and his father were, there's no greater blow than losing your child." He'd made the observation without thinking. But then it hit him what he'd done. He'd admitted out loud the depth of his own soul-shattering loss.

Noah didn't even like confronting Beth and Molly's deaths in the privacy of his own nightmares. He couldn't believe he'd alluded to his personal tragedy in such a matter-of-fact way. Almost as if he were developing a measure of detachment and objectivity about it.

Immediately he felt guilty.

Unfortunately, this was one of those times when Caroline was too perceptive for Noah's comfort. "You don't like to talk about them much, do you? Your wife and daughter."

The blackness began to descend on him, the terrible weight that pressed down with suffocating force whenever memories fought their way too close to the surface.

He clamped his back teeth together. "No." He certainly couldn't deny it.

Caroline drifted closer, invading that buffer zone of space Noah preferred to keep between him and the rest of the world. "Through missing-children's organizations I've met a number of parents whose outcomes weren't as lucky as mine was. Who eventually found out their children had died."

Children. Died. Noah had to force himself not to shudder at the horror of it. You weren't supposed to use those words in the same sentence.

"What I learned from them is that it's okay to talk about loved ones who die. That most parents actually derive comfort from hearing their lost child's name, or sharing memories, or even telling total strangers what their child was like.'' Her eyes shone with an intensity born of compassion and her own pain. ''Maybe it's a way to keep part of the child alive, to make sure the memories live on. To validate the child's existence, rather than pretend he or she was never born.''

Caroline watched him steadily, unlike most people whose gazes kept slipping away from his because they didn't really want to get a good look at what he was feeling inside. She was standing so close to him now that her eyes filled Noah's vision. Her pupils were huge, dark as midnight, glowing with an inner luminescence that might have been a rescue beacon...or the glare of oncoming headlights.

Stay away! Don't come any closer!

A premonition of danger seized Noah, stronger than any he'd encountered in his work. He had to fight the urge to back away from her. He didn't want to listen, didn't want to face the meaning of her words....

''I can't understand what you're going through, Noah. No one can.'' Caroline took hold of his hand. The contact was like a sizzling jolt of electricity. ''But it might help to talk about your feelings. To talk about your wife and daughter.''

Noah felt paralyzed, as if frozen in the headlights of oncoming destruction. His heart was racing a mile a minute.

Caroline no doubt read the resistance in his rigid muscles and the viselike set of his jaw. With a sad, one-sided smile she gave his hand a final squeeze. ''I'm sorry. It's none of my business. I shouldn't have said all that.'' She uncurled her fingers and moved away from him. ''But if you ever feel like telling me sometime, I'd love to hear what your little girl was like.''

Noah stood bolted to the carpet. If he'd been capable of movement, he would have thrown up an arm to ward off that blinding, terrifying light rushing straight toward him through the blackness.

A harsh sound filled his ears, and it took him a split second to recognize it as his own voice.

"Her name was Molly," he rasped. "My daughter. My wife's name was Beth."

Caroline tilted her head when she looked at him. Noah would have preferred a thousand lashes from a whip to the gentle sympathy he saw glittering in her eyes. "You must have loved them both very much," she said softly.

That out-of-control vehicle was bearing down on him now, horn blasting, tires screeching, a sickening prelude to the splintering crash of metal and the scream of shattering glass.

"I loved them," Noah said, prying each one of those words from his throat like a steel shard. "I'm also the one who killed them."

Chapter 6

Caroline decided she couldn't possibly have heard Noah correctly.

Then she looked more closely at the anguish carved across the rugged, merciless landscape of his features, and recognized the true meaning behind his shocking statement.

Noah blamed himself for the deaths of his wife and daughter.

"What happened?" Caroline didn't stop to consider whether she had the right to ask.

His fists were clenched against his solid thighs as if he wanted to punch someone. "We were coming home from the county fair over in Carleton." He spoke in a monotone that sounded as if he was reading from a police report. "It was pitch-dark out. Way past Molly's bedtime, but this was a special occasion." Noah's mouth was the only part of him that moved. "I was driving."

Caroline's mind raced ahead. Dear God. Now she could see where this twisty road was leading. *Noah, Noah, it wasn't your fault!*

"We were singing silly songs. Beth and Molly started playing some game that had us all laughing. I turned around to make a funny face at Molly in the back seat. I only took my eyes off the road for a second, but it was long enough—" His Adam's apple bobbed up and down in a harsh convulsion. "When I looked forward again there were headlights coming straight at us. A drunk driver had veered across the center line of the road. I swerved immediately, but it was...it was too late."

"Oh, Noah." Caroline laid her hand on his arm. It felt like trying to comfort a stone statue.

"The other driver died at the hospital. Beth and Molly— they never even made it that far."

"I'm so sorry." Caroline longed to put her arms around him, but knew the gesture would be unwelcome. "What about you? Were you badly injured?"

He took an impatient swipe at the air, as if he was swatting a fly. "A couple of broken ribs." A sour laugh erupted from his throat. "They said I was incredibly lucky. We were all buckled in, yet I was the only one who survived." He grimaced. "Ironic, isn't it? Two innocent people died, but the person whose fault it was lived."

"No, he didn't." Caroline dug her nails into his sleeve for emphasis. "The accident was the drunk driver's fault. And you said he died."

Torment and self-loathing roughened Noah's voice. "*I* was to blame. If I hadn't taken my eyes off the road—"

"You couldn't have known some drunk was going to come along right at that second!" Caroline exclaimed.

A muscle twitched near Noah's temple. "If I'd reacted more quickly, or handled the car differently—"

"The outcome might have been the same. You did the best you could. That's all anyone could have done."

"It wasn't good enough." His jaw shifted slightly, like a dead bolt locking the door on further debate.

Over the past three years, Caroline had gotten used to banging on closed doors. "Noah, it's only natural to feel guilty that you survived and they didn't. But you can't seriously believe you're responsible for their deaths in the same way as that drunk driver, can you?"

To her dismay, she saw that he could.

A minute ago she'd wanted to hug him. Now she wanted to shake some sense into him. "Do you think you can somehow make up for what happened by punishing yourself with guilt for the rest of your life? Is that it?"

The dangerous gleam in Noah's eye warned Caroline that she'd gone too far. Well, in for a penny, in for a pound. "It wasn't your fault Beth and Molly died. You've got to let go of this idea that you're somehow to blame, or you'll never be able to come to terms with what happened."

His deadly calm reply didn't mask the angry currents simmering below its surface. "Thanks. But if I wanted psychoanalysis, I'd go see a shrink."

Even though Caroline realized Noah was only lashing out at her because of his pain, his words still hurt. She let go of his arm. But she wouldn't let go of the subject. "Beth and Molly wouldn't want you to keep torturing yourself like this."

Noah's bitter gaze seared into her like a high-intensity cobalt laser. "Easy enough for you to say." He hoisted his chin in the direction of Ethan's room. "After all, you got your kid back."

With that parting shot, he swung around and strode out to the garage.

From Ruby's desk inside the front window of the sheriff's substation, Noah watched Rollie Fletcher tie his mule to a lamppost across the street. Rollie was one of Eagle River's more colorful characters—a combination middle-aged hippie and nineteenth-century gold prospector. For as long as Noah had lived here, and probably a lot longer than that, Rollie had been trying to strike it rich on one played-out mining claim or another. He used the mule to haul his supplies out to his campsite on Deer Creek. Noah had warned him more than once about tying his animal to public property, pointing out the nuisance this created—a nuisance Rollie never bothered to clean up. I should probably go over there and write him a ticket, Noah thought.

It was a measure of the sorry state he was in that he didn't bother.

He hadn't slept a wink all night. He just lay there, stiff as a corpse, staring at the insides of his eyelids. Thinking about Beth and Molly. About Caroline.

He couldn't believe how deep she'd managed to dig inside him yesterday evening. All the way down to the blackness, the pain, the guilt. If Noah had thought living under the same roof with her had been a trial before, he couldn't imagine what it was going to be like from now—

The door swung open and Ruby breezed through it. A puzzled frown crimped the edges of her mouth. "How come all the lights are—" She flipped on the light switch and looked even more bewildered when she spotted Noah sitting behind her desk. "Why're *you* on duty instead of Allen?" she demanded.

"I decided to come in early, so I sent him home." Allen, one of Noah's deputies, wasn't exactly thrilled about his current assignment to the graveyard shift.

Ruby propped a hand on one skinny hip. "Well, what are you doing sitting alone in the dark?"

"It's 7:00 a.m. I wouldn't exactly call it dark."

"Not light enough to see what you're doing, though." She bustled around her desk and got a good look at Noah. "Wow, you look like something out of that horror movie I watched on video last night. Maybe I should turn the lights back off."

"Very funny." Noah stood aside to make room for her. "I didn't sleep well, that's all. And by the way, what are *you* doing in so early?"

To his astonishment, Ruby turned the same improbable red shade as her hair. "I've got work to catch up on."

"What work? You're so far ahead of me I can barely keep up."

"Computer work."

"Oh?"

Her mouth compressed into a tiny straight line. Like an unblinking cursor.

Comprehension dawned. "Ruby, you're not still carrying on that romance over the Internet, are you?"

"What if I am?" She defiantly jabbed a button with one of her long, lacquered talons and the computer whirred into life.

"Ruby, don't you read the newspapers? That kind of stuff can be dangerous! You might be revealing all your intimate secrets to some lunatic."

"My intimate secrets are *my* business, thank you." Her nails clicked rapidly over the keyboard like a string of fire-crackers.

Noah gave up. First a mule tied to a lamppost, then a cyber-smitten secretary. It was too much to deal with so early in the morning. "I'll be in my office," he said.

"Better make some coffee fast," she advised over her shoulder. "You look like you could use it."

What Noah could use was a transfer to another case. To another town. Maybe to a whole other line of work entirely. He closed the door of his office and slumped down behind his desk.

He'd always been dedicated to his job. Ever since the accident, in fact, his job had become his salvation. It was the one area of his life Noah could focus on with enough concentration to blot out the other areas for a while. To forget how the rest of his life had blown up in his face, maiming him forever.

As long as his brain cells were occupied with work, they didn't have time to torture him with those headlights, rushing at him out of the blackness, destroying his world in a deafening explosion of metal and glass....

Noah sprang from his chair and forced his hands to go through the motions of making coffee. Measure the beans, grind the beans, pour the fresh grounds into a paper filter...

But now his work involved Caroline Tate. A woman who'd unnerved him from the first moment he'd laid eyes on her and felt that startling pull of attraction. A woman whose presence in his home was a constant reminder of everything he'd lost.

A woman who kept forcing Noah to dredge up the memories and the pain and the sense of overpowering loss he'd buried in that deep, dark hole in his subconsciousness just so he could keep functioning.

So whenever Noah tried to focus on this case, he wound up thinking about Caroline instead. Seeing her amazing green eyes. Hearing her voice. *Beth and Molly wouldn't want you to keep on torturing yourself like this....*

But Noah's guilt and his grief were all he had left of them. How could he let go?

He was coming back down the hall after filling the coffeepot with water when Ruby sang out, "Someone to see you, Sergeant Garrett." Uh-oh. He must still be in the doghouse. Ruby never addressed him by rank.

He came out into the front part of the substation and found Ellie Conover, the minister's twenty-something daughter, perched on one of the visitor chairs near Ruby's desk. When Ellie stood up, Noah saw she was clutching one of the police-sketch fliers of the man Ethan had seen arguing with his father several days before Jeff's death.

Alertness nudged aside some of that slow-witted, draggy feeling. "Morning, Ellie. How can I help you?"

"Well..." She twirled a strand of brown hair around one finger. "I was hoping I might be able to help *you*, actually." She glanced dubiously at the wrinkled flier in her hand.

"The sheriff's department always appreciates any help we get from the public," Noah assured her.

"Well..." Ellie was an earnest, sober young woman whose spare time was devoted to good works. Anytime someone needed a volunteer for a worthy cause, Ellie would be the first to stick up her hand. "It's just that I'd hate to get someone in trouble. He seemed like a nice enough person. I mean, you can't judge people by their appearances...."

Noah decided it was time to lasso this rambling conversation. "Are you referring to the drawing on that flier?" He pointed. "Have you seen that person somewhere?"

Ellie chewed her lip unhappily and didn't answer. Noah sat her back down and eased into the chair next to her. "Let me explain that I don't actually suspect this man of anything," he said. "I just want to ask him a few questions, that's all. It doesn't mean you'd be getting him in trouble by telling me what you know about him."

Now she was nibbling on the ends of her hair. Noah noticed her fingernails appeared to have gotten the same treatment. She sighed. "Well, as you may know, I volunteer quite a bit at the local food bank. Handing out donated food to the needy."

Noah nodded his encouragement.

"This man..." She glanced one last time at the picture as if begging him to forgive her. "I think I may have seen him at the food bank a few times last week."

Noah tried not to show his excitement. "*Think* you saw him? Or *know?*"

She sighed again, her eyes troubled. "*Know* I saw him. It's the same man. I mean, he didn't look *exactly* like this picture, but...see this scar?" Below the unkempt fringe of hair, above one deep-set eye, Ethan had described a jagged scar bisecting the man's eyebrow. "The man I saw at the food bank had a scar just like that."

"Do you know his name?"

Ellie started to shake her head, then hesitated. "Buck," she said reluctantly. "He called himself Buck."

"Was that a first name? Last name?"

This time she shook her head more decisively. "I don't know. Just Buck."

"He was a—" Noah searched for the right word "—a customer at the food bank?"

"That's right." Ellie nodded. "He'd come in the morning, usually. He liked beef stew, so I'd try to set aside some cans for him."

"When did you first see him?"

She squinted at the ceiling as if the answer might be printed up there. "Hmm, a little over a week ago, I guess. He came three or four days in a row."

"When's the last time you saw him?"

When she looked back at Noah, Ellie was chewing her lip again. Her hands were knotted tightly in her lap, crushing the flier into a ball. "The last time I saw him," she said unhappily, "was the day poor Jeff at the gas station died."

Noah felt a satisfying click as one more piece of the puzzle snapped into place. "You did the right thing coming in, Ellie." He escorted her to the door.

"I'd just hate for anyone to get in trouble because of me." She paused at the sidewalk. "I really can't believe Buck could have…hurt anyone. He acted so—so polite.…"

Well, no one said killers couldn't have good manners. What had Ethan heard his father yelling at this Buck character? "You can't do this."

Do what?

Something involving money, Ethan had said. And Noah suspected he might be getting a clearer picture of exactly what it was.

Caroline stumbled through the dark woods in a panic. Gnarled branches snaked out to claw her face and tear her clothes. Rocks erupted from the earth directly in her path to trip her and slow her progress. Scratched, bruised, her aching lungs screaming for air, she forced her tortured muscles to keep moving her forward, but the air was as dark and viscous as molasses.

Ethan, Ethan!

Somewhere up ahead the monster had her son. She had to catch up, had to stop him before it was too late, but which way had they gone? The woods were pitch-black…they could be anywhere.…

She whirled one way and then another, frantically searching for a sign. Chest on fire, heart thundering in her ears, fear coursing through her bloodstream…

Close by, a twig cracked.

Caroline snapped awake.

Her heart was still thundering in her ears. *Something* had awakened her. Was someone in the house? Still fighting off the clinging vestiges of the nightmare, she instinctively fumbled to switch off the reading lamp next to the couch where she'd fallen asleep.

Now the darkness was for real.

She strained her ears for any further sound, but heard nothing beyond her own labored breathing and the bass-drum beat of her pulse. Had someone come here after Ethan? Was that what her subconsciousness had been trying to warn her of with that terrifying dream?

Cautiously, Caroline slipped off the couch and tiptoed across the living room. She cursed herself for not locating some sort of weapon before turning off the light. But the element of surprise was all she had going for her. At least now the intruder might not realize someone inside the house was awake.

She sidled along the wall dividing the living room from the hallway. She paused at the entrance. Not a sound. Inch by inch, she poked her head into the hallway. No sign of movement. Not here, anyway.

Taking a deep breath, Caroline crept into the hall. She turned instinctively toward the stairs, toward Ethan's bedroom.

Someone grabbed her from behind.

The deep breath that would have exploded in a scream was cut off by the strong hand clamped over her mouth. Caroline thrashed like a wild animal caught in a trap, incoherent moans fighting their way from her throat. She tried to bite, tried to stomp her foot on his instep, tried to wrestle free, but he was simply too powerful, his reflexes too quick for her.

She felt his breath next to her ear and recoiled in revulsion. Then she flung her head backward, hoping to make cracking contact with his skull. She missed. Once more she felt his hot, moist breath, and now realized he was saying something.

Caroline didn't care what it was. She kept struggling. All

at once he peeled his rough fingers from her mouth. Her oxygen-starved lungs hauled in a quick gust of air to fuel a scream. In that brief span of time she finally heard what he was trying to tell her.

"For cryin' out loud, Caroline. It's me!"

She continued to flail against him for the few befuddled seconds it took her panic-stricken brain to absorb the fact that her assailant was Noah.

Air rushed from her lungs, not in a scream but in a deflated whoosh. Relief washed over her, stealing the strength from her limbs. She collapsed in his arms.

"You!" she said breathlessly.

His arms tightened around her as she sagged toward the floor. "For God's sake, Caroline, what are you doing skulking around in the dark?" Irritation was etched in his voice, but she could hear relief there as well.

"I...heard a noise. Thought it was...someone coming after...Ethan." Her rapid breathing was making her lightheaded. Either that, or Noah was holding her too tight.

"It didn't occur to you it was just me coming home?" His hands shifted a little. He probably wasn't aware how close they were to her breasts.

"I fell asleep on the couch. I was...having a nightmare. About the killer kidnapping Ethan." She shivered. The hallway was dark as her nightmare. She couldn't see Noah's face at all. But she could picture every hard, compelling line of it. "It must have been the sound of your car that woke me up." She clutched his shoulders to pull herself straighter. "Hey, what the heck did you grab me for, anyway?"

"What else was I supposed to do? I drive up, see a faint light on in the house, and by the time I get to the door someone's turned it off." He hissed a stream of air through his teeth. "For all I knew I was walking into an ambush."

"Oh." Caroline relaxed her grip on his shoulders a little. But she kept her hands where they were. "Well, I figured if it was the killer, I'd be an easy target, sitting there with the light on."

"Good thinking." Noah eased his hands partway down her back. "Except then I came into a completely dark house and heard someone moving around in the living room. I assumed it was someone who wasn't supposed to be there." He slid his hands back up again.

"How could you hear me?" Caroline asked indignantly. "I thought I was as quiet as a mouse."

"Mice aren't all that quiet." She heard a smile creep into his voice. "Besides, I've got good hearing."

There was something unsettling about having this conversation in total darkness. Unsettling...yet somehow exciting. She'd been right. It *was* nice to lean on Noah.

"Why are you home so late, anyway?" This time Caroline didn't care if she sounded like a worried wife.

Noah paused a second before replying. "I got tied up with work." His fingers were kneading her flesh. Very gently, probably unconsciously.

Caroline brought her face close to his. "Baloney," she said.

He jerked his head back a little. "Huh?"

"You were trying to avoid me, because of the big fight we had last night." Though "fight" was hardly the word for the bitter, wrenching, gut-twisting scene that had taken place in Jeff's living room. Noah hadn't spoken one word to Caroline the whole way home. "That's why you were gone when I got up this morning," she said. "That's why you didn't come home until you thought I'd be sound asleep."

"But you're not asleep." His voice was a low rumble as he brought his head close to hers again. His fingers resumed their delicious, lulling massage of her spine. "Why is that?"

"I was...waiting up for you."

"Oh?"

Tingling pleasure oozed through her limbs like warm honey. It dimly dawned on Caroline that they were standing here in the dark hallway locked in what amounted to a rather close embrace. For some reason that fact didn't bother her. Not at all.

"I wanted to apologize for last night," she said. Her words

came out a tiny bit slurred, as if she were drugged. Maybe she was. "I shouldn't have said those things to you. About the way you're dealing with Beth and Molly's deaths. I had no right to criticize you. I shouldn't have stuck my big nose in where it didn't belong."

She sensed Noah processing this, considering whether or not to accept her apology and put the incident behind them.

His response was hardly what she'd expected. "Your nose isn't all that big," he said gruffly, bringing his face close to nuzzle his nose against hers. His warm breath caressed her lips. A stab of fierce longing speared through Caroline, catching her off guard. "I...overreacted," Noah said. "You were only trying to help. I shouldn't have flown off the handle like that."

His mouth couldn't have been more than one inch from hers. Caroline was starting to feel dizzy again. It was amazing how complete darkness heightened the rest of your senses while it deprived you of sight. She could smell tantalizing traces of aftershave and male sweat rising off Noah's collar, could hear his slow breathing as a steady contrast to her own. It was almost as if she could feel the blood coursing through his body, warming her skin with its throbbing rhythm.

A moment ago it had seemed that they were standing awfully close together. Now Caroline felt as if she couldn't get close enough. "No, it was my fault," she said. Goodness, was that really her voice, so throaty and filled with yearning? "You were right, I can't possibly know what you're going through."

"Caroline."

"I had no right to make judgments. I shouldn't have—"

"Caroline," he said again, and this time something in his voice hauled her up short.

She swallowed. Heat flamed across her cheeks. "Yes?" she whispered.

"Kiss me."

Oh, sweet heaven...

Without giving one second's thought to the consequences, Caroline complied. Though Noah may have beaten her to it.

All she knew was that their lips were somehow fused together and her arms were circled around his neck as she hung on for dear life.

His mouth moved over hers with a barely controlled, near-desperate hunger, as if he were starving for the taste of her. Caroline knew just how he felt. Her entire being was focused on kissing Noah Garrett as if her very survival depended on it. Desire coursed through her, replacing the blood in her veins and the air in her lungs, turning her limbs molten.

When his tongue coaxed her lips apart she welcomed it gladly, eagerly, melding their mouths together in even more intimate contact. Her breasts were crushed against the rock-hard wall of his chest. He tangled his fingers so tightly through her hair that Caroline's scalp hurt. Nothing had ever felt this good in her whole life.

The delicious sandpaper roughness of his jaw rasped against her skin. "Ah, Caro..." His abbreviated version of her name came out sounding like an endearment trapped between their lips. He dragged his hands in circles around her back, coming seductively close to her breasts but never quite touching them. Caroline was astonished by how much she wanted him to. She'd never before felt so reckless, so...so...carried away. Even while a voice in the distant reaches of her brain was hollering that this was a mistake, her body was insisting that nothing had ever felt so right.

She twined her tongue around his as Noah deepened their kiss. His mouth was tender and hard at the same time. Caroline felt the same conflict in the taut bowstring of muscle beneath his shirt, as if he were straining against invisible handcuffs.

She lifted her hands to the base of his skull, sliding her fingers through his hair. If only she could banish the tortured thoughts that swirled beneath them....

It took her a moment to locate the source of the purring sound coming from her own throat. Noah widened his stance, cupping her bottom to draw her more snugly between his thighs. Twin bolts of shock and desire crashed through Caroline when the hard bulge beneath his belt buckle nudged her abdomen. She'd had little experience with men except for Jeff, and Noah's bold display of male passion startled her. For the first time she fully comprehended where this kiss might lead, what a dangerous path she was treading.

Then all at once it felt as if she'd stepped off a cliff. Noah simply wasn't there anymore. Caroline popped open her eyes in bewilderment. Well, okay, he was still *there*. A trace of moonlight filtering through the trees helped her seek out Noah's wide-shouldered outline looming above her in the dark. Except now a gap of several feet separated her from him.

"Caroline." This time her name didn't sound like an endearment. More like a warning. "I—I'm sorry. I didn't mean—" She could see an arm swipe across his brow. "I shouldn't have let that happen." He sounded as shaken as she was.

Caroline pressed quivering fingertips to her lips. Her mouth felt bruised. Not to mention her ego. For one crazy, frenzied moment she'd been ready to...never mind. It was humiliating enough to be rejected so abruptly. Even when she knew it was for the best.

Thank goodness at least one of them had had sense enough to stop.

"It's all right," she assured him quickly. "It was as much my fault as yours." If only there were some magic way to instantly transport herself to the privacy of her room. Her face was burning.

She heard Noah groping his way along the hall. She squeezed her eyes shut against the sudden blaze of light. If only she didn't have to open them, to face Noah, to look into his eyes and read whatever was there.

When Caroline heard him draw near again, she screwed up her courage and did all three at once. Noah's shirt and tie were rumpled, his hair spiked up every-which-way where she'd run her fingers through it. Instinctively, her gaze dropped to his mouth. Something hot tightened in her belly when she imagined *her* mouth there.

Sweet mercy, how she'd wanted him! How she *still* wanted

him, even though his laser-blue eyes were boring into her with such glaring guilt and self-recrimination they made Caroline feel as if she'd done something wrong.

Well, she had, hadn't she? Something stupid. Reckless. Something she could never allow to happen again, now that she knew how rapidly her feelings could overpower her better judgment.

"Gee, I guess now we've kissed and made up," she said, trying to make light of what had just passed between them. "Does this mean you forgive me for trying to interfere in your life?"

Noah studied her for so long, with that dazed look imprinted upon his rugged features, that Caroline wanted to squirm. "There's nothing to forgive," he said finally.

"Then we're friends again?" she asked brightly, already backing toward the staircase.

"Sure." Noah dragged his fingers through his hair, as if trying to rake away the memory of her touch. "Friends." He pronounced it the way he might have said, "Cockroaches." Not too convincing.

But Caroline didn't want convincing. Maybe she and Noah hadn't exactly been friends before, but whatever it was they had been, tonight they'd definitely crossed the line into something else. A dangerous new territory she wanted no part of. Emotional quicksand.

She didn't like the way Noah had made her feel, didn't like the way he'd made her forget all the reasons she didn't want a man in her life. Caroline's feelings and instincts where men were concerned were completely untrustworthy. Hadn't she proven that by marrying Jeff?

Once before she'd made the mistake of letting a man sweep her off her feet. And she'd paid for that terrible error with years of heartache. She wasn't about to make the same mistake again. Especially when it wasn't just her own happiness at stake. It wouldn't be fair to Ethan to let another man into their lives, someone Ethan might grow attached to, someone who would end up letting them both down.

Though Caroline couldn't imagine Noah doing that to anyone.

Not that her unreliable instincts even mattered. Because Noah had made it as clear as humanly possible that he was as gun-shy about involvement as Caroline was.

All she had to do was look at his face right now. His stony features were haggard with regret, even though Caroline had felt the indisputable proof that he'd wanted her as much as she'd wanted him.

"I'm going upstairs to bed now." She bit her tongue, but it was too late to rephrase that. In the cooling aftermath of their torrid embrace, the word *bed* came loaded with suggestive connotations.

"See you in the morning," Noah told her. Although Caroline would lay odds he was planning another predawn escape.

Which suited her just fine. Clearly the less time she spent in the vicinity of Noah's tempting arms and sexy mouth, the better.

"Good night," Caroline told him. Though she knew it wasn't going to be. She flew up the stairs as if she had rockets attached to her heels, eager for the safe refuge of her room and the blissful oblivion of sleep.

It was a long, long time, though, before she finally closed her eyes.

Chapter 7

Noah sat cooling his heels in the branch manager's office at the Tamarack County Bank. His thoughts, however, were far away from interest rates and minimum monthly balances. His mind was filled with Caroline.

He couldn't believe he'd been fool enough to kiss her last night. As if having her in his house hadn't created enough trouble already. It shook Noah up, her uncanny ability to crawl inside his head and poke around through the dark, cobwebbed corners in there. His emotional attic contained an awful lot of stuff Noah had no desire to sort through. He'd packed it away for a reason.

Then along came Caroline, with her sympathetic eyes and compassionate touch, dragging everything out into the open. Making Noah feel again, after he'd finally gotten his feelings securely stored away where they couldn't destroy him.

Kiss me. How the hell could he have said that to her? Why didn't he just ask her to pour more kerosene on a blazing, out-of-control fire?

Then, though he fought it, Noah recalled the excitement that had lunged through him when she'd wrapped her arms around his neck. He felt her soft, warm, sexy curves straining against him, driving him wild, urging him into forbidden territory. Once again he heard soft moans humming in the slender column of her throat and tasted her mouth—sweet and giving and eager beneath his.

Heat flooded Noah's loins, making him stir uncomfortably in the bank manager's guest chair. But it also answered the question of how he could have said what he did. He lusted after Caroline Tate with a fierce hunger that set his blood boiling and tortured him with seductive images of her beautiful, naked body writhing under him in bed.

But that's all it was. Lust. Noah would get over it as soon as he wrapped up this case and put Caroline and her son on the plane to Baltimore. Yessir, this troublesome physical craving would dissipate as rapidly as a white plume of jet contrail streaking across the sky.

That's what Noah kept telling himself, anyway.

Quincy Medford, the middle-aged bank manager, bustled back into his office and handed a computer printout to Noah. "Here are the records you wanted." He lowered his prosperous bulk behind his desk. "Sorry I couldn't let you see 'em before, but without a court order..."

"I understand." Just this morning Noah had gotten a judge to approve his official request to examine the bank records of Jeff Tucker, aka Jefferson Randolph Tate. He wasn't sure what the records might show, but since money had apparently played a role in Jeff's death, it was probably smart to examine the role it had played during the last several months of his life.

"You looking for anything in particular?" Quincy leaned forward, curiosity gleaming behind his thick-lensed glasses, thumbs twiddling on top of his desk. Like everyone else in town, he seemed to covet even a bit part in this real-life drama.

"Not really." Noah scanned the pages in front of him, which showed all the checks Jeff had written recently, plus the deposits he'd made to his checking account. "What about his savings account?"

"Didn't have one." Quincy straightened the cuff of his shirt. His college pinkie ring winked at Noah. "No need to, really. As you can see for yourself, he pretty much used up one paycheck by the time another one came along."

Noah skimmed down the columns of dates and figures. "Those appear to be his only deposits. His paychecks. And there's nothing out-of-the-ordinary about the checks he's written—rent, utility companies, car insurance...." He folded away the printout to study more closely later. But nothing odd had leaped off the page during his initial survey. No checks made out to a loan shark, for example. His bank records indicated that Jeff Tate, while not exactly what you'd call well-off, had managed his own finances with considerably more success than he'd managed his father's furniture business.

"Well, it looks like our victim had his financial house in order." Noah rose to his feet. "Guess it would show on here if he ever bounced checks or anything like that, huh?"

"Never happened." Quincy came around his desk as if he thought Noah might need an escort to find his way out of the bank. Clearly he was reluctant to see his brief role in the investigation end. "No, Jeff Tucker—sorry, *Tate*—was pretty conscientious about that." Quincy stroked his bulldog chin and nodded sagely. "Of course, he had good reason to be. Considering he was a kidnapper, he'd be pretty anxious to avoid even the slightest risk of brushing up against the law."

The Private Eye Musing Out Loud. That might have been the title of the portrait Quincy was posing for. Noah briefly considered turning this whole case over to the bank manager. Let Caroline Tate go and live in *his* house.

"Well, thanks for this." Noah rolled the printout into a tube and tapped his palm with it.

"I'll admit, it did make me wonder why he was so desperate for money all of a sudden." *The Private Eye, Still Musing.*

Then Quincy's comment sunk in. Noah clutched the printout tighter. "What do you mean, desperate for money?"

From behind his glasses, Quincy's nearsighted tortoise-like eyes blinked at Noah. "Well...the loan," he said slowly. "The loan he came in and applied for."

"When was this?" Noah crossed his arms and broadened his stance to block the door. He didn't actually think Quincy might make a run for it without answering, but if there was a new lead lurking somewhere in this office, Noah sure as heck wasn't going to let it escape.

"Well, let me think." Quincy massaged his balding pate as if to stimulate his memory. "Last week, I guess. I'll have to check my files to be certain."

"What did he want the loan for?"

"All he would tell me was that it was to pay off some unexpected personal expenses. He wouldn't be any more specific than that." Quincy shrugged the padded shoulders of his three-piece suit. "That's one of the reasons I had to turn him down."

"What were the other reasons?"

"Come on, Noah." The bank manager gestured at the printout. "You've seen for yourself how much money Jeff made, how he was barely meeting expenses as it was. How could he have afforded the monthly payment on a twenty-thousand-dollar loan?"

"Twenty thousand dollars? That's how much he wanted?"

Quincy nodded. "Like I said, I asked what it was for, but he wouldn't give me a straight answer." His face brightened. Noah could almost see a lightbulb go on over his head. "Hey, maybe he wanted it to take the kid out of the country, so he could start over someplace else, where no one could find them."

"Maybe," Noah said. But what would have prompted Jeff to make a sudden move when he'd lived safely in Eagle River with his stolen son for nearly three years?

"What day was it you turned him down?" Noah asked. He expected Quincy to mutter something about checking his files. It turned out not to be necessary, however.

Discomfort sidled across Quincy's florid features. "Funny

coincidence," he replied with a sickly smile that said it wasn't funny at all. "It just so happens that I turned him down for that loan the morning of the day he died."

Click. Another piece of the puzzle fell into place. Unfortunately, Noah still couldn't quite make out what the final picture was supposed to look like.

"How'd Jeff react when you turned him down?" he asked.

"Well, about like you'd expect, I guess. He wasn't too happy." Quincy beat a retreat behind his desk. Apparently he'd lost some of his enthusiasm for assisting the investigation, now that he himself might have a distant, indirect link to the case.

Noah followed him back across the room. "Was he surprised? Upset? Angry?"

"Angry? No, he didn't act angry." Quincy shuffled through some papers as if he'd suddenly remembered pressing business that demanded his immediate attention.

"How did he behave, then? What was his demeanor?"

"Demeanor?" Noah felt like he was talking to a parrot.

"The way he acted. How he looked," he explained patiently, even though he knew Quincy understood what he meant.

"Hmm." With Noah hovering over his desk, the bank manager finally had no choice but to set his papers aside. "Actually, now that you mention it, it did strike me as kind of odd—the way he looked when I told him he couldn't have the money."

"And how was that?"

Quincy tapped his pen against the desk while he considered his answer. "Scared," he said finally. "He looked scared."

Noah had never thought of himself as a coward. But that's what he would be, wouldn't he, if he found another excuse not to go home tonight until it was nearly bedtime?

With the Tate case occupying so many work hours, he could easily hunt up a stack of routine paperwork to keep him at the office all evening. He wouldn't have to face Caroline across the dinner table, or struggle to make polite chitchat while they both pretended that kiss last night hadn't happened. Best of all, he wouldn't have to twist himself in knots fighting off his desire for her—the desire that gripped him like a raging fever whenever he came within a hundred yards of her.

The demands of his job offered him an easy way out. Unfortunately, it was also the coward's way out. So at five-thirty Noah left his office, stopped off to pick up a large pepperoni from the local pizza joint, and drove home. It felt strange to think there were people there waiting for him. Strange, but not entirely unpleasant.

When he drove up he found Ethan outside in the driveway, tossing a softball up and down and looking bored. "Hi, Sergeant." He caught the ball in his mitt one last time and jogged over to the Jeep. "Did you find that guy—oops! Sorry." Instant sunburn stained his cheeks. "My mom says I shouldn't keep pestering you about finding the guy who might have hurt my dad."

"Well, your mom probably worries about being pushy." Noah ferried the cardboard pizza box out of the car. "But you've got a right to know whether or not I'm doing my job. So you go right ahead and ask, son."

Son. He called plenty of boys that. It was just an expression, that was all. A convenient way to address kids. If Noah had ever had a son of his own, he probably would have had some other nickname for him. Champ, maybe. Sport or tiger—something like that. Son almost sounded too formal.

But for just a second there, it made Noah imagine Ethan as his son. Not that he could ever replace Ethan's real father in the boy's life. Noah was acutely aware that human beings weren't replaceable. But a kid needed a father of some sort.

Of course, there was only one way that Noah would ever become Ethan's father. And that was never going to happen.

Ethan looked relieved by Noah's reassurance. "Well...*did* you find that guy yet?" He squinted against the still-bright sun.

"Nope. Haven't found him." At Ethan's downcast expression, Noah nearly promised he would, though. But Noah wasn't in the habit of making promises he might not be able to keep. It wouldn't be fair to Ethan. "These things sometimes take a while," he explained. "But I'm working as hard as I can to find out what happened to your dad." He peered into Ethan's dejected face. "I guess now it's my turn to be pushy, and ask if you remember anything more about the day your dad died."

Ethan shook his head at the ground. "It's like I fell asleep for a long, long time. I just can't remember what happened."

Noah hesitated, then ruffled the boy's blond hair the way he'd seen Caroline do. "Don't worry about it. I know you're doing the best you can, and that's all anyone can ask."

You did the best you could. That's all anyone could have done. Caroline's voice. Talking about the accident. But that wasn't the same thing at all.

The rich aroma of pizza suddenly made Noah queasy. He set the box on the roof of the Jeep. "How about playing some catch?" he suggested.

Ethan looked at the ball in his mitt, then at Noah. "Okay, I guess."

"I'm kind of rusty at it, so you'll have to bear with me." Until the accident, Noah had been a pretty fair second baseman on the Sheriff's Department team. But he hadn't picked up a softball since.

The two of them backed apart, so Ethan was across the driveway and Noah next to the house. Ethan drew back his arm and lobbed a long, slow arc that practically dropped right into Noah's hands. "Hey, you're pretty good," he called.

Ethan hunched his shoulders as if to shrug off Noah's praise, but he stood a little straighter. "Okay, here goes." Noah pitched the ball back to him.

Ethan had to dodge sideways a couple of paces to snag it with his mitt. "You're pretty good, too," he said dutifully.

Noah laughed. "Don't flatter me, kid. I warned you I was rusty." Something loosened inside his chest. He was also rusty at laughing. It surprised him, though, how good it felt.

They tossed the ball back and forth a couple more times. "I bet it's not quite so boring being stuck way out here," Noah commented, "now that you've got your own stuff around."

"I guess." Ethan's mouth canted sideways. "My mom didn't want to let me take my stuff out of the boxes. She said we were gonna go back to Baltimore soon, so I'd just have to pack it up again."

Noah felt a slight lurch in the pit of his stomach, like an elevator dropping. He knew they were going back to Baltimore soon. He wanted them to go. So why did he feel semi-queasy again?

Judging from the way Ethan jutted his lower lip unhappily, the youngster wasn't exactly thrilled about the prospect. "I wish we could stay in Eagle River," he grumbled. "My mom says we live in Baltimore, but I can hardly even remember it."

This was a can of worms Noah refused even to consider opening. It wasn't his place.

"So, what'd you do all day?" he asked Ethan. He used to prompt Molly with the same question. She would entertain him with a detailed recitation starting with "I woke up" and ending with "Then I hugged my daddy when he got home." *Oh, my curly-haired angel, I miss you so much....*

Ethan wasn't nearly as chatty as Molly had been. "Watched TV. Ate lunch. Rode my bike up and down the driveway."

Noah yanked himself back to the present and frowned. "You didn't go all the way out to the road, did you?"

"Nah. My mom told me not to."

"She explain why?"

Ethan made a face. "Not ezactly."

Noah sympathized with Caroline's desire not to frighten Ethan. But the boy would be safer if he understood the danger he could be in. Noah chose his words carefully. "The thing is, Ethan, you might have seen something when your dad got hurt that could help me put a bad guy in jail. Something you just can't remember right now."

"I'm trying to, though."

"I know you are. The problem is, the bad guy might have figured that out, too. He might be worried you're gonna be able to help me find him." Noah returned Ethan's throw. "And unfortunately, if he ever got the chance, he might try to do something to stop you."

The ball hit the ground at Ethan's feet and bounced into the woods. "You mean *kill* me?" His eyes were as huge and round as silver dollars.

Noah winced. "That's not going to happen," he said hastily. "Not as long as you and your mom stay out of sight. That's why it's important not to ride your bike all the way out to the road, so no one will know you're staying here."

Ethan's freckles stood out against his pale cheeks like a light spattering of paint. Noah almost wished the boy hadn't been smart enough to put two and two together. Well, he was his mother's son, after all. Noah should have known the kid wouldn't let him get away with sugarcoating the truth.

"Come ȯn, throw me the ball," he said. "I need all the practice I can get."

Ethan ducked into the trees to retrieve the softball. But the unpleasant jolt he'd just received must have thrown off his aim a little. Noah made a leaping grab as the ball came toward him, but it sailed right over his head...

...and smashed through the living-room window.

The cymbal crash of broken glass echoed in the few seconds of silence that followed. Then came the drumbeat of footsteps inside the house, growing louder.

Noah barely had time to note the horrified guilt on Ethan's face before Caroline flew out the front door. She clutched a baseball bat—Ethan's, no doubt—in her right hand. Her left was bunched into a white-knuckled fist that clearly meant business. The fierce determination on her tense, pretty face was awesome to behold.

Once she caught sight of Ethan, then whipped her head around to where Noah was standing, her grimace of fear dissolved into a near swoon of relief. "Oh!" She pounded her fist to her heart and sagged against one of the posts at the top of the front steps. "I thought..."

She was breathing too fast to complete her sentence. Not that she needed to. It hardly required a professional detective to deduce that the explosion of shattering glass had terrified her that someone was trying to harm her son.

Noah stepped toward her, sparing a quick glance at Ethan. The boy stood frozen to the gravel, ghost-white with remorse for all the commotion he'd caused.

"Hey, good thinking," Noah told Caroline, pointing at the bat dangling from her hand. "Now we can have a *real* game."

From the corner of his vision he saw Ethan cover a snicker with his hand. Caroline just stared at him, her eyes as lovely and brilliant as the world's most expensive emeralds. "What?" She levered her gaze down to see where he was pointing. "This?" She lifted the bat as if she'd never seen it before. "Gosh, I don't even remember picking it up."

Noah extracted it from her limp fingers before she dropped it on her foot. "Unfortunately, now we seem to be missing the softball." Somehow his fingers got all tangled up with hers for a few seconds.

Caroline's silky hair floated above her shoulders as she whirled to inspect the broken window. The sun's golden rays made the strands shimmer. Noah liked it when she wore her hair long and loose like that. She looked less businesslike, more...unrestrained. She was wearing a blouse Noah had never seen before, some kind of soft, fil.ny lavender material with tiny pearl buttons down the front. It was impossible not to envision his fingers slowly traveling down that row, unhitching each button from its delicate little loop....

Noah's groin tightened.

Dismay pleated Caroline's forehead. "Ethan, did you do this?" She pointed at the window. What was left of it, anyway.

Ethan hung his head and punched his mitt a couple of times. "Yeah."

"It was an accident," Noah said quickly. "No big deal. I

was my fault as much as his.'' At Caroline's dubious frown, he insisted, ''I should have caught the ball.''

''Hmm.'' She didn't look too convinced, but her frown turned into a subdued smile that told Noah she appreciated his lifting the blame from Ethan's shoulders. ''Well, come on inside, then. Dinner's about ready.''

Noah's glance traveled to the roof of the Jeep. Caroline's followed. ''Oh, dear,'' she said when she saw the pizza. ''I guess we should have coordinated our dinner plans.''

''No problem.'' Noah walked over and retrieved the cardboard box. ''Pizza reheats.'' He signaled Ethan with a jerk of his head. ''Come on, slugger. Let's go chow down.''

Ethan shuffled across the driveway. ''Sorry I broke the window,'' he mumbled.

''You can help me fix it tomorrow, after I buy a new pane of glass.''

Ethan rubbed his nose with the back of his mitt. ''I could pay for it out of my allowance,'' he said. Then uncertainty fell across his face. '''Cept, I'm not sure if my mom's gonna give me one.''

Noah's heart went out to him. Poor kid. Each day brought new realizations of how his life was going to be different without his dad. ''Tell you what.'' He dropped a hand on the back of Ethan's neck and gave him a good-natured shake. ''You help me fix the window and we'll call it even, all right?''

Ethan peered up at him through the long lashes he'd inherited from his mother. ''You're not mad?''

''Who, me? Nah.'' They climbed the front steps together. ''Accidents happen. This one was pretty minor in the grand scheme of things.''

Caroline was waiting for them by the front door. As Noah and Ethan came inside, Noah locked glances with her over the top of Ethan's head. Gratitude shone in her eyes. Her lips curved into sort of a wistful slant, drawing Noah's attention to her mouth.

A primitive urge slammed into his gut like a hard throw to

home plate. He just hoped Caroline couldn't read what was probably in *his* eyes.

It stunned him, how much he wanted to kiss her again.

Stir crazy. That's what she must be. Cooped up in this isolated house all day long, stranded without transportation. Anxious to get back to Baltimore, back to work, back to her interrupted life with Ethan.

Caroline had been stirring up a storm, no doubt about it. The remains of the dinner she had spent all afternoon preparing had barely been cleared from the table before she was hunting through the cupboards for a mixing bowl so she could bake a loaf of banana bread.

She refused to consider the possibility that this frenzy of culinary activity was a subconscious effort to expend her energies on something more productive than wasted fantasies about a certain gorgeous sheriff's investigator.

So what if Noah was a terrific kisser? So what if he was wonderful with her son? Caroline's heart had led her astray once before, and she wasn't about to follow it blindly again.

Her heart? Who was she kidding? Her hormones were equally at fault. Unfortunately, she wasn't having much luck bringing them under control. Every time she relived that hot, hungry kiss she and Noah had shared in the dark last night...

Caroline's knees went weak. She leaned against the counter and vigorously whipped the bread batter with a wooden spoon.

As soon as they'd helped clean up after dinner, Noah and Ethan had retreated to the living room. Caroline had heard them in there a while ago, working to temporarily tape up the broken window with cardboard. Even though a solid pane of glass wouldn't stop a killer from breaking in, she would still feel better when Noah had replaced it tomorrow.

She was sliding the loaf pan into the oven when she heard Noah's footsteps behind her. "All finished," he said as he came into the kitchen.

Caroline closed the oven door and turned around, unable to squelch that little kick of anticipation she'd started to feel whenever Noah entered the room. He quickly yanked up his gaze. Unless Caroline was mistaken, he'd been enjoying a rear view of her bending over the oven.

The realization added to the heat on her cheeks. "Where's Ethan?" she asked.

"He volunteered to sweep up the broken glass." Noah scooped a dribble of batter from the mixing bowl and popped it into his mouth. "He's a good kid."

Caroline nearly made a tart retort about how she couldn't take much credit for that recently, thanks to Jeff. But she bit her tongue. Let it go, she thought. Jeff's gone and you have Ethan back. That's all that matters. The only person who'll suffer if you let this resentment keep surfacing is yourself. And probably Ethan.

Noah leaned against the counter. He'd changed into jeans and a cranberry polo shirt. This was the most casual Caroline had ever seen him dressed. His shirt clung to the muscular contours of his chest, reminding her of how she'd done the same thing herself last night.

She fanned her face with her hand. Boy, the oven sure heated the place up.

Noah's short sleeves revealed powerful biceps and a dusting of dark hair along his sturdy forearms. "I learned something interesting today," he said, fingering some more batter from the bowl. When he popped it into his mouth, Caroline's own mouth watered. Almost as if she could taste him herself.

She cranked on the faucet, grabbed the bowl and blasted a rush of water into it.

Noah spoke over the noise. "I found out Jeff applied for a bank loan not long before he died."

Caroline immediately switched off the water. "What for?" He had her full attention now, and not just because of his irresistible sex appeal.

"He wouldn't tell the bank." Noah's blue eyes watched her steadily. "But the bank manager told me they turned him down for a loan the same day he died."

Caroline dried her hands. "What does that mean?" she asked slowly.

"I'm not sure. But I've got a theory."

"Which is?"

Grim creases bracketed his mouth. "I think he was being blackmailed."

Caroline's jaw dropped. "Jeff? *Blackmailed?*"

"Well, he possessed one of the necessary ingredients for blackmail. A big secret he was desperate to keep hidden."

Caroline twisted the towel in her hands. "You mean the fact that he'd kidnapped Ethan."

"Something came up suddenly that had him scrambling for money. Twenty thousand dollars, to be exact." Noah ticked off a couple of points on his fingers. "Jeff asked his boss for a raise *and* applied for a loan shortly before he died."

"But he didn't get either one."

"No. And something else." He ticked off point number three. "I also found out that this Buck character apparently left town the same day Jeff was killed."

Caroline crinkled her brow. "Buck? Who's he?"

"Sorry." Noah gave his head a sharp shake, as if annoyed with himself. "I learned that's the name of the stranger Ethan overheard arguing with Jeff."

Caroline drew in a startled breath. "You *found* him?"

"Not yet." Noah eased the towel from her fingers. Caroline had practically knotted it into a rope. "But I found someone who recognized him and knew him by that name. My guess is that Buck was a transient. A drifter."

"And you think he was blackmailing Jeff?"

"Somehow he must have discovered Jeff's secret." Noah hung up the towel. "There was a lot of publicity when Ethan disappeared, wasn't there?"

Caroline gave a short, hard laugh. "You can say that again. And not just right after he disappeared. For three years I did everything possible to keep his face in front of the public. Television, newspapers, milk cartons, the whole bit." The memory of her terrible, hopeless crusade was like a ghost come back to haunt her. "I distributed enough fliers to wallpaper the entire country."

Maybe Noah saw that ghost flit through her expression. He grazed the back of one finger along Caroline's jaw in a strangely moving gesture of sympathy. "Buck must have spotted a picture of Ethan somewhere, and for some reason it stuck in his mind so that he recognized him here in Eagle River."

Despite Noah's tender touch, anger bubbled up inside Caroline. "I'd say old Buck made a serious error in judgment, wouldn't you?" She spat out the words bitterly. "Too bad he didn't try to weasel money out of *me*, instead. I'd have gladly paid him a heck of a lot more than Jeff could ever have come up with." She gouged her nails into her palms. "What's wrong with people like that, anyway?" she demanded. "How could that awful man try to make money off a missing child instead of helping return him to his mother?"

Noah settled an arm around Caroline's shoulders. Under other circumstances she would have been surprised... disconcerted...tempted to let her body respond to his. But right now she was too worked up.

"Believe me," Noah assured her, "in my line of work I ask myself that kind of question all the time." He squeezed her shoulders. "Unfortunately, there's no logical explanation for why some people do the rotten things they do."

"Do you think he killed Jeff?" Caroline asked in a low voice.

"I think it's possible." While he laid out his theory, Noah slid his hand up and down her arm, warming her with the gentle friction. Caroline wondered if he was even aware he was doing it. "Ethan heard Jeff and Buck arguing about money. Jeff then tried to get money—fast. Let's assume that the same day the bank turned Jeff down for a loan, Buck showed up at the gas station demanding his blackmail payment. When Jeff told him he couldn't come up with the money, Buck was furious. He threatened Jeff, forced him to open the safe and the cash register, then helped himself to the contents."

Caroline's stomach flipped over when she envisioned what must have come next. "Maybe Buck intended to kill Jeff to cover up the robbery," Noah speculated grimly. "Or maybe the two of them got into a physical fight and he killed Jeff by accident. Either way—"

A brittle cascade of noise made both of them jerk their heads toward the doorway. Ethan stood just inside the kitchen, his thin, rigid body trembling as if he were fighting to stand upright in a hurricane. His features were contorted, flushed with agitation. In one hand he clutched a broom. From the other dangled a metal dustpan. The last few shards of glass spilled off it, hitting the floor with tinkly, discordant notes.

Oh, no, moaned a voice inside Caroline's head. He must have overheard...

Ethan's brown eyes were as hard and round as polished agates. "I hate him!" he shouted. He dropped the dustpan. Spittle beaded at one corner of his mouth. "He killed my dad! I hate him! I hate him! I *hate* him!"

The broom crashed to the floor as he whirled and bolted down the hallway.

Chapter 8

Noah was just dumping the last specks of shattered glass into the trash bag beneath the sink when Caroline came back. She looked pale. Upset. Beautiful.

"How's Ethan?" he asked, storing the broom and dustpan in the corner.

She sank into a chair at the table and plunged her fingers through her hair. "He wouldn't open the door to his room. He just kept saying, 'Leave me alone.'" Hurt trembled in her voice.

Noah sat down beside her. "Guess that's all you can do, then. For now." He could imagine how helpless Caroline must feel. Instinct urged him to scoot a little closer, to draw her head down onto his shoulder, wrap his arms around her and offer what comfort he could.

But instinct had been Noah's traitorous enemy ever since Caroline had stepped off that plane from Baltimore and turned his life upside down. This time, Noah's better judgment won out. He didn't touch her.

"I think it's probably a good sign, that Ethan's angry."

Caroline gazed at him with vulnerable, hopeful eyes that made Noah ache to give her what she wanted. "That's one of the stages people go through after they've suffered a tragic loss," she went on. "Shock, denial, anger, then finally acceptance." She nodded as if she'd succeeded at convincing herself. "So the fact that Ethan is furious at the man who killed his father means he's making progress in accepting Jeff's death."

A sharp, crushing memory flashed through Noah. The memory of the night when he'd returned to his house alone, after Beth and Molly's funeral. He remembered pain slamming through him, rage turning his vision red. Wood splintering, glass crashing, fabric ripping like the sound of his heart being torn out of him.

It came back to him in a sickening rush, that frantic need to smash things before he turned that destructive urge upon himself.

Unfortunately, in Noah's case, acceptance hadn't followed anger. He hoped it would be different for Ethan. But then, why shouldn't it be? Ethan hadn't been the person responsible for his father's death.

The blackness descended over Noah once more, smothering and oppressive. Headlights stabbing through the night, bearing down on him...

His chair scraped back as he shoved himself to his feet. Caroline sprang up at the same moment, confusing him. Did she see those headlights, too?

"Oh, gosh! My banana bread!" She grabbed a pair of pot holders and leaped for the oven. Heat whooshed out like the breath of a furnace. She settled the pan on top of the stove, shut the oven door and stood there fanning herself with a pot holder. "A little well-done, but not burned, thank goodness. I completely forgot about it!"

Strands of cornsilk hair swirled back from her temples. Her face was rosy from the heat. Noah was seized by a profound hunger that had nothing to do with the appetizing smell drifting through the kitchen.

But something else gnawed at the pit of his stomach, too.

Uneasiness about how natural it felt, having her here. About the way she'd fitted herself into his life like a puzzle piece he hadn't even known was missing, and made his house feel almost like a home again.

Noah deliberately positioned himself so the table was between them. "Caroline, you really don't have to do all this."

That delectable little spot between her eyebrows puckered in bewilderment. "All what?"

"All this—" He rotated his hand in frustration, like a spinning tire stuck in mud. "All this—cooking."

Caroline continued to regard him blankly.

"Like that fantastic dinner you fixed tonight," Noah said. He realized he must sound like an ungrateful idiot. But he had to put a stop to these cozy meals together before he got used to them. Next thing he knew, she'd be packing a lunch for him every morning.

Caroline frowned uncertainly. "Ethan and I have to eat, too. It's no trouble to make enough for three."

"Well...the banana bread, then." Noah speared a finger at the pan as if pointing out an incriminating piece of evidence. "You shouldn't have gone to all that trouble."

Caroline narrowed her eyes at him. "The bananas were overripe," she said slowly, like a teacher talking to a dull-witted pupil. "They would have gone to waste if I hadn't used them."

Noah felt himself floundering. He couldn't even put his finger on exactly what was bugging him. But he was too stubborn to quit, now that he'd made a big deal about it.

"It isn't just the cooking. It's the—the—flowers." He gestured at the newly plucked bouquet of wildflowers in the center of the table. "And the cleaning." He whipped open the refrigerator like Houdini revealing the amazing disappearance of someone he'd just locked into it. "This morning when I was getting out the milk, I noticed you'd gone through and thrown out all my leftovers."

Caroline arched an eyebrow. "From what I could see, most

of them dated from sometime near the start of the last Ice Age.'' Her chin jutted forward a defensive fraction of an inch.

''I know.'' Noah held up his palm. ''And I appreciate the fact that you tossed them out.'' He let the refrigerator door swing shut. ''But it's not necessary. You're supposed to be my—my *guest*.'' That wasn't quite the right word, but he couldn't come up with a better one. ''It makes me feel guilty, all the work you go to.''

''Oh, really?'' A faint glow that might have been comprehension lit up Caroline's eyes. She fixed Noah with a look that made him feel like a germ under a microscope. ''Is that what's making you feel guilty?''

''Yes. No. I mean—'' He scrubbed his fingers through his hair in exasperation. What the hell did he mean, anyway? He wasn't even sure himself any longer.

Caroline came around the table. Noah had to fight the desire to retreat backward. He didn't care for that penetrating, analytic expression of hers one bit. ''I think it's more than that,'' she said. ''Look, as long as Ethan and I are stuck here, I'm thrilled to have something to do to keep myself busy all day. Other than hovering over Ethan, which he hates.'' Her lips clamped into a tight line, as if she were trying to keep her chin from quivering.

Noah said hastily, ''I just don't want you to feel obligated to—''

''It's because I'm trespassing on your wife's territory, isn't it?'' A dab of color blazed on each perfect cheekbone. ''You resent it, don't you? That I've made myself at home in her kitchen.''

''No!'' He grabbed Caroline's shoulders, torn between thrusting her away and hauling her into his arms. He forced his muscles to unclench. ''This—isn't her kitchen. This isn't the same house I lived in with Beth and Molly.'' He released his grip.

If Caroline had been startled by his rough handling of her, she didn't show it. ''But I'm still trespassing,'' she said thoughtfully, her gaze never leaving his face. "Someplace you don't want me to go."

Noah thought of all those fences he'd erected to barricade his heart. About how Caroline kept finding ways to slip through them, no matter how quickly he kept hammering new boards into place. Trespassing.

"Yeah," he said finally. "I guess you could call it that."

Though she tried to hide it, Noah glimpsed the injured look that flashed through her eyes. For a second she wore the same hurt expression as when she'd reported how Ethan had told her to leave him alone.

Then something fragile in her features hardened, like delicate blown glass. "Look, this whole arrangement certainly wasn't my idea." She gave her chair an abrupt shove to push it under the table. "I'm not any happier about this situation than you are. All I'm trying to do is make the best of it."

"Caroline, I'm sorry. I realize this is difficult for both of—"

"For whatever it's worth, I'm not trying to take your wife's place. That's the last thing I'd ever want." She blinked rapidly, lashes fluttering like agitated butterflies. "Believe me, I never want to be anyone's wife again." Her lips twisted with what she may have intended as scorn. But the overall effect was the opposite. "Here." She dug into one pocket of her slacks and fished out a folded slip of paper. "Here's a shopping list for tomorrow. We're almost out of food." She flung it onto the kitchen table and made for the doorway.

"Caroline, wait." Noah moved to stop her, but she dodged neatly around him.

An uncomfortable mixture of yearning and remorse filled him as he listened to her footsteps pattering up the stairs. He had to anchor his hands to the edge of the table to keep himself from following.

He wanted to go after her. To tell Caroline that he hadn't meant what he'd said about trespassing. But he *had* meant it. Hadn't he?

* * *

Around five in the afternoon a couple of days later, Noah
crossed his hands behind his head, leaned back in his chair
and propped his feet on an open desk drawer. Let's see, if he
had to make a guess, he would predict that cold pizza and an
ever colder reception were both on the menu for dinner tonight. His prediction was based on what he'd been served last
night when he got home.

Well, he had no one to blame but himself, did he? Hadn't
he told Caroline in so many words that he had no appetite for
the delicious meals and welcoming atmosphere she'd created?

Except now he was forced to admit to himself how much
he actually missed sitting down to dinner with her and Ethan
in that warm, cozy kitchen.

Noah wasn't exactly looking forward to another evening of
indigestion and awkward silences. So he was relieved when
Zack Hastings stuck his head into the office.

"Ozzie wants to talk to you," Noah's deputy informed him.
"Says that character on the Wanted poster was hanging around
his bar last week." Zack meant the sketch of Buck.

Ozzie Baines ran the Mineshaft Saloon. Five minutes later
Noah's rear end was planted on one of Ozzie's barstools. The
smell of stale beer and old cigarette smoke hung on the murky
air. From the back room came the crack of billiard balls. Except for one lone drinker at the far end of the bar and a couple
who looked like tourists sitting by the front window, Noah
and Ozzie had the place to themselves. Happy Hour in Eagle
River was a pretty low-key affair.

Noah tapped his finger on the sketch he'd laid on top of the
bar. "You ever hear this guy mention his name?"

"Nah." Ozzie continued mopping the well-worn wood with
a damp rag. "He come round here a coupla times, nursed a
shot of my bottom-dollar whiskey for about an hour, then left.
Looked to me like he was hopin' if he hung around long
enough, someone might come in and buy a round for the house
so he'd get himself a free drink."

Noah sipped the faint taste of guilt along with the beer Ozzie had poured him. He made a mental note to insist on paying

for it when he left. "Anyone ever buy him a drink? Maybe sit down and talk with him for a while?"

Ozzie shrugged. With his sagging jowls and bloodshot eyes, he resembled a tall, skinny basset hound. "Last time he come in here was the day Rollie Fletcher was showin' off that gold nugget he found. Rollie come in here to celebrate, swore everyone sitting at the bar to secrecy about his big find. Like that would do any good." Ozzie snorted. "I remember thinking if Rollie weren't so blasted cheap, that fella mighta finally got himself a free drink after all." The bar owner cracked a cynical smile. "Course, to hear him tell it, pretty soon *he* was gonna be the one buying drinks for everyone."

"Who? You mean this guy on the poster?"

Ozzie nodded while he emptied an ashtray full of peanut shells. "Yup. Claimed he was gonna come into some big money any day now."

"He say how?" Blackmail, Noah was thinking.

"Nah. He was just blowin' hot air, that's what I figured." The front door admitted a welcome sweep of daylight along with two new customers. One of them was Andy Johnson, a local carpenter and the son of Irene, who owned the diner.

Andy bellied up to the bar next to Noah. "Hey, Sarge."

"Andy."

"Ozzie, give us a coupla cold ones, huh?" While Ozzie busied himself getting the beer, Andy drummed his fingers on the bar, tapped his foot, swiveled his head around to check out the other customers. Andy usually seemed to have a surplus of nervous energy, as if electricity ran through his internal wiring.

Eventually his gaze landed on the police sketch in front of Noah. "Hey, it's the Buck Man," he said, grabbing a handful of peanuts from the nearest bowl.

Noah sat up straighter. "You know this guy?" he asked, pointing at the drawing.

Andy shrugged. "Saw him in here once or twice." He cracked a peanut between his thumb and forefinger and popped the shelled nuts into his mouth.

"You know his name?" Noah mentally crossed his fingers.

"Buckman, he told me. That's why I called him the Buck Man. Buck...Man. Buckman. Get it?" He chomped noisily.

"I get it," Noah said. A little fizz of excitement crept into his bloodstream. "That his last name?"

"Guess so." Crunch, crunch.

"You know his first name?"

"Nope." Andy reached thirstily for the beers Ozzie had just set on the bar. "Hey, nice talking to you, Sarge." He carried the beers over to the table where his buddy was sitting.

Ozzie wiped up the damp rings left behind. "You think this guy's the killer?" He flicked his rag at the poster.

"I think he might have some useful information," Noah answered carefully. He eased off the bar stool and drew out his wallet. "You be sure and give me a call if he shows up here again, will you?"

"You bet. Hey, put that away. Your money's no good here."

Noah dropped a couple of bills next to his half-finished beer. "Consider it payment for your help, then. I sure appreciate it."

"Always glad to do my duty, just like any other public-minded citizen." The *ka-ching!* of Ozzie's old-fashioned cash register rang in Noah's ears as he stepped out of the darkened bar. He blinked as if it was high noon outside instead of approaching dinnertime. All over Eagle River casseroles were sliding into ovens, tables were being set, good smells were coming out of kitchens.

Not from Noah Garrett's kitchen, though. It was back to microwave dinners and warmed-up leftovers for him.

With a sigh, he walked back to the substation so he could send out the name Buckman to the jurisdictions where he'd already distributed the sketch. Ruby waved a yellow message slip at him as soon as he came through the door.

Noah frowned at it. "Who's Mrs. Glass?"

Ruby resumed typing at machine-gun speed. "She claims to be a friend of yours. Said you knew her number."

Glass. The only thing that name brought to mind was—

Good grief. The pane of glass he'd bought yesterday to fix the broken window at home. This cryptic message must be Caroline's way of asking him to call her without leaving her real name.

Noah hustled into his office and closed the door. He hoped nothing was wrong. But why would she need to get in touch with him?

He listened to his own answering machine pick up. Obviously Caroline wouldn't answer the phone unless she knew it was him.

"Caroline? It's me. It's okay to pick up the phone. Are you there? Hello?"

He kept up his one-sided conversation until the machine cut him off. Hmm. If Caroline had wanted to talk to him, why hadn't she answered? Unless...

"See you tomorrow," he told his startled secretary as he rushed past her desk.

"You're leaving? But what about—" The door swinging shut cut off the rest of Ruby's puzzled question.

This is stupid, Noah assured himself as he roared off in the Jeep. You don't even know for certain that Caroline left that message. Maybe there really *is* a Mrs. Glass, and you've just forgotten her.

But then why hadn't Caroline picked up the phone?

Noah stepped a little harder on the gas.

Maybe she's still mad. Maybe she doesn't want to talk to you.

There were any number of maybes. And one or two of them sent a chill up his spine.

Noah was halfway home before he noticed the car following him. He'd spotted the beat-up compact sedan back in town. Hadn't recognized it at the time. But it had made the same turns he had, stayed the same distance behind him for the last half mile, even though Noah was recklessly breaking the speed limit.

The car's persistent, somehow ominous presence in his rearview mirror added to his uneasy feeling that something was wrong.

Up ahead was a dirt road that led to a couple of vacation cabins up in the mountains. Noah made a sharp right turn into it and screeched to a halt. He leaped out of the Jeep and concealed himself behind some trees.

Sure enough, the other car nosed around the turn moments later. It skidded on the gravel when the driver braked suddenly to avoid hitting the Jeep parked in the road. Noah catapulted from his hiding place and had his fingers on the car door handle before the other vehicle even came to a complete stop.

The driver squawked as Noah yanked him out of his seat and shoved him up against the side of the car.

"Lost?" he inquired through clenched teeth.

"Hey, easy, easy!" His pursuer was a kid in his twenties, vaguely familiar, with a mop of red hair and a sly, superior twist to his mouth that Noah didn't like very much. "I just wanted to ask you a few questions, is all. I'm a reporter."

"That so?" Noah tightened fistfuls of the kid's shirt. "They teach you how to tail people in journalism school? 'Cause maybe you ought to go back for a refresher course."

Now the kid looked nervous. Noah had to give him credit, though. He didn't back down. "Look, I've been phoning your office for days trying to get information on the Tate murder investigation." He hoisted his chin to an indignant angle. "You never return my calls."

Noah visualized all those yellow message slips drifting into his wastepaper basket like autumn leaves. "I've got better things to do with my time than answer questions for reporters."

In truth, Noah hadn't been bothered much by the press after the initial flurry of excitement about this case had died down. The big-city news media, attracted by the human-interest angle, had soon gone back home to cover newer, more sensational crimes. As for local coverage, the *Eagle River Gazette* only came out once a week and was mainly devoted to high-school sports scores and supermarket specials.

Noah thought he might recognize this kid from the paper over in Carleton, the county seat. He'd spotted him at the sheriff's press conference, straining eagerly for attention like the know-it-all kid in math class frantically waving his hand to get the teacher to call on him.

"I don't have time for an interview," Noah said, releasing the kid's shirt. "Get back in your car and drive away. Now."

"Just one question, then." Noah responded with a glare that probably would have made the kid back up, except his car was in the way. "I tried to contact Caroline Tate back in Baltimore," he continued quickly, "to ask how she and her son are doing. And you know what?"

Noah fought to maintain a bland expression.

"According to my sources, Ms. Tate and her son never went back to Baltimore." Triumph flared in his pale eyes. "So I asked myself, where could they be? And I decided you'd be the person to ask." That sly look was back now. "I mean, since you're in charge of the case and all, you must know the location of a potentially important witness. The boy, I mean. Ethan." He arched his brows to convey innocence. "Has his memory come back, by the way?"

White-hot anger surged through Noah, all out of proportion to the situation. The kid was only doing his job, after all. But it was anger born of fear. Fear that something could have happened to Caroline and Ethan.

After all, if Jimmy Olson here had discovered they hadn't gone back to Baltimore, the killer could have found out, too. And come looking for them.

Maybe that was why Caroline hadn't answered the phone....

"Get in your car," Noah said with a calm he was far from feeling. "Back it up. Drive away from here." He pushed his face close to the reporter's. "If I catch you following me again, I'll throw you in jail. Got that?"

The kid sidled toward the car door. "Haven't you ever heard of freedom of the press?" he mumbled under his breath.

Noah made a sound in his throat. The kid scrambled into

the car. Seconds later its tires were spinning on the gravel as
he peeled out of there.

Noah waited for as long as he could stand it, to make sure
the reporter was really gone. He couldn't risk letting the kid
outsmart him, follow him home, discover Caroline and Ethan
there.

That's if they still *were* there.

All at once Noah couldn't wait one second longer. He
shoved the Jeep into gear, whipped it around and took off for
home at a speed he would have arrested anyone else for.

He hadn't been able to protect Beth and Molly. Was he
about to fail Caroline and Ethan in the same terrible way?

Caroline blinked back tears as she studied the framed photograph in her hands. An attractive woman around thirty, with
sparkling eyes and curly brown hair, had her arms wrapped
around a little girl who looked about four. The little girl resembled a bright-eyed cherub, with long golden ringlets and
rosy cheeks. Her beaming smile revealed two big dimples and
a narrow gap between her front baby teeth. She was adorable.

Caroline hadn't meant to snoop through Noah's desk, hadn't
meant to find this picture of Beth and Molly hidden away at
the back of a bottom drawer. She'd come into the room Noah
used for an office looking for a calculator, so she could occupy
herself this evening toying with some business projections for
her company.

When she hadn't found a calculator on top of his desk, she'd
peeked into one of the top drawers, which had been cracked
open a tiny bit anyway. Then she'd gone ahead and pulled it
all the way out. Before she knew it, she'd been rooting through
all the drawers, searching impatiently, thinking he had to have
a calculator in there somewhere.

Then she'd discovered the picture of Beth and Molly. So
Noah hadn't got rid of every single reminder of his lost wife
and child! Obviously, however, he still couldn't bear to look
at them. Sympathy and sorrow squeezed Caroline's heart. As
long as Noah continued to blame himself for their deaths, this

beautiful photograph would stay shut away, out of sight. Noah would never be able to get past his devastating loss and move on with his life.

How terribly sad, Caroline thought. He would make such a wonderful husband for some lucky woman. A fabulous father for some lucky child.

Not for her and Ethan, though. What if Caroline had him pegged all wrong? What if she let Noah become an important part of their lives, only to have him turn out to be another Jeff? Ethan had already lost one father. Caroline would never, ever let that happen again.

Not that she would ever have to make that decision, of course. Noah might be physically attracted to her, but he could hardly have made it plainer that he wanted no meaningful involvement with her or any other woman. He'd clearly posted his emotions as out of bounds. No trespassing.

It was just so difficult to remain aloof from him, when—

"Caroline?" The bang of the front door made her jump. Holy cow, it was Noah! He was going to discover her in his office, rummaging through his private possessions, her incriminating fingerprints smeared all over the picture he would be furious to know she'd found.

Quick as a wink she slid the picture back into the drawer and eased it shut.

"Caroline, where are you?"

Oh, Lord, what should she do? There wasn't time to make sure she'd put everything back exactly the way it had been. Noah was so darned observant, it would take him about half a second to notice someone had gone through his desk.

"Caroline!" His footsteps pounded down the hall. "Ethan!"

Yikes! As soon as he passed the doorway he would catch sight of her out of the corner of his eye, trapped behind his desk like a prisoner in the dock.

Caroline dropped to her knees and ducked her head. Some irrational, childish instinct had made her do it, and now she really was trapped if Noah came in here. How on earth was she going to explain crouching down behind his desk? *Oh, I was, um, looking for something I dropped.* Except what had she been doing in here in the first place?

Relief washed over her when she heard his footsteps pass by. Goodness, what was he yelling about, anyway?

Now he was pounding up the stairs. "Caroline! Ethan! Are you here?"

"Where *else* would we be?" she muttered under her breath.

Then she realized this was her chance. She scooted out from behind the desk, casting one final look to make sure she hadn't left any drawers open—oops, that top one had been open just a crack. She hastily adjusted it, then hurried out of the office as fast as tiptoeing allowed.

"Noah?" She made herself walk slower, breathe slower. But she couldn't do much about her heart rate. "Noah, I'm down here," she called from the foot of the steps. She caught a glimpse of him disappearing down the upstairs hallway.

Immediately he turned and came thundering down the staircase.

"Is something wrong?" she asked, alarmed by the look on his face. "You seem kind of—*oof!*" Her question was cut off when Noah squeezed all the air from her lungs in a big bear hug. Caroline was shocked and delighted at the same time. What on earth had brought this on?

For a moment she allowed herself to savor the exquisite sensation of Noah's arms around her. He held her so close to his chest that she could feel his heart thumping through the layers of clothing that separated them. Maybe it was because he was holding her so tight, but it almost felt like his arms were shaking.

She could barely breathe with her face pressed into the front of his shirt. She crinkled her nose, puzzled. The faint smell of cigarette smoke clung to his clothes. Even so, Caroline's oxygen-deprived senses were aroused by the sexy masculine scent that had already become familiar to her. Even blindfolded, she would have known it was Noah holding her.

Tentatively, she slid her hands beneath his jacket, around

his waist, tracing the edge of his belt with her fingertips. She had just gathered the courage to venture beneath the tooled leather when Noah grasped her shoulders and thrust her backward.

"You didn't answer the phone," he said. Beneath his accusing tone Caroline detected relief and something else she couldn't quite identify.

"Answer what phone? *This* one?" She dropped her hands from his waist. "Well, of course not. We don't want people to know I'm here, remember?"

His eyes darted back and forth across her face, as if he were trying to memorize her features for a police sketch. "Why didn't you pick up when you heard my voice come on the answering machine?"

"When?" Caroline didn't know which confused her more—Noah's questions or his strange behavior.

"Just a little while ago. Here." He took hold of her hand and towed her into the office where she'd been hiding from him only minutes earlier. He punched a button on the machine that sat on his desk. Caroline tried not to look guilty.

Noah's recorded voice emerged, sounding baffled at first, progressing to concern, then skirting outright fear toward the end. "Caroline? If you're there, for God's sake pick up the phone!"

He punched another button when the message ended. "Didn't you hear all that when I called?"

Caroline found Noah's exasperation rather touching. Clearly he'd been awfully worried about her. Though she still had no idea why. "Ethan and I ate dinner early, then went for a walk in the woods," she explained. "Your call must have come while we were outside."

"Where is Ethan, anyway?" Noah craned his neck to see past Caroline, as if hoping to spot Ethan right behind her. That worried crease between his dark brows was back.

"Up in his room." Caroline pointed at the ceiling and sighed. "I think he's going through some more of the stuff we brought back from Jeff's the other night."

"He didn't answer me just now when I called."

"He's got the door shut. He probably didn't hear you."

"Who's Mrs. Glass?"

"Mrs.—? Oh." Caroline's cheeks grew warm. "That was just my clever attempt to leave you a message to call me. I forgot to put butter on my shopping list the other day. I wanted to ask if you could stop off and pick some up on your way home." Now his dazed expression was starting to worry *her.* She tugged on his hand. "Noah, what's all this about?"

"Butter?" He tightened his grip as if he thought she were about to run away. "This whole thing was about butter?"

"*What* whole thing?" She experimented with wiggling her fingers loose. Nope. "I don't have the slightest idea what you're talking about."

Noah groaned. "Caroline." He pulled her to him again and freed her fingers so he could plunge both hands through her hair. "Caroline, you scared the pants off me! I thought something had—that someone—oh, hell." He closed his eyes as if struggling for control.

When he opened them, what Caroline saw there took her breath away. "I was afraid something had happened to you," he said in a low voice.

Then he hauled off and kissed her. Like a man given a second chance to do it right.

Chapter 9

She was warm and lovely and alive, and she was kissing Noah back with all the sweet, hot urgency he himself could no longer control.

He couldn't believe how good Caroline felt in his arms, her soft curves molded against him, her mouth straining eagerly beneath his. Her shimmering hair flowed across his fingers like the finest silk. With his hands gently cupping her head, Noah could feel the excited flutter of her pulse in the slender column of her throat.

Between her parted lips he found her tongue with his. A hunger surged through him that swept away the boundaries of his previous experience. With a certainty that was part elation, part despair, Noah realized that no matter how long or how often he kissed Caroline Tate, he would never get enough of her.

"Mmm." He dragged his lips from hers to explore the soft, sensual curve of her neck. In the open V of her blouse collar he found the sexy hollow that had fascinated him from the first. Just as he'd thought. His mouth was a perfect fit.

Caroline's head fell backward. Noah buried his face in her hair, inhaling that elusive, maddening fragrance of hers that would drift tantalizingly across his consciousness at odd moments of the day, distracting and tormenting him like a ghostly temptress who wouldn't leave him alone. "You smell so good," he whispered into the perfect, delicate shell of her ear. He nibbled her earlobe. "Mmm, you taste so good, too...."

A shiver passed through Caroline's body, making her tremble like a slender willow in the breeze. Noah drew his hands slowly down her back, curving them around the narrow span of her waist, the enticing swell of her hips. He wanted to acquaint himself intimately with every soft, gorgeous square inch of her. He ached with the desperate need to protect her. To cherish her. To make her his.

His hands traveled upward to encounter her breasts. A tiny whimper of pleasure escaped her throat, arousing him as intensely as the soft, yielding flesh beneath his fingers. A white-hot flare of desire ignited in his loins, burning away whatever lingering reluctance might have warned him to slow down.

He backed into his desk with a bump, sending miscellaneous items clattering and rolling across the top. He hoisted himself halfway onto the edge, bracing himself so he could coax Caroline into the angle formed by his thighs. She sucked in a sharp breath as he nestled her intimately against him in a bold demonstration of how much he wanted her. Her face was so close to his that a sea of green filled Noah's vision when she stared at him with those wide, magnificent eyes.

He let himself be lured into their depths. *Let* himself? Who was he kidding? He was as eager to plunge in as a man on fire would be to dive into a swimming pool. He drew Caroline closer...closer...until he saw her eyes drift shut and felt her arms come around his neck. Their lips reunited in a delicious fusion that was even hotter, more frenzied than before.

She tasted like the sweetest, most intoxicating nectar on earth. In some distant, detached corner of his mind Noah was startled by his own greedy, out-of-control thirst. Caroline responded to him with her mouth, her hands, her entire body as if she was driven by the same fierce, reckless craving he was.

She rubbed herself seductively against him, sending shards of excruciating pleasure splintering through him. She teased her fingers through his hair, tortured him with her lips. Oh, man, did he want her! In a thousand different ways he couldn't even begin to imagine. The world seemed to tilt on its axis, swirling around Noah, blurring everything except for the acutely clear, increasingly painful fact that he wanted this woman in his bed. Now.

"Caroline," he growled hoarsely as soon as he could pry his mouth away from hers. Then he couldn't stop himself from dragging his lips along her jawline...down her creamy, smooth throat...to savor that exquisite hollow at the base of her neck once more....

In between kisses he managed to groan, "Caro...I want...to make...love with you."

Beneath his lips the purring in her throat went silent. Her hands stilled their intimate caresses. And something grew taut inside her.

Caution took a moment to gain control over passion. Desire ebbed slowly from Noah's belly, not enough to extinguish the fiery need inside him, but just enough to leave him chilled. And feeling empty.

He lifted his head so he could see what was in her eyes. As her expression came into focus, dread seeped into the pit of his stomach. "Caroline? What's wrong?"

She pushed her hair back from one side of her face. The fingers of her other hand fluttered against his shoulder in a little tap dance of indecision. "I—" She swallowed with a dry clicking sound. Her lips were red...lush...swollen and moist from his kisses. A fresh spear of desire shot through him, even though he sensed its target was now out of reach.

Caroline's gaze broke from his, darting everywhere like a nervous butterfly. Finally her eyes met Noah's again. "I don't think we—I mean—" She broke off, flustered. This was a side of her Noah hadn't seen before. Caroline never hesitated to say what was on her mind. The fact that she was having trouble finding words hardly seemed like a good sign.

Her discomfort was contagious. All at once the fact that Noah was still holding her in his arms, that he'd just been kissing her with bruising, mindless passion—that he'd wanted to take her to bed, for Pete's sake—seemed the height of stupidity. Of recklessness. Of presumption.

A huge mistake, in other words.

But damn it, he still wanted her.

He loosened his hold. "It's okay, Caroline. We don't have to take this any further." A voice inside his head warned they'd already taken it too far. Too bad the rest of his anatomy wasn't listening.

She was still nestled between his thighs, her hands resting lightly on his arms. "It isn't that I don't...return your feelings." She licked her lips. An uncomfortable stirring in his groin made Noah push himself off the edge of his desk to stand upright. Caroline took the opportunity to back away from him a little. A subtle maneuver, but unmistakable. She wanted to extricate herself from their embrace, but didn't know how to do it without embarrassment.

Noah decided to spare them both. He pressed a kiss to her forehead, brushing aside several golden strands of hair that clung to his mouth. Then he released her and stepped aside. "You don't have to explain. I understand."

"No, you don't." He was surprised when she didn't take the face-saving escape route he offered. Then again, he shouldn't have been. Caroline never took the easy way out.

"Please, I don't want you to think I'm trying to be...coy. A tease." She straightened her blouse. Noah imagined his handprints all over it. "After all, we're both adults. Responsible adults. We ought to be able to...make love if we feel like it." Her cheeks turned even pinker.

Despite the awkwardness of the situation and the insistent throbbing below his belt buckle, Noah was amused by the way she stumbled over the words *make love*. Here she was, a sophisticated, successful businesswoman, who'd been married,

borne a child and been to hell and back. And she still had
trouble referring to that most intimate act between a man and
a woman.

"I didn't mean to pressure you," Noah said. "It was inexcusable." Something else struck him as vaguely ludicrous.
Moments ago he'd been as turned on as he could ever remember being in his life. He and Caroline had been about as physically close as two people could be without actually merging
into one. Yet they'd both remained fully clothed. Hardly a
button was out of place on Caroline's blouse, while Noah himself was still wearing his jacket and tie as if all set to head
off to work.

How could their embrace have felt as erotic and exciting as
if they'd both been writhing around stark naked on the desk
top?

Ouch. Noah thought about staples and pencils and other
hard, sharp objects. Just as well Caroline had called a halt to
the whole thing.

So why did he feel such an enormous letdown?

Pure biology, he assured himself. That's all it was. The male
body responded to certain stimuli in certain specific ways, and
if nature wasn't allowed to take its course, well, certain physical consequences were inevitable.

But that didn't explain the hollow sensation in his chest.

"You weren't pressuring me," Caroline said, fiddling with
one of the buttons Noah hadn't gotten around to undoing. "I
was equally responsible. Equally...enthusiastic." A self-
conscious smile touched her lips. "And I—well, I certainly
won't deny I'm attracted to you. At...a number of levels."
Her mouth twisted wryly. "I'm sure that's obvious. So it was
only natural for you to assume that we—that I—um, that this
attraction would proceed to its logical conclusion."

Noah could see what she was doing. Trying to analyze the
incredible explosion of desire and need and sheer physical
pleasure that had just occurred between them. Trying to pi-
geonhole their feelings into rational little slots with labels in

an effort to tame and control them. Trying to bring order out of chaos.

Problem was, feelings weren't always so easily sorted out and labeled. Noah knew that better than anyone.

"Logical conclusion?" he echoed, stepping across the distance that separated them. It took all of his willpower not to touch her again. "You mean, sleeping together? Having sex? Doing the wild thing?" He didn't know what perverse imp was making him spell it out in such blunt terms. Maybe he was trying to torture himself with what he'd missed out on. Or maybe he just wanted to see her blush again.

Feisty sparks glittered in her eyes. "Yes. Making love." The way she said those two words sent heat flowing through his belly again.

Noah fisted his hands to keep from reaching for her. "Don't worry about it. I'm hardly some hormone-charged teenager with only one thing on his mind." At least part of that was true, anyway. "You were right to put the brakes on. There are...ethical considerations here, if not legal ones." He forced himself to move away from her. Around his desk, so it formed an obstacle to any dumb impulses he might have. "After all, you're the mother of a witness in a murder I'm investigating. If it ever comes to a trial, I can just imagine what a defense lawyer would make out of an affair between us."

"An affair." Her lip curled as if she didn't like the taste of the term very much. "Yes. Well, you see, I can't afford to have affairs. Not with you, or with anyone else. Because of Ethan."

Noah was momentarily distracted by the unpleasant vision of Caroline having an affair with someone else. "What do you mean?" he finally asked.

She paced back and forth in front of his desk, hands moving as if she were plucking thoughts out of the air. She would have made a great college professor, Noah decided. Always analyzing, struggling to form abstract feelings into words.

It was one of the qualities he found most endearing about her. But also one of the most unsettling.

"I can't let myself get involved with anyone again. Ever." That pronouncement appeared to strike her as a shade melodramatic. She pursed her mouth. "Well, not until Ethan's grown up, anyway."

"You think you have to devote yourself entirely to him from now on?" Not that Noah was trying to change Caroline's mind about involvement or anything. But such obsessive devotion to her son didn't sound particularly healthy.

"It's not just that. I'll admit, now that I have him back, it's hard not to keep him within hugging distance twenty-four hours a day." A wistful smile illuminated her face. "But I know that would drive Ethan crazy. I don't intend to turn into a smothering, overprotective parent." Steel glinted in her eyes. "But I'm not going to take the risk of letting Ethan suffer another devastating loss, either."

Noah picked up a stray pencil and tapped it on the desk. "What kind of loss are you talking about, exactly?"

"Another loss like his father's death." Caroline straightened her spine. She went on almost defiantly, "Any man who became part of my life would become part of Ethan's as well. And any man I'd be interested in would be someone Ethan could look up to. Someone who could become a father figure to him."

"I see." Though he tried to dodge the fact, Noah had to admit how much that role would appeal to him. Ethan was a good kid. Noah would have been proud to have a son like him...if only things had turned out differently.

"Jeff wasn't much of a husband, but he loved Ethan. And Ethan loved him." Sadness clouded Caroline's pretty features. Noah knew she was mourning not the loss of the ex-husband who'd betrayed her, but of the man she'd once believed him to be. "Jeff's death has been an awful blow to Ethan. One that'll affect him the rest of his life." Her gaze seemed to edge away from Noah's while she said, "I won't risk letting Ethan become attached to someone else that way. There are all types of losses besides death. And no guarantees that any man I...got involved with would stick around permanently to be a father to my son.''

Noah's instinctive reaction was to deny that. To point out that any man lucky enough to be part of Caroline's life would be the world's biggest fool to walk away from her and her son. To swear that *he* would never be such a fool.

Then he got a grip on himself. Exactly what kind of promise would he be making? How had a discussion of sex turned into a debate about happily-ever-after? Caroline was spelling it out as clearly as she could for him, that she wasn't interested in committing herself to a relationship. And after barely one week's acquaintance, Noah clearly recognized she wasn't the type of woman to sleep with a man she wasn't committed to.

You didn't have to be a math genius to figure out that equation.

Fine. There would be no romps in the hay, no frolicking between the sheets.

But even as he tried to make light of what he would be missing, Noah knew deep down inside that making love with Caroline would have meant a lot more than that.

Maybe that was the biggest reason of all to be thankful she'd pulled away from him. Strangely, though, gratitude didn't seem to be one of the emotions churning in his gut right now.

''Well, you're certainly right about one thing,'' he said, pretending to straighten his desk by shoving objects around in a random arrangement. ''Life sure doesn't come with any guarantees.'' No way to ask for your money back, no way to exchange it for a brand-new one if the life you'd originally been handed abruptly destructed right before your eyes.

Noah saw those headlights again, racing toward him out of the darkness. For some reason they seemed dimmer this time, or maybe the night was less black.

He felt Caroline's clear-eyed scrutiny tracking the aimless movements of his hands. Both of them had had their blissful visions of the future shattered—those innocent dreams of the rose-strewn path of life that was supposed to follow the magical words, "I do." Caroline had lost her dream to disillusionment and betrayal. Noah had lost his to a deafening explosion of glass and steel on a quiet country road.

No guarantees in life. Yet Caroline seemed to have made it her mission to convince Noah to take risks again, with all her encouragement about facing his past, overcoming his grief and moving on with his life. He could see by the troubled look on her face that she'd just mentally collided with the rather large, inconvenient contradiction in her philosophy. How could Caroline justify a refusal to take risks in her own life, when she seemed bent on persuading Noah that's exactly what *he* ought to do?

With a sigh, he decided they could both use some time alone. "Think I'll go grab a quick shower before I eat." Noah was careful to keep his distance from her as he came around his desk and headed for the door.

Caroline trailed after him. She still looked troubled, but there was relief mixed in her expression as well. "There's still some pizza in the refrigerator you can heat up."

"Perfect," Noah replied with more gusto than he actually felt. Food wasn't what he hungered for at the moment.

Cold pizza was a perfect choice, though. A perfect match for the cold shower he planned to be standing under within the next thirty seconds.

No matter how hard she tried to focus on something else, all day long Caroline's thoughts kept spinning back to last night. While fixing lunch she became absorbed by the memory of how delicious Noah's mouth had felt melded against hers, how eagerly their tongues had sought each other. She emerged from her daydream to find herself spreading mayonnaise on *both* sides of the sandwich bread.

After lunch she decided to work on some business projections, calculator or no. But somehow her attention wandered off and she couldn't stop remembering how Noah's strong, sensual hands had caressed her, aroused her, made her ache for him. When she snapped back to the present, she saw she'd pencilled little hearts all over her neat rows of figures.

While she filled the tea kettle for an afternoon cup of tea, beneath the rushing water she heard Noah whispering, "Caro, I want to make love with you...." By the time she switched on the stove she was caught up in an incredibly erotic fantasy about what might have happened if she'd replied, "Yes, Noah, yes..."

It wasn't until Ethan came into the kitchen with his hands clamped over his ears that Caroline realized the steaming tea kettle was shrieking.

She'd told Noah the reason she couldn't make love with him was because of Ethan—because she couldn't risk hurting her son by becoming involved with a man who might eventually walk out on them.

That part was true. But it was only part of the truth.

The rest of it was that Caroline was afraid if she made love with Noah Garrett, she might very well fall in love with him, too.

There were a dozen reasons why a relationship between them was impossible. Her desire to protect Ethan and her dismal track record with men. Noah's guilt about his wife and child. The fact that they lived three thousand miles apart, for heaven's sake! It would be sheer insanity to give her heart to a man who would only wind up breaking it.

Noah was a wonderful man. But Caroline didn't want a man in her life, ever again. No matter how decent he was. How honest and hardworking and handsome. Or sexy. Even if he made her toes curl up and her spine tingle and her knees turn to mush whenever he walked into the room. Even if—

There, she'd gone and done it again! Gotten completely sidetracked from the task at hand by skipping off into some tempting, treacherous fantasy. Caroline slapped her palm against the banister in frustration. She'd reached the top of the staircase, but she couldn't for the life of her remember why she'd come up here.

Maybe it was something she'd wanted from her room. But

when she passed the closed door to Ethan's, she hesitated. He'd been spending an awful lot of time in there lately. Maybe she could cajole him into joining her for a short walk before it was time to start dinner.

Caroline raised her hand to knock, then frowned. She canted her head to bring her ear next to the door. Had she just imagined she'd heard something, or—

She heard it again, and this time the sound was unmistakable. Her heart constricted with a pang. Ordinarily she tried to respect Ethan's privacy, but the need to rush to his side at once was irresistible.

She opened the door and hurried across the room, nearly tripping over a scattering of objects Ethan had pulled out of the boxes they'd brought from Jeff's house. Ethan lay sprawled across the bed, face buried in the pillow. His shoulders heaved with sobs.

"Honey…" Caroline lowered herself beside him and patted his back helplessly. Ethan stiffened at her touch, then dissolved into another storm of muffled sobs.

Caroline's heart felt as if it would crack right in two. "Sweetheart, do you want to talk about it? Can you tell me what's wrong?"

Brilliant question, replied a scathing inner voice. *His father just died. What do you think he's crying about?*

She scooted closer and hoisted Ethan into her arms. Even in the midst of this emotional crisis, she was filled with awe by the incredible miracle that had brought him back to her again. While his sobs subsided against her blouse, she stroked his hair over and over, committing each precious strand to memory. Once more she felt that fierce thrust of determination, that overwhelming urge to protect him from all the hurts in the world.

She would never, *ever* let her darling boy suffer through a nightmare like this again.

Ethan sniffled and drew back a little. He sat up next to Caroline, swinging his feet over the side of the bed and staring down at the floor.

She took his hand in hers, desperately searching for words of comfort.

Ethan rubbed his nose and mumbled something.

"What was that, sweetheart?"

He sniffed. "Boys aren't s'posed to cry."

Caroline bit down on a smile. "Who told you that?"

"Dad."

"Oh." Caroline nodded. "I see." Just the sort of fatherly wisdom Jeff would dispense. Of course, growing up with Randolph Tate for a father, it was no wonder Jeff's ideas of appropriate male and female behavior occasionally seemed rooted in a previous century. "Well, you know what?"

"What?" He wiped one eye with his fist.

Caroline squeezed his hand. "I think it's just fine for boys to cry."

"You do?" He lifted his tear-stained face and glanced at her.

"Sure." Seeing his mournful expression, Caroline had to fight the urge to burst out blubbering herself. "Everybody feels like crying sometimes. There's nothing wrong with that." She gently lifted a tear from his cheek with one knuckle. "What's bad is when you try to keep what you're feeling bottled up inside you. When you do, everything gets all tangled up in knots."

"It does?" He hiccupped.

"Yup." Caroline touched the tip of his freckled nose for emphasis. "So it's much better to cry and get it all out of your system."

"Huh." His puffy brown eyes remained skeptical. "I bet *Noah* doesn't cry."

"Well...maybe not." Hadn't she seen proof that Noah was exactly the type of man to hold everything inside, to turn his pain against himself? "I'll bet he feels like crying sometimes, though."

"Like if he doesn't catch some bad guy he's after?"

Caroline gave her son a rueful smile. "Maybe."

Ethan's chin began to tremble again.

Caroline wrapped her arm around him. "Sweetie, what is it?"

"I wish I could help him catch the bad guy who hurt Dad." Ethan's eyes brimmed with tears again. "I try and try to remember what happened, but I just—just can't!" His throat closed up so that his voice climbed to a heartbreaking squeak.

"Oh, Ethan." Caroline brought her other arm around him and hugged him close, rocking back and forth on the edge of the bed. It absolutely killed her to watch her child go through such misery, such guilt. "You're doing the best you can. That's all anyone can ask. Don't feel bad about not remembering stuff."

"I found our boat." She had to loosen her embrace a little in order to hear what Ethan was saying.

"What boat, honey?"

He pointed to one of the objects Caroline had nearly tripped over in her haste to comfort him. It was a simple, crudely built wooden boat that looked like it would probably capsize and sink within the first ten seconds of its maiden voyage. "Dad and me made it this winter. I found a picture in a book and he helped me build it."

Viewing it through her son's eyes, Caroline was able to see the poor, pathetic little boat as a magnificent seagoing vessel with pennants proudly waving from her masts. "It's a wonderful boat," she said softly.

"Dad promised we could take it down to the river and try it out when the weather got warm." Ethan's voice quivered. "But then he had to work on Saturday and Sunday for a while, and I had to go to school the other days, so we still haven't gone." He gulped. "Now we won't—ever."

Caroline fought to maintain her composure. "Does your boat have a name?" she asked through clenched teeth.

Ethan shook his head morosely.

"Well, a boat should have a name." She reached down and picked it up off the floor. "What if we name this boat after your dad? The *Jefferson Randolph Tate*." She pointed to the bow. "We could paint the name right here."

Ethan perked up with interest. "Could we?"

"Of course! Then you and I can take it to a river, and maybe you can read a poem that reminds you of your dad. Then we'll launch the boat, and it'll be sort of a memorial to him."

Ethan tilted his head to an uncertain angle. "But I don't know any poems."

"I'll help you find one."

"You will?"

"Uh-huh." She handed the boat to Ethan. "I think your dad would like that, don't you?"

"I guess so." Ethan ran his fingers over the boat's rough edges, its amateurish angles. His face brightened a little. "Yeah. I'm pretty sure my dad would like it."

"Good!" Caroline sent up a quick prayer that the darn boat wouldn't sink as soon as it hit water. She ruffled Ethan's hair. "Hey, how about if you and I go outside for a quick game of catch before I start fixing dinner?"

Ethan looked doubtful. "You know how to play catch?"

"You bet!" She huffed on her nails, then buffed them modestly on the front of her blouse. "Just call me Sandy Colfax."

"*Mom.*" Ethan rolled his eyes in disgust. "It's Sandy *Koufax.*"

"Oh. Well, that's what I meant. Come on." She grabbed his baseball mitt from the floor and put it on. "Let's see you toss a few right here, huh?" She punched her fist into the mitt.

"Mom?"

"Yes, honey?"

"It goes on your *other* hand." But he retrieved his softball from beneath the bed and followed his mother good-naturedly downstairs.

It was hard enough for Caroline to curb her desire for Noah when he *wasn't* around. When he surprised her by showing up for dinner that evening, she discovered that ignoring the feelings he stirred inside her was downright impossible in his actual presence.

Each time he glanced at her with those guarded blue eyes, his gaze seemed charged with meaning. Whenever their hands accidentally brushed while passing things around the table, the electricity that sizzled along Caroline's skin nearly made her drop whatever she was holding. The vivid mutual awareness of the passion that had seized them last night made the temperature in the kitchen seem to creep upward all through dinner.

Though she kept putting food into her mouth, Caroline didn't taste a bite.

I will not fall in love with him, she swore to herself. I won't. I can't!

Then Noah would pass her one of those meaningful looks across the table, and something would melt inside her.

She couldn't go on like this. Every day spent under Noah's roof made it more and more difficult to keep him at a distance, both emotionally and physically. How long would it be before her frazzled nerves and overcharged hormones wore down her resistance to him completely?

She desperately wanted a man she could never have. And the longer she stayed here with him, the more she wanted him.

The answer seemed simple. Then why was it so difficult to put into action?

What finally gave Caroline the courage was Ethan. The more she pondered this afternoon's tearful scene, the more she realized that putting their lives on hold like this wasn't doing her son any good. Though well-intentioned, Noah had imprisoned Ethan in an emotional pressure cooker. Her son's continuing inability to remember what he might have witnessed the day his father died was torturing him. Caroline couldn't permit the situation to continue any longer.

So she hovered nervously outside the kitchen, waiting for Noah to finish washing the dinner dishes. Ethan was in the living room watching a baseball game on TV. When she heard the loud slurp of dishwater going down the drain, she forced herself to enter the kitchen.

Noah was drying his hands on a towel. He gave Caroline

one of his subdued, unconsciously sexy smiles when he saw her. "Hi." He hung the towel on a hook. "I was just going to go watch the game with Ethan. Care to join us?"

Her mouth was dry. "No, thank you. I—I want to talk to you." Her words came out more abruptly than she'd intended. But at least she'd got them out.

Noah arched his brows in inquiry. He pulled out a chair and motioned for Caroline to sit down.

She ignored the gesture. "It won't take long. I just want to let you know that I've come to a decision."

"Oh?" He rested his hands casually on the back of the chair. But Caroline noticed his knuckles were white.

"Yes." She moistened her lips. "Ethan and I have been here for a week now. And he still hasn't remembered anything more about Jeff's murder."

Something flashed across Noah's expression, like the sudden awareness of a man who sees a locomotive bearing down on him.

"It's time for us to move on with our lives." Caroline jerked up her chin. Before Noah could interrupt, she announced in a rush, "I'm taking Ethan back home to Baltimore tomorrow."

Chapter 10

"**I** wish you wouldn't." Noah was making every effort to sound calm. Reasonable. When what he really wanted was to holler that Caroline and Ethan would step on a plane tomorrow over his dead body.

He didn't kid himself that the panicky sensation in his chest was simply because an important witness was about to hightail it clear across country. Noah was a realist. He refused to shirk from facts. And the unfortunate fact was that, somewhere along the way, this case had gotten personal. Maybe it had been from the very beginning.

"As I told you before," she said, "I'll do everything I can to cooperate with your investigation."

Noah studied Caroline for a moment. She was wearing the pretty mint green blouse that accentuated her eyes. Those gorgeous, unforgettable eyes Noah was sure he would never see again if she got on a plane tomorrow.

"If Ethan remembers anything more about the day his father died, I'll contact you right away."

"Caroline, let's give him a couple more days, all right?"

Noah said, even though he knew a couple of days might not make any difference. "It'd be so much easier for both of you if you don't have to drag him all the way back here later on."

"Easy?" She emitted a short laugh. "You call this *easy?* Living cooped up here like prisoners? Trapped here without a car? Afraid to show our faces in town?" She gestured at the refrigerator. "I can't even run out and buy groceries, for heaven's sake! And I'm tired of wearing the same clothes over and over. Not to mention what this—this house arrest is doing to Ethan."

Noah came around the table. "I know it's been tough on him—"

"No. You don't." Her hair swirled around her shoulders as she shook her head emphatically. "He's tormented by guilt because he can't remember what he might have witnessed when Jeff was killed."

"It's not his fault—"

"Noah, he's a little boy!" Her face, twisted in anguish, was a poignant plea for understanding. "All he knows is that he's letting his dad down. That it's his fault the bad guy has gotten away."

Noah grasped her shoulders. "Caroline, that's not true! Ethan's got no reason to feel guilty."

"How do you expect him to feel? He knows you're counting on him to remember something. He respects and admires you, Noah." She seemed reluctant to say it. "He feels like he's letting you down, too."

Speechless, Noah could only hope Caroline was way off base here. The last thing he wanted was to make Ethan feel guilty.

She splayed her hands on his chest as if preparing to push him away. "Ethan needs to escape from this—this pressure cooker you've put him in. He needs to move on, to get started with our new life together. We both do!" Determination vibrated through her body. "Instead, we're stuck here in this limbo, waiting for something to happen that probably never will!"

Every instinct inside Noah urged him to grip her tighter, to hang on and never let go. Caroline had gotten under his skin in a way he wouldn't have believed possible a week ago. Even though living under the same roof with her had become a daily battle against his own desires, he couldn't help hoping she would change her mind and stay a little longer. He was like an addict, craving the one dangerous pleasure that was worst for him.

He tried to chalk it up to hormones. It had been so long since he'd shared his home with a woman, it was no wonder he was so eager to share his bed with her, too. Probably any woman would have had the same disturbing effect on him. Even a woman he hadn't felt this weird sense of connection to. Even a woman who wasn't as caring and courageous, as intelligent and independent as Caroline Tate.

Even a woman who wasn't as beautiful. As passionate.

Hormones, that's all this powerful attraction was. Because anything else felt like betrayal.

Noah curled his fingers into her flesh and kneaded her shoulders. "I realize this has been an extremely difficult situation for both of you." Not to mention what a strain it had been for him. "But what I said before still holds true. It'll be good for Ethan to feel like he helped capture his father's killer. We have to give him that chance."

"We *have* given him that chance. But with each day that goes by, that chance becomes smaller and smaller. How much longer do you expect us to stay here?" she asked. "Forever?"

Noah's hands stilled on her shoulders. That slight hesitation before she'd said "forever" had revealed more than she'd intended to, he was sure.

But that word wasn't in Noah's vocabulary anymore. Not after he'd found out that forever could be cut cruelly short by one swift, merciless stroke of fate.

Caroline's gaze darted back and forth across his face as if she was searching for something. "No," she said after the silence had lasted for a dozen awkward seconds. "I didn't think so." She dropped her hands from his chest. Some of the tension in her seemed to dissolve. Though Noah got the crazy impression that what she was letting go of was hope.

What did she want from him, anyway? She'd spelled it out in letters as loud as neon that she was as gun-shy about involvement as he was. Why was she studying him with that look of disappointment, as if he'd let her down somehow?

Maybe it would be best if he did put them on that plane tomorrow. That's what common sense told him, anyway.

"Go ahead and make the reservations," he said.

Caroline's eyes widened.

"But do me one favor."

Her expression turned wary. "What?"

"Make them for three days from now." Noah squeezed her arms briefly. "Please."

Despair dragged down the corners of her mouth. "Noah, it's no use. Putting it off isn't going to change—"

"Look, this new lead might turn out to—"

"What new lead?" Her head came up in a hurry.

"His name," he said. "Buckman. I sent it out to all the law-enforcement agencies in the north part of the state, so that'll make it easier for—"

"Wait a second." She was shaking her head as if dazed from a blow. "Are you saying you found out his name? This mysterious Buck character? The man you think might have killed Jeff?"

Noah nodded. Somehow his hand had tunneled its way into her hair. Soft, silky, spilling over his fingers like warm butterscotch... "I found a witness in town who recognized his picture. He only knew his last name, but—"

Caroline held up her palm to silence him. "When did this happen?"

"Er...yesterday."

"*Yesterday?*" She sounded incredulous. "Why didn't you tell me before?"

"Well, I meant to, but then when I got home last night..." He cleared his throat, remembering the frantic drive...the chilling fear when he hadn't found them in the house right away...the wild, frenzied embrace that had seared all thoughts of the case right out of his mind. "Guess I got distracted," he said. "And forgot to tell you." He wound a corkscrew of her long hair around his finger.

Caroline's cheeks turned pink. Clearly she was recalling what had distracted him. Her long lashes screened her expression when she lowered her eyes for a moment. Her breasts rose and fell in a sigh. "You really think there's a chance of finding this person soon?"

Noah didn't want to make any promises. But he did want her to stay. Badly. "I think the odds are a lot higher, now that we know his name."

Caroline worried her lip. "But we don't even know for sure this Buckman had anything to do with Jeff's death."

"Not for sure, but it all fits." Noah untangled his fingers from the gossamer strands of her hair so he could tick off points of evidence. "The owner of the bar where he hung out told me Buckman bragged he was going to come into money. Meanwhile, Jeff was desperately scrambling to get some."

"Because Buckman was blackmailing him."

Noah tapped his belly. "Call it gut instinct. But I'm convinced that's what was going on. Especially since Buckman apparently disappeared the day Jeff was killed."

Caroline stared at the floor, rubbing her temples. "If he did kill Jeff," she said when she finally looked up, "I don't want him to get away with it."

"No. Of course not." Noah sensed this was a turning point. Up until now Caroline had cared about catching the killer primarily for Ethan's sake. But now that they had a name to attach to him, the concept of justice wasn't quite so abstract anymore.

Which might mean she would be willing to delay her return home a little while longer. "When we locate this Buckman," Noah pointed out, "I'll need Ethan to identify him as the man he saw arguing with his father." He shrugged, as if Caroline's travel plans were a matter of indifference to him. "I'd just hate for you to have to turn right around and fly all the way back from Baltimore.''

She pinned him with one of those too-perceptive looks of hers. ''Don't you mean, *if* you find him?''

''I prefer to think positive.''

She made a sound that was half laughter, half sigh. Man, she was pretty! It was all Noah could do not to plunge his fingers through her hair again, tilt back her head, bring her mouth up to his....

''Wishful thinking,'' she said, startling him with her apparent ability to read his mind.

''Huh?'' *Clever retort, Garrett.*

''You call it thinking positive.'' She folded her arms and gave him a skeptical look, drumming her fingers. ''I just hope it isn't merely wishful thinking. That you'll find this Buckman guy soon.''

''Give me two more days to find him.'' Whew! She hadn't read his mind after all. ''There's something else to consider, too.''

''What's that?'' Caroline was giving him the same look she might give a high-pressure used-car salesman.

''There's a chance that seeing Buckman again might jar something loose in Ethan's memory.'' Noah grimaced. ''Maybe he saw the guy do more than argue with his father.''

Caroline sucked in a quick breath. She let it out slowly. ''Maybe,'' she said, ''there are some things it's best not to remember.''

''That doesn't sound like you.'' Noah wagged a scolding finger. ''I thought you were big on facing the past.''

Her lips crimped into a rueful line, as if to say *you caught me.* ''Don't you know the rules go out the window when it comes to your own child?''

''Yeah,'' Noah said. ''I know.''

Caroline bit her lip. She reached across the gap that separated them and squeezed his hand. ''Okay, you win. I'll make the reservations for three days from now.''

Noah flipped over her palm and idly traced its lines with

his finger, making her shiver. Love line...life line...which was which?

Even if he'd believed in that stuff, it hardly mattered. Because whatever future Caroline's palm foretold didn't include him.

She had her destiny, and he had his. It seemed both of them, by choice, were destined to be alone.

For the first time since Beth and Molly had died, Noah wondered whether he'd made the right choice.

On impulse, he lifted Caroline's palm and pressed a kiss into her soft, warm flesh. He wasn't sure which one of them he'd startled the most. She stared up at him with those huge, luminous eyes that saw too much, sometimes, for Noah's comfort.

Right now they revealed plenty, too. In their troubled, jade green depths Noah saw regret. Longing. Resignation. As if Caroline accepted that whatever it was she was looking for, Noah couldn't give it to her.

"I'll go call the airline," she said, gently detaching her hand from his.

He let her go, and listened to her footsteps recede down the hallway. The first steps of the journey that would take her out of his life for good.

Three more days.

Noah had a feeling they were going to be both the longest and the shortest three days of his life.

"I think you're really going to like living in Baltimore again, honey." Seated on the floor of Ethan's room, Caroline was helping her son pack for their trip home the next day. "Remember the aquarium? Your dad and I used to take you there when you were little."

Ethan shrugged. "I remember...playing with a starfish," he said grudgingly. "I guess."

"Yes! In the children's tidepool exhibit," Caroline said brightly. "I think there's even a picture of it in our photo album."

Ethan hadn't exactly been thrilled when Caroline had informed him yesterday that they had plane reservations to go home. Well, why should he have been? As far as Ethan was concerned, home was here in Eagle River.

Caroline had to admit she'd developed a surprising affection for the place herself—what little she'd seen of it, anyway. But this picturesque little town wasn't where she belonged. Baltimore was where she had her business. Her home. Friends she cared about.

Eagle River only had...Noah.

She pushed the thought of him out of her mind. She'd had plenty of practice at it over the last couple of days. By now it should have been easy. But it wasn't.

She wriggled Ethan's baseball mitt from his reluctant fingers and stowed it in one of the cardboard boxes she planned to check on the plane as luggage. "And you know what else there is in Baltimore? The Babe Ruth Museum! How about if the two of us go there next weekend?"

Another shrug. "''Kay."

Nice try, Caroline. Better try again. "Or else we could take in a baseball game. Would you like that?"

Amazingly enough, Ethan perked up. "The Orioles are my dad's and my favorite team!"

"Well...great! It's a date, then." Caroline's spirits lifted a little. Now that the time had nearly come when she and Ethan would actually start to rebuild their life together, she was plagued by anxious bouts of uncertainty. What if Ethan didn't like living with her again?

"When we go to the game, can we get hot dogs with lots of mustard? And sodas? And popcorn?"

Uh-oh. If Ethan was going to make a habit of mooning at her like this with such irresistible hopefulness in his big brown eyes, Caroline was going to have a tough time denying him anything.

She grabbed him, mussing his hair and tickling him till he squealed. "You drive a hard bargain, mister." She kissed the top of his head before letting him go. "I don't want to hear any complaints when you get a stomachache."

"*Mom.*" He blew a disdainful sound through his lips. "I won't get a stomachache."

"You'd better not." A fresh gust of love soared inside her, sweeping away her doubts. She and Ethan were going to be fine on their own.

Just the two of them.

Really.

Their last day together.

The last time Caroline would hear Noah's car pull up in the driveway, and know that moments later he would come through the door and greet her with one of those devastating, low-key smiles that made her heart flutter.

The last evening the three of them would sit around the dinner table, just like a real family, with Noah complimenting her cooking and sending a delicious thrill along her skin whenever their hands brushed together.

The last night they would sleep under the same roof. Except Caroline was afraid she wasn't going to sleep at all.

She'd tucked Ethan into bed hours ago. She and Noah had already said their good-nights.

For the last time.

Before coming up to bed, Caroline hadn't bothered to ask Noah if there were any new leads in the case. Or if the elusive Buckman had surfaced somewhere, giving her and Ethan a reason to remain here a while longer. Noah would have told her if anything like that had happened.

The somber expression on his dark, brooding features had spoken more eloquently than words, anyway.

This was it, then. The end of the road for them.

Though it was after midnight and their flight to Baltimore left in less than twelve hours, Caroline couldn't keep her eyes closed. She would force them shut, but then images would start dancing on the back of her eyelids. Sounds would whisper through the darkness. Vivid memories would make her skin crawl with desire.

Noah, his handsome, haunted face filling her vision as he lowered his head to kiss her. His voice, growling seductively in her ear, arousing her with his warm breath. *Caro...I want to make love with you...*

His mouth and hands moving over her flesh, seeking, caressing, bringing her to life. The taut hardness of his body pressing into her, shocking her, exciting her, making her want him even more...

"Oh, sweet heaven," Caroline moaned into her pillow. Once again her eyes were wide open, her heart pounding, her skin on fire.

Against her own better judgment, she'd let herself become way too involved with Noah. Now she was going to have to suffer the consequences.

She couldn't believe how much she dreaded walking onto that plane tomorrow. Turning her back on Noah for the last time. Turning her back on what they might have shared together, if only...

"If only what?" she demanded of her pillow. "If only we were both different people? If only we hadn't both suffered such sorrow and disillusionment in the past?"

She flipped onto her back and stared blindly at the ceiling. "If all that were true, we never would have met in the first place." She pounded her fist into the mattress. "So quit tearing your heart out over something that was never meant to be."

Her self-directed pep talk failed to achieve its purpose. She still couldn't sleep.

Well, this was a waste of time. Caroline switched on the bedside lamp. Rather than toss and turn till she was exhausted, she might as well accomplish something useful.

She fought her way out of the tangled sheets and located her purse. When the going got tough, Caroline Tate made lists. Let's see...what were the first items she ought to take care of once they got back to Baltimore? Enroll Ethan in school for next fall. Take him to the doctor for a thorough physical exam. Consult a child psychologist about how to navigate the rocky emotional road ahead of them.

Then there were all those business-related matters she would have to catch up on...

"Drat," she muttered. "I know I had a pencil in here." She tossed the purse onto the bed with disgust. Hmm. She could go back to trying to sleep, or else...

Moments later she was groping her way down the stairs on tiptoe. Noah had pencils in his office. Paper, too. He wouldn't mind if she—

Caroline halted at the base of the steps. Had she forgotten to turn off the kitchen light before going to bed? Puzzled, she padded down the hall on bare feet.

"Oh!" She pulled up short in the kitchen doorway. "You're up late."

Noah sat at the table, papers and file folders spread out in front of him. His dark hair was tousled as if he'd been plowing his hands through it in frustration. The front of his shirt was completely unbuttoned, his sleeves rolled up to expose sturdy forearms.

He looked about as rumpled as Caroline had ever seen him. Rumpled...and incredibly sexy. She pulled out a chair and sat down across from him, trying not to stare at the broad expanse of muscles revealed by his open shirt. A sprinkling of dark hair matched that on his arms.

Chasing criminals certainly kept him in fine shape, she observed with a wistful pang.

"What are you doing up?" he asked, taking a sip of something steaming from a mug. His eyes, watching her over the rim, were guarded. All at once she was vividly aware she was wearing nothing but a thin nightgown.

"Couldn't sleep," she explained. "I came down in search of pencil and paper so I could make a list of all the things I need to take care of once we get back to Baltimore." She offered him a self-conscious smile. "Jittery about tomorrow, I guess."

"Not afraid of flying, are you?" He set down his mug.

"No, it's not the plane trip. Just…everything else." *Embarking on a new life with my son. Looking out the window while the plane takes off, straining for a glimpse of you inside the terminal, knowing I'll probably never see you again…*

Her heart moaned as if someone had tightened a vise around it.

Noah pushed a pencil and paper in her direction. "Help yourself."

"Thanks." She didn't move to take them. All at once she couldn't think of anything worth writing down.

"Would you like some coffee?" he asked, touching his mug. "It's decaffeinated."

Caroline was about to decline, when a foolish voice inside her head whispered that this would give her an excuse to sit here with Noah a while longer. "No, don't get up," she told him. "I'll get it." She opened the cupboard and took out a cup. "After all, I do know my way around this kitchen pretty well by now."

"Yes." He nudged a bottle toward her when she sat down. "Here. This'll make up for the missing caffeine."

She studied the label of the coffee-flavored liqueur. Why not? *Go crazy, Caroline. After all, it's your last night with the man of your dreams.*

The man you'll be dreaming about for the rest of your life.

She splashed a dollop into her coffee. "What are you doing up so late?" She sipped her drink. Mmm. Yummy.

Noah spread his hands to encompass the disarray on the table. "Going over my notes on this case one more time. Witness statements. Trying to figure out if there isn't something I've missed."

"I'm sure there isn't."

Noah dragged a hand through his hair. "What if my theory about what happened is wrong? What if Jeff's death didn't have anything to do with Buckman or blackmail?"

"You'll find out the truth. Eventually." Caroline had never

seen Noah so unsure of himself before. He always acted with such calm conviction, such inner certainty.

He reached across the table and covered her hand with his. "What if the killer isn't some drifter? What if he's someone with the cleverness and resources to track down Ethan once you've gone back to Baltimore?"

Caroline shuddered. All at once she felt a chill, even with the warmth Noah's touch had ignited inside her. "Noah, we can't keep hiding here forever." There was that word again. Forever. Why did it seem so charged with meaning whenever it was spoken between them?

She took a deep breath. "You know I would never do anything to put Ethan in danger. But I refuse to raise my son in an atmosphere of fear. I have to believe that the chances of the killer posing a threat to him in Baltimore are so remote as to be nonexistent."

In the harsh glare of the kitchen light, the shadows beneath Noah's eyes made him look haggard. Tormented. Caroline wished she knew how to smooth the creases from his troubled brow, to banish the ghosts that haunted him.

"I'd never forgive myself if anything happened to either one of you," he said hoarsely.

She curled her fingers through his and gripped his hand. Tight. "You've done the best you could," she assured him. "That's all anyone can ask."

"It's not good enough." Noah's mouth hardened into a grim line.

"It has to be."

They sat there across the table from each other, eyes riveted together, hands clutched in an almost desperate link.

"Sometimes," Caroline said softly, "no matter how hard we try, it simply isn't possible to protect the people we love from harm."

The fiery blue of Noah's eyes intensified, though Caroline had the impression he was looking straight through her instead of directly at her. "I think that knowledge is probably even tougher to live with than guilt," she said.

His thumb stroked the back of her hand, but absently. The rugged lines of his face shifted into a faraway expression. Caroline envisioned the framed photo hidden away in his desk drawer, and knew what he was seeing.

Noah lifted his hand from hers. Withdrawing. Lost to her now.

The liqueur began to burble in Caroline's stomach like acid. She pushed back her chair. "I suppose I should try to get some sleep." Even though she knew it would be hopeless. Her senses were too full of Noah to allow her any rest.

She paused in the doorway, looking back to burn this image of him into her memory. She didn't want to remember him the way he would be tomorrow, surrounded by mobs of people at the airport...bidding her an awkward, impersonal, rushed goodbye over the sound of their boarding announcement...jostled by passengers hurrying to catch their flights.

She would much rather remember him the way he looked now, here in the cozy kitchen where they'd shared so many meals and meaningful discussions, under the roof where he'd offered her and her child shelter and a place to be safe.

Noah, a lock of dark brown hair slashing across his forehead. His turbulent eyes, blazing across the room at her from beneath his furrowed brow. The intriguing cleft in his chin that Caroline's fingers yearned to trace. His square, resolute jaw. His mouth, which could so unexpectedly flicker into a crooked smile that was like the sun coming out from behind the clouds.

His mouth, which had known hers so intimately and whispered the promise of unspeakable pleasures to come. Except they wouldn't be sharing any more intimate pleasures together.

A sharp pain jabbed at Caroline's breastbone. She hadn't meant to care for Noah Garrett. But she did.

"I'll miss you," she said quietly. She had to fight to keep her voice from quavering. Better walk away now, before she humiliated herself.

She forced herself to turn.

A loud clatter from behind froze Caroline in her tracks. She turned back to the kitchen again.

Noah was on his feet, his chair tipped onto the floor. He clutched the edge of the table with both hands, muscles rippling along his forearms as if he were physically restraining himself from moving. His brow gleamed with sweat.

"I'll miss you, too," he said in a low, strangled voice. "Caro…"

Impossible to say which of them moved first. All Caroline knew was that she was running back across the linoleum and Noah was coming around the table, rushing forward to meet her, and then they were…

In each other's arms.

Chapter 11

Mouths and hands and limbs came together in a frantic, frenzied jumble. Noah couldn't even tell where his body left off and Caroline's began, they were merged together with such desperate fusion. As if they would never let go of each other.

He fisted his hands in her hair, pulling her even closer. His tongue sought hers, found it, plundered the hot, sweet recesses of her mouth like a man dying of thirst. She was velvet and steel, fire and ice, pleasure and pain.

She was Noah's anchor in a swirling universe.

His hands couldn't settle on any one place. First her hair, then the narrow curve of her waist, then the gentle, seductive swell of her hips. He cupped her against him, boldly demonstrating the hard proof of his desire.

With a moan of longing, her head fell back. Noah buried his lips in the base of her throat, in that irresistible notch that had beckoned him since the first day he'd met her. So prim and proper she'd looked that day in her Pilgrim gray outfit. Now she was writhing in his arms, arousing shocking desires with her mouth and hands, clad in nothing but a cotton nightgown that provided the flimsiest of barricades to her body.

Not that she seemed intent on barricading him. Noah's hands traveled freely up her spine, caressing the lithe, arching muscles of her back, kneading the lush, pliant flesh of her breasts.

She certainly wasn't responding to him in a prim and proper manner. Beneath his thumbs her nipples were as hard as pebbles. She gasped sharply, then dissolved against him with a moan of unmistakable pleasure. Her fingers clenched in his hair. The pulse in her throat beat rapidly against Noah's lips like a trapped butterfly.

She twined one long, sleek leg around his. Then slowly inched it upward.

Noah let out a muffled groan. All the pent-up desire he'd been fighting so hard to restrain since Caroline had come to live under his roof threatened to explode right here in the middle of the kitchen. This wasn't the tender, slow-paced seduction that had tortured his imagination for so long.

This was a wild, unrestrained free-for-all.

He seized her face between his hands. "Caro..." He couldn't even finish the rest of his question before she was nodding rapidly, her nose bumping against his with an eagerness that matched his.

"Yes," she whispered between his lips. "Oh, yes..."

She didn't need to say it twice. With a surge of joy and desire, Noah swept her up into his arms. He was amazed by how right she felt there. How easy it was to carry her. She seemed weightless in his arms. Or perhaps the urgency of his need for her had endowed him with superhuman strength.

As he strode down the darkened hall, trying not to trip in his haste, Noah became aware of another urge. The urge to protect her. Holding her like this, with her arms wrapped tightly around his neck, her head resting against his chest, stirred some deep, primitive instinct inside him.

As he kicked shut the door to his bedroom, he was filled

with the fierce realization that he would willingly sacrifice his own life to save hers. To save the life of the child she loved.

He laid his precious cargo on the bed with more gentleness than either of them had displayed so far. "Do you mind if I turn on a light?" he asked, his voice an unfamiliar rasp. "I want to see you. To see us. Together."

This would be his first and last chance. His only chance. Tonight's memories would have to last a lifetime. Noah wanted them as complete, as vivid as possible.

In the faint starlight filtering through the window, he could barely make out Caroline's delicate features, even though her hands held his face close to hers.

"Yes," she murmured. "I mean—no, I don't mind."

Still, he detected reluctance. "I've got an idea." He snapped his fingers and hauled himself into a sitting position. "Candles." He reached for the drawer in his nightstand.

"You keep candles in your bedroom?" Caroline asked with a half breathless, half teasing note in her voice. "Why, Sergeant Garrett, you astonish me."

"For blackouts," he replied, fumbling in the drawer for the matches he kept there. "You know, when the electricity goes out." He struck a match, and a flame sprang to life.

"I should have known," she murmured.

Even though his hands refused to stay quite steady, Noah managed to light the candle and drip melted wax onto the chipped saucer he kept for this purpose. As soon as a coin-sized blob of liquid had accumulated, he stuck the base of the candle into it. In moments, when the wax hardened, it would hold the candle upright.

He set the saucer on the nightstand. Then he turned to look at Caroline.

Her hair was fanned across his pillow like a shimmering curtain, alive with the flickering glow of candlelight. Noah caught up a few strands and pressed them to his lips. "Like silk..." he muttered. He smelled the floral scent of shampoo clinging to her hair. He was determined to savor every second of their time together, to acquaint himself fully with every square inch of her.

Because after tonight he wouldn't have another chance to commit her to memory.

Caroline lifted her hand. Her fingers were cool against his cheek. Her eyes gazed up at him with such longing, such understanding...

"You have the most beautiful eyes I've ever seen," Noah said gruffly. He wasn't used to paying compliments. He hoped he didn't sound like he was trying to come off as Mr. Suave or something.

But the simple sincerity of his statement must have come through his voice. Caroline's eyes misted. She blinked rapidly to clear them. "Thank you," she whispered. "I like your eyes, too."

"*My* eyes?" Noah made a scoffing sound. "They're bloodshot, probably."

"No." She ran her fingertips lightly along his eyebrows, like a blind person acquainting herself with his features. "You have very...compelling eyes. Honest eyes."

He shifted himself so he was lying on top of her, bracing his weight with his elbows. "And what do you see in my eyes right now?"

Caroline's eyes flared wide open, pupils dilating into dark pools. "Noah..." she whispered.

Then he was kissing her again, reveling in the excitement and tenderness she aroused inside him with each flick of her tongue, each stroke of her hand, each muffled moan of encouragement and delight.

Heat poured through his loins like molten lava, racing along its unchanneled course, obliterating every obstacle in its path. He sought Caroline's breast beneath her nightgown, and all at once that thin cotton layer became an intolerable barrier. He fumbled for the hem and coaxed the fabric upward, over her thighs, her hips, her slender, straining torso.

He adjusted his position to allow room to remove the garment over her head. Caroline shimmied out of it with an unconsciously erotic, fluid movement that nearly made Noah seize her right then and there and be done with it. Instead, he forced his trembling hands to take her slowly, to worship her, to seduce her until she was as hot and liquid with need as he was.

He eased her back onto the pillow, kissing her hair, her eyelids, the sweet hollow of her neck. Branding her with his mouth. Making her his.

His mouth traveled a roundabout route across her creamy flesh, along the valley between her breasts. When he finally captured her nipple between his roaming lips, she gasped sharply, arching her back. Noah swirled his tongue around the taut, rosy peak, eliciting whimpers of pleasure that reflected his own mounting excitement.

Don't rush! Make it last! warned the final coherent part of Noah's brain. He didn't want this to end. He wanted it to go on and on, over and over. Forever.

He raised himself on his forearms to give them both some breathing space, to delay as long as possible the moment when it would be finished. The candlelight rippled along Caroline's smooth skin, burnishing it with gold. "You're so lovely," he said, nearly stumbling over the words. If he hadn't meant them so earnestly, he never would have been able to get them out. He was much better at conveying his feelings by action than by poetry.

Miraculously, Caroline seemed moved by his clumsy compliment. Her lips parted as her luminous eyes took on an even brighter sparkle. She reached for him, grasping the collar of his open shirt with both hands and pulling him down to her again. Her lips danced a slow waltz over his, leaving him dizzy.

When she splayed her hands across his bare chest, Noah was positive she could feel his heart pumping a mile a minute. The sound of it filled his own ears as she slid her hands toward his collarbone, beneath his shirt so she could maneuver it off his shoulders. She managed to get it halfway off, so the sleeves were pinning his arms to his sides like a straitjacket, before

Noah couldn't stand to wait one second longer and whipped it off himself.

"Mmm." Caroline flicked her tongue across her lower lip while she stared hungrily at the naked contours of his chest. Noah felt a painful throb in the region of his zipper and knew he wouldn't be able to hold back much longer.

He reached down, but Caroline brushed his hand gently aside and lowered his zipper herself. The sexy humming in her throat while she slowly tugged it open nearly drove Noah crazy.

The release was exquisite, the relief only temporary. Desire churned through him, setting his blood on fire, turning him feverish with raging need. This exquisite agony went way beyond anything he'd ever experienced before. Into uncharted territory.

"Caro, honey, I want this to be good for you...." Maybe he could cool himself down a bit by focusing on her pleasure instead of his.

Nope.

"It is," Caroline reassured him softly. "Oh, darling, it is!" She reached for him again.

Pleasure spiraled through him like an out-of-control rocket, making him shudder. He shucked off his pants in a hurry, then stretched out beside Caroline.

Her lace panties were the only barrier between them now. Noah crooked his finger inside the elastic and tugged as gently as he could manage. Caroline assisted him, sliding the panties down over her hips and wriggling out of them with a sinuous motion that almost drove Noah over the edge.

He slid his hand along the lush, naked landscape of her body, exploring the unfamiliar, intensely exciting terrain. She was so soft and warm, so vibrant and alive! Her eager responsiveness stoked Noah's desire even hotter and higher. He loved the little catch in her throat when he curved his palm over her breast. And he loved the way her eyes flared into pools of jade when he brought his hand lower, between her thighs, to ease open the delicate, quivering petals of her flesh.

"Noah," she gasped. "Please, darling…now…"

Come to think of it, there were a *lot* of things he loved about Caroline.

"What's your rush?" he teased, stroking the velvety folds as she arched against his hand. "We've got all night." Though he knew he wasn't going to last much longer.

All night. And that was all they had. This one night. Because in the morning a plane would carry her away from him forever.

Pressure seemed to clamp down on Noah's chest, an anvil of regret. They had no future, and the past was off-limits for tonight. All he could hope for was to lose himself in the present.

He hoisted himself above her, nudging into her as gently as he knew how, to give her time to get used to him. With excruciating slowness he eased himself inside her. He watched her eyes, saw them flicker with candlelight and passion. They grew huge as he finally sheathed himself in her sweet warm softness.

Caroline made a little sighing sound like "Ohh…" Her eyelashes fluttered shut. She wrapped her legs around Noah, holding him snugly.

When they began to move together, it felt as natural to Noah as breathing. Except breathing had never felt this good. Nothing had. Ever.

Caroline's eyes were open again now, so that Noah could see the reflection of his own incredible pleasure there. They blurred into a beautiful green sea when he lowered his mouth to hers. Sliding, stroking, thrusting…their tongues performed a sensual joust that mimicked the rhythm of their bodies.

The tempo of their movements increased. Noah felt a different kind of pressure building inside him, an urgency of sensation and need that surged through his blood, set fire to his skin and made him forget everything else in the universe besides this warm, sexy, wonderful woman joined to him here in his bed.

"Caro," he groaned, clamping his jaws together as if that

could hold back the oncoming tide. "Honey, I—I can't... wait...much...longer...."

Her breath against his face made his skin even hotter. "That...makes...two of us," she panted. Seconds later he felt a tremor pass through her body. Her fingertips gouged into his shoulder blades, intensifying his own excitement.

"Oh, Noah!" she cried out, her eyes huge and glittering.

He watched spasms of pleasure ripple across her beautiful face while she writhed beneath him. Even as Noah tried heroically to hold back just a few seconds longer, something exploded inside him, sending white-hot lightning bolts of release and pure, glorious, physical sensation crashing through him again and again.

He thought he called out her name. He thought he could read her lips crooning, "Yes, yes...." Except he couldn't hear anything above the tumultuous roar in his head. As if a chaotic, swirling flood were toppling him end over end, sweeping him onward to oblivion.

At last the room stopped whirling. Noah's vision cleared. Sound returned. Something inside his chest had broken loose and shifted, so that he would never be the same as he'd been before.

Because of Caroline.

"I must be crushing you." With limbs that felt weighted by lead, Noah dragged himself from his position sprawled on top of her and collapsed back against the mattress. He slid an arm beneath Caroline's shoulders and cradled her against him.

"I *was* having kind of a hard time catching my breath." She traced his chest muscles with the tip of her finger. "Though that might have been from something else."

Noah grinned. "You wanton woman, you."

"Not anymore." She arched her eyebrows suggestively. "I *got* what I wanted."

He chuckled. "You and me both." He hugged her closer and pressed an affectionate kiss to her temple. Her hair was damp with sweat, her skin glistening as the candle flame danced over it.

There was that sharp pressure in his chest again, as if his heart had swelled too big to fit behind his ribs.

Caroline slung her arm across his midsection and snuggled against him. Man, she felt good beside him!

"Every ounce of strength has been drained from my body," she said limply. "I feel like a wet noodle."

Noah skated his hands across her bare skin, poking and prodding like a doctor during an exam. "No, you don't."

When she laughed, the sound tickled his ears. "You know, you're pretty funny when you've got your clothes off."

"Gee, thanks."

"I *meant*—" she nipped his earlobe "—your sense of humor." She propped herself on one elbow to get a better look at him. The frank admiration Noah saw on her face while she studied him in the wavering light stirred a response from his body.

"Oho, what's this?" She skimmed her hand down his sweat-slickened torso.

"Cut that out," Noah said, hoping she wouldn't.

"Cut what out?" She arranged her features in an expression of such angelic innocence, he could practically see her halo.

But her fingers worked devilish magic. Noah swallowed. "Uh, Caroline…"

"Mmm?"

"It's kind of soon to…I mean, I'm not sure I can…oh, wow."

Caroline twined her bare leg around his and nibbled on his earlobe again. "I'm sure you can rise to the occasion," she whispered.

She was right.

Caroline snapped awake to the smell of smoke. Where was she? It was pitch-dark, she was chilled to the bone, and the only sound she could hear was…

Someone breathing next to her.

She jerked quickly backward and nearly fell off the edge of

something. A…bed? Oh. That's right. Noah's bed, to be exact. While Caroline groped for the covers, it all came back to her.

Every blushing, skin-tingling detail of their lovemaking.

Now she detected a faint waxy odor, too. The candle must have burned out after they'd fallen asleep, exhausted. Wrapped in each other's arms, too heated by the lingering remnants of their passion to need any sheets or blankets over them.

Except now Caroline was cold.

She crawled back across the mattress, inch by cautious inch, toward the warmth of Noah's body. He didn't exactly snore, she decided, but there was no mistaking the fact he was sound asleep.

With one exploring toe she succeeded at locating the edge of a blanket. Slowly, so as not to waken him, she dragged it closer until she could tug it up with her hand. Brr! She didn't want to disturb Noah's sleep, but couldn't stand the thought of him lying there in the cold. Ever-so-gently, she tucked the blanket over him as well.

As soon as she huddled up against his back for warmth, Noah rolled over and flopped his arm around her waist. He was still asleep. Only now Caroline was trapped.

Once she'd taken care of her immediate concern, getting warm, a different kind of chill seeped inside her. One that wouldn't be so easily banished by a fuzzy blanket and a sexy warm male bundled up beside her.

"Oh, Noah," she whispered forlornly to the darkness. What time was it? One o'clock in the morning? Two? Either way, it was only a matter of hours until she would have to say goodbye to him, probably forever. By this time tomorrow she would be three thousand miles away from him. Not that geography was the problem. It was a different kind of distance that separated them. The impassable chasm between two wounded hearts.

Caroline wasn't naive enough to believe that making love with her had healed the pain and guilt of Noah's past. He'd finally surrendered to a simple biological equation, that was all. Take two lonely adults, confine them under the same roof in a high-stress situation, add a large dose of mutual attraction, and *voilà!* The results were completely predictable.

Caroline knew he cared about her. About Ethan, too, for that matter. But until Noah could come to terms with the tragedy that had claimed his wife and child, the pain and guilt of his past would prevent him from building a future with a new family.

Why did that knowledge hurt so much? Especially when Caroline herself had vowed to steer clear of relationships from now on. Even if she'd been willing to risk her own heart again, she would never risk Ethan's happiness by bringing a new father into his life.

Fathers, unfortunately, didn't come with guarantees. Ethan had suffered enough already. Even if Noah leaped out of bed this second, threw himself at Caroline's feet and proclaimed his undying love, she would still have to turn away and walk out of his life. To make sure that he never walked out of hers.

Caroline covered her face in the darkness. A tear leaked from the corner of her eye. Darn it! Leaving Noah would be even harder now. Why had she ignored her better judgment and let him make love to her?

Let him? mocked the realist inside her. *I'd say your role was a little more active than that. Or was that some other woman kissing him, moaning with delight, whispering naughty things in his ear?*

Caroline yanked her hands from her face as if her cheeks had burned them. Could that have been her? Playing the seductress? Teasing Noah, touching him in the most intimate ways possible, seducing him even as he'd seduced her with his greedy mouth, his skillful hands...

Desire coiled into a tight knot in her abdomen when she relived the incredible, uninhibited bliss of melding their bodies into one.

Bliss she would never know again.

Dear heaven, this was torture! Lying here encircled by Noah's strong arm, by the erotic masculine smell of him, by the deep, reassuring cadence of his breathing. Measuring this one night of perfect rapture against all the cold, lonely, endless nights to come.

Caroline's heart throbbed with an empty ache that was nearly unbearable. She turned her head into his chest, filling her lungs with the precious, now-familiar scent that would haunt her forever.

This would be her one and only chance to say what was in her heart.

Her lips barely moved against his skin. "I love you, Noah," she told him silently.

Now it was time to leave him.

Sneaking out of bed was a tricky proposition, thanks to that heavy, muscular arm draped across her. Somehow Caroline managed to wriggle out from beneath it without eliciting a groan of protest. The moment she drew away from Noah's sheltering warmth she was cold, even before she slithered out from beneath the blanket and hit the floor with her bare feet.

At least the tears couldn't hinder her vision any more than the darkness itself. Caroline groped around on the floor, trying to recreate the earlier sequence of events, which she hoped would point her in the most likely direction to find her nightgown and panties.

Recalling those events did not improve the chaotic state of her emotions.

Her fingers encountered a rumpled heap of cotton. Aha! Here was her nightgown, at least. Now if she could only locate—

"Where'd you go?"

The sleepy rumble of Noah's voice made Caroline start. She clutched the nightgown over her naked breasts, over her pounding heart.

"I'm...right here." The glowing digits of the bedside alarm clock backlit him faintly, so she could just make out his broad-shouldered profile. He was propped up on one arm, positioned so that he seemed to be staring right at her. Even though Caroline knew she must be nearly invisible, she felt self-conscious under his scrutiny.

"You're not leaving, are you?"

For a second, wild exhilaration leaped inside her. He didn't want her to leave tomorrow!

"I was hoping you'd stay the rest of the night."

Oh. He wasn't talking about her going back to Baltimore. He meant, was she leaving his bed, his room, right now.

Caroline tried to shake off the cold splash of disappointment that doused her. What would it matter, even if Noah wanted her to stay here for good? She couldn't.

"I—should go back to my own room." She felt around on the floor with growing frustration. Where *were* those darn panties, anyway? "I don't think it's a good idea to be in bed together when Ethan wakes up in the morning."

"Hmm." She heard a faint rasp that sounded like Noah was rubbing his jaw. "You're right, of course." The bed creaked as he shifted his muscular bulk. "What are you doing down there, anyway?"

"Trying to find my…undergarments," she mumbled.

"Oh." She thought she detected amusement in that one syllable. "Probably make it easier if I turned on the light."

"No—"

Too late. Light exploded into the room. Even though its source was only the small bedside reading lamp, compared to the cloaking darkness Caroline felt as if he'd turned a spotlight on her.

She blinked, uncomfortably aware of her nakedness and how she must look with her hair a tangled mess, her mouth swollen from their kisses. The bunched-up nightgown in her hand didn't conceal much.

When her eyes adjusted to the sudden brightness, she saw Noah was watching her with exactly the close intensity she'd feared. The sheet slanted across his hips, stark white in contrast to his darker skin. If Caroline hadn't known him better, she would have suspected he'd strategically arranged it for maximum erotic appeal. The sheet's position boldly revealed his fabulous chest, bulging biceps, and one perfectly sculpted, muscular leg stretched out on the mattress.

The rest of his sexy physique was left to the imagination. Except Caroline didn't *need* to imagine it anymore.

All at once she felt light-headed. She'd never in her life picked up one of those magazines featuring nude male models, but Noah would have been a prime candidate for a centerfold, she was sure. Or maybe one of those calendars. Beefcakes of Law Enforcement...

Get a grip, she scolded her hormones. Time to get out of here before she did something she would regret.

She finally spotted her panties in a lacy heap on top of Noah's discarded trousers. When she scooped them up she had a sudden vivid image of her own fingers tugging down his zipper, teasing him, tormenting him....

Oooh, boy. Caroline gulped. She was shocked by the un-suspected side of her nature Noah had brought out. He'd jok-ingly called her a wanton woman, but that's exactly what she'd felt like with him.

Yet it had all felt so natural, so right....

His eyes glowed with frank admiration, creating their own candlelight. "You're a beautiful woman, Caroline."

She didn't feel so wanton now. She felt shy, awkwardly pleased. How on earth was she going to get dressed with him watching her like that?

"And you're even more beautiful on the inside, where it really counts." He flung the sheet aside and rose from the bed, seemingly oblivious to his nakedness.

Caroline, on the other hand, was extremely conscious of it. He bracketed her shoulders with his hands and stood so close that their bare toes were touching. She kept her wadded-up nightclothes between them, like a basketball she was preparing to shoot. The heat from his body enveloped her.

"Morning's a few hours off," he said into her hair. By sliding her eyes all the way to one side Caroline could read the alarm clock. Nearly two-thirty. Noah worked his hands along her bare arms, kneading, caressing, cajoling. "Can't you stay a little while longer?"

She could tell it was hard for him to ask. It was even harder for her to say no. "Ethan might wake up in the middle of the night and come looking for me." Though he'd never done so before. "I—want him to be able to find me. But not here."

The real reason was that Caroline was scared to stay. Scared of the feelings that making love with Noah had finally forced her to admit to herself. Scared she might embarrass them both in a tender, unguarded moment.

Scared that just sleeping in his arms for a few more hours would make stepping on that plane tomorrow even more heart-breaking than it was already going to be.

Except that today *was* tomorrow. Or tomorrow was today. Either way, the day was finally here when she and Noah would part company for good.

If he was disappointed by her answer, he concealed it. "Of course. I understand."

She was a mother, and that had to come first. Always.

Noah pressed a kiss to her forehead. Caroline wondered whether she would always feel the tender brand of his lips there, a lingering reminder of what she'd walked away from. What they'd *both* walked away from.

He squeezed her shoulders briefly, then let her go. No games, no wheedling, no sly, sensual touches to convince her to stay. That was the kind of honest, straightforward, no-nonsense man Noah was. He respected her decision and wouldn't try to coax her into changing her mind.

Which was just as well. Now that there was nothing to prevent her from walking out the door, Caroline had to fight an overwhelming impulse to throw her arms around his sturdy, comforting, sexy-smelling neck and hang on for dear life.

Somehow she managed to get dressed, hopping up and down on one foot like a drunk flamingo while she pulled on her panties. It didn't help to have Noah sitting on the edge of the bed, watching her reverse striptease act.

"I feel like I should walk you back to your room," he said when she was finished.

"No! I mean, that won't be necessary." Then she saw by the wry uptilt of his mouth that he was kidding.

"I could put on a bathrobe," he offered.

Caroline jammed her hands through her hair, trying to rake the disheveled mess into some semblance of order. "Really, I can find my own way. No problem." What would Ethan think if he found them tiptoeing down the hall together in their nightclothes?

Maybe he was too young to know about sex. Had Jeff ever sat down and given him that birds-and-bees lecture? Or was Caroline going to have the privilege of sharing that awkward rite of passage with her son? He was only eight years old. Still, in this day and age kids were exposed to mature subject matter sooner than they used to be. Was there some tactful way she could ask Ethan if he and Jeff had ever had that particular father-son talk?

All at once, the enormity of the task ahead of her came lumbering toward Caroline like a steamroller. Raising a child by herself was going to be a huge challenge. She would have to be both mother and father to Ethan, even though she didn't know the first thing about baseball or building boats or—or any of that other traditionally guy stuff.

Stop it, she warned herself. You're just trying to rationalize wanting a man in your life.

Only not just *a* man. *This* man. The one striding buck naked across the room toward her, with a look of purpose on his face and a look of renewed arousal on his—

"Here." Noah brushed past her and pulled open a dresser drawer. "Take this." He placed a flashlight in her hand. "Since you won't let me escort you personally." He wrapped her fingers around it. "This way you won't have to turn on any lights and risk waking up Ethan."

"Thank you." Caroline willed him to keep his fingers curled around hers, to maintain this last precious link between them. "I...guess I'd better go."

Don't let me go!

With silent deliberation, he crooked a finger beneath her chin and tilted her face up to his. The kiss he gave her was almost chaste, as sweet and cautious as if it had been the first kiss for both of them.

All too soon it was over. Noah's chest heaved once as he dropped his hands and stepped back from her. Unchaining her. Setting her adrift.

Caroline willed back tears as she took one final look at his face. At those handsome, honest features that had become so dear to her. Roughened now by the shadow of whiskers, harsh with longing, carved with regret.

The face of the man she loved. The man she could never have.

"Good night," she whispered just before her throat closed up tight. Good-bye, she thought.

Without waiting for Noah to echo her words, she turned and took hold of the doorknob. She blinked frantically while she struggled with it, vowing not to cry in front of him. What was wrong with this darn thing, anyway? Talk about awkward exits...

Noah reached past her and turned the lock. Caroline closed her eyes and drew in a long, shaky breath, filling her senses with the heat and smell of him. Then she opened the door, switched on the flashlight and fled.

Without looking at Noah again.

He was fully dressed the next time she saw him, hair still damp from his shower. Caroline herself had been awake for hours. At the crack of dawn she'd given up hoping for sleep and had come downstairs to fix one last breakfast for the three of them.

The rattling of plates and skillets wound her nerves to an even tighter pitch, but at least it gave her something to do. She heard Noah go into his shower, then heard the phone ring just after he'd shut off the water.

Should she go ahead and answer it? After all, Noah would be driving her and Ethan to the airport in less than two hours. What did it matter now if someone found out they'd been staying here?

Never mind. She heard the thud of bare feet sprinting for the phone and knew Noah would answer it.

Less than two hours...

Spirits sagging, Caroline forced herself to go through the motions of cooking. She checked her watch every thirty seconds. At last she decided it was time to wake up Ethan.

She adjusted the stove burner to low. When she turned around, Noah was standing in the doorway.

Caroline caught her breath. Coming face-to-face with him was like slamming headfirst into a granite wall. All the incredible memories of what they'd said and done to each other last night came back in a rush. Desire exploded in the pit of her stomach, an intense hunger that would never be satisfied.

Noah held her gaze steadily, so that Caroline knew he was remembering the same things. But there was an added element in his eyes, an excitement she didn't understand.

He stepped into the kitchen, breaking the spell between them. "That was the sheriff over in Marshall County on the phone a few minutes ago." Noah rounded the table as if he meant to seize Caroline and whirl her through the air.

Instead, he halted two feet away, eyes gleaming with triumph. "They've got Buckman in custody."

Chapter 12

"They picked him up on some minor theft charge four days ago," Noah explained between bites of omelet. "Apparently he strolled out of a convenience store with a bottle of wine he didn't bother paying for."

Across the table, Caroline plucked little pieces off a paper napkin. "So he's been in jail all this time?"

"He was scheduled to go to court this afternoon. Judge probably would have released him." Noah swallowed some coffee. "The information I sent out regarding his name must have been floating around the Marshall County sheriff's office for a few days before anyone checked it out. It was a stroke of luck they discovered we were looking for him before they let him go."

"Mmm." Caroline had reduced her napkin to a pile of confetti. That worried pucker between her eyebrows was back. Noah hadn't exactly expected her to jump for joy when he told her about Buckman, but he'd thought she'd be pleased that her ex-husband's probable killer had been caught. Now they wouldn't have to worry about him coming after Ethan.

Instead, she'd turned uncharacteristically silent. Maybe because she realized this new development was going to throw a monkey wrench in her plans to return home today. Or maybe her withdrawn behavior had to do with last night. With those wild, passionate hours they'd spent in bed together.

She seemed reluctant to meet Noah's eyes. Did she regret what they'd done?

Noah himself had been troubled by second thoughts ever since Caroline had left him in the wee hours of the morning. Man, it had been tough to let her go! But he hadn't had the right to pressure her to stay. Not when Caroline had made it clear she wanted no emotional strings tying her to any man. No promises, no commitments. Even if Noah had been willing to make them.

Once Caroline had gone, the bed Noah had slept alone in for four years had seemed impossibly lonely. Empty. And way too big for just one person.

It had reminded him of those awful nights after Beth had died when, blissfully forgetful in the mists of slumber, Noah would roll over and sling his arm around his sleeping wife. Except his arm encountered only the empty mattress. Beth wasn't there anymore. She would never lie beside him again.

The shock of finding her gone would snap Noah wide awake and send the terrible, raw truth crashing down on him all over again. Beth. Molly. Both gone forever.

He wouldn't get another wink of sleep for the rest of the night.

Gradually he'd grown accustomed to sleeping alone. He'd stopped reaching for Beth in the darkness. He'd blotted out all memory of how pleasant it was to wake up next to the familiar body of the woman he loved, to have a quick drowsy chat in the middle of the night if they both happened to stir awake at the same time. He'd forced himself to forget how enjoyable it was to cuddle and watch the sun come up together, to make playful, passionate love whenever the spirit moved them.

But once Caroline had left him last night and Noah had

crawled back into his empty bed, all those memories had come
crashing down again. Along with a nagging guilt that was like
a profound ache in his soul.

How could he have betrayed Beth by finding joy with another woman? From the moment Noah's mouth had first collided with Caroline's last night, he hadn't thought of his late
wife even once. Not until about two seconds after Caroline
had left and Noah started to miss her.

Then it all rushed back, the anguish of missing Beth, of
yearning for her lost presence with such ferocious intensity
that Noah halfway believed he could bring her and Molly back
by sheer force of his will.

He blamed himself for their deaths. Now he blamed himself
for betraying their memories.

"I've got to go," he said abruptly, pushing his plate away
without finishing the delicious bacon-and-cheese omelet Caroline had fixed for him. "I told the Marshall County sheriff
I'd be there as soon as I could."

Caroline rose from the table when he did. "How long does
it take to drive there?"

"Maybe an hour."

"Hmm." The furrow between her brows deepened. She was
wearing the same outfit she'd had on the first day Noah had
met her, the gray dress with the burgundy blazer. Her traveling
clothes, apparently.

For a second he was seized by the powerful memory of
tasting that delicate hollow above the neckline, feeling Caroline's pulse flutter beneath his tongue, dragging his mouth
down the sweet, soft trail between her breasts—

His body instinctively responded with a sharp, unmistakable
throb that jolted Noah back to the present. "I guess you realize
this means a delay in your travel plans," he said, reaching for
the sport coat he'd draped over a chair. "For one thing, I can't
drive you to the airport this morning." He slung the coat over
his shoulder. "And of course, now that we've found Buckman,
I'll need Ethan to identify him."

"Yes. Certainly." Caroline absently fingered a stray wisp

of hair. She seemed distracted. Distant. As if she was already pulling away from him. "I'll call the airline and postpone our reservations."

Noah moved toward the back door, increasing the distance between them when what he really wanted was to hold her as close as possible. So their hearts were beating right next to each other. So their bodies fit snugly, perfectly together, like two missing pieces of a puzzle that had finally found each other. So that all he had to do to kiss her was lower his mouth and—

He slapped the cuffs on his runaway imagination. Now, what had they just been discussing? Oh, yeah. "After I interview Buckman and determine he's the guy we're looking for, I'll arrange to have him brought back here to Eagle River." Noah patted his pockets, making sure he had his notepad. "Once Ethan identifies him, you can go ahead and rebook your flight."

"I...guess there won't be any reason for us to stick around here after that." Caroline linked her fingers together and hunched her shoulders with a bright smile. "After Ethan identifies him, I mean." Her cheerfulness seemed forced. Her smile carried a hint of a question mark.

Only Noah couldn't quite figure out what she was asking. "No need for you to stay after that," he agreed. "I know you're anxious to get home."

"Yes." Whatever warmth there'd been behind Caroline's smile faded. A shutter seemed to drop behind her eyes, like a window shade yanked down to block an intruder. As if she was shutting Noah out.

All at once he couldn't stand it anymore, this barrier that had sprung up between them since last night. For the last half hour they'd been warily circling each other like two clumsy dancers, holding each other at a stiff arm's length, trying not to step on each other's toes, watching their feet instead of each other.

Last night Noah had felt as close to Caroline as he had to anyone in his life. Closer than he'd thought he would ever feel

to another human being again. He missed that feeling. He
wanted it back.

Her eyes widened with faint alarm as Noah took three long
strides across the kitchen. She didn't flinch, though, even when
he made his intentions clear. Her arms slipped around his waist
like a reflex when Noah drew her into his embrace.

There, this was much better. Like a nice, easy slow dance.
He nuzzled his cheek on top of Caroline's head and closed his
eyes, allowing himself to imagine the two of them joined like
this forever.

But he'd pledged himself forever to a woman once before,
hadn't he? Built a life with her. Made a baby. And then lit-
erally driven Beth and Molly to their deaths.

How could he allow himself to find happiness again, to
move on with his life, when *their* lives had been cut so cruelly
short? Thanks to him.

A clamp tightened around Noah's heart. He loosened his
hold on Caroline just enough so he could look down into her
face. "About last night..." he began. Then he stopped without
the foggiest idea of what to say. That for a few hours she'd
made him feel whole again? That he would never, ever forget
her as long as he lived?

Her eyes watched him expectantly. Searching. But Noah
knew that whatever she was looking for, he couldn't offer it
to her. All he had to offer was the truth.

"For whatever it's worth," he said, gliding his hand down
the long, luxurious sweep of her hair, "I want you to know
that last night meant something to me. Something very special."

Caroline summoned a smile. "I'd say it's worth quite a lot,
hearing you say that."

"I just...didn't want you to think it was only about sex."

Her smile wavered as she lifted her hand to his cheek. "I
didn't think that," she murmured. "I know you too well ever
to think that."

She did know him. Better than he knew himself sometimes,
Noah thought. He'd often found her perceptiveness discon-

certing, the way she could see past the stoic, controlled armor he wore in front of the world. At first he'd resented the way she kept probing into his private pain, ignoring all those Keep Out signs he'd posted to warn people away.

But she'd made Noah feel something besides grief and guilt for the first time in four years. And for that, he would always be grateful.

He leaned his forehead against hers. Those luminous green eyes that would haunt him forever filled his vision. He brushed his mouth across her hair, her eyelids, the tip of her nose. Then he kissed her tenderly, hoping to convey some of the feelings it was too dangerous to express out loud.

She clung to him for just a fraction of a second when he finally broke their kiss. Then she stepped back and let him go. "Good luck with Buckman," she said.

"I'll call you after I talk to him." Noah hesitated with his hand on the doorknob, reluctant to leave, wanting to say more.

Except they'd already said whatever there was to say, hadn't they?

Everything except goodbye.

Caroline watched Noah close the door behind him, then listened to his footsteps crunch across the gravel toward his Jeep. She pressed her fingertips to her mouth, as if that way she could hold on a little longer to the taste and heat of his farewell kiss.

She'd done her best to brace herself emotionally for the fact that she would probably never see Noah again after this morning. Now that she and Ethan wouldn't be flying back to Baltimore today after all, she felt as if someone had yanked the rug out from under her. Startled. Disoriented. Not sure which way to fall.

When she turned to clear the dishes from the table, she found Ethan hovering in the kitchen doorway. "Good morning, sleepyhead! I was just about to come wake you." She ferried the remains of Noah's omelet to the sink. "What would you like for breakfast? Eggs? Pancakes? French..."

Caroline's cheerful menu trailed off when she did a double take and absorbed Ethan's expression. He hadn't budged from the doorway. His feet were planted at an aggressive stance, his fists bunched at his sides as if he were preparing to stand up to the school-yard bully.

His eyes tracked her every move, as round and hard as brown marbles. Accusingly. To her dismay, Caroline realized the red blotches on her son's pale cheeks were those of anger.

"Ethan?" She dropped the silverware she was carrying and hastened toward him. "Honey, what is it? What's wr—"

Ethan backed away from her. Caroline was so shocked she froze. His freckles stood out against the pinched, white bridge of his nose. The spikes of his uncombed blond hair trembled.

"I saw you," he said in a strangled voice. Then anger shored up his words. "I saw you *kissing* him!" He nearly spat out the accusation.

Oh, dear. Caroline flushed with embarrassment and concern. "Ethan, honey, what you saw was just—"

"I don't *want* him to be my dad!"

Calm, Caroline. Just stay calm. "Sweetheart, Noah isn't going to—"

"My dad's *dead!*"

Caroline reached out, her heart aching for her son. "I know."

Ethan shook off her hand. "That guy's *never* going to be my dad! Never!" His chin quivered. "I *hate* him!"

"Oh, Ethan, you don't mean—"

"Lemme go! Just leave me alone."

Caroline caught a flash of angry tears in his eyes as he whirled away. His sneakers pounded down the hall and up the stairs. Moments later she heard a door slam.

She felt sick to her stomach. Chilled to the bone. How could she have let this happen?

She lowered herself into the nearest chair before her shaky legs buckled. Dear heaven, this was exactly why she'd vowed not to let a man into her life again!

Her one concern above all others was to make Ethan feel

loved and secure. To build up his trust and confidence in their future together. To make sure he knew that he was more important to her than anyone else on earth.

The past few years had turned the foundations of Ethan's universe to quicksand. First his parents had gotten divorced. Then he'd been abruptly whisked away from his home and told that his mother was dead. Now he'd just lost his father, and had to adjust to the idea of having a mother again.

Her poor confused child must be worried sick that none of the adults in his life were ever going to stick around! No wonder he viewed Noah as a threat, as a rival for his mother's affections. When Ethan had accidentally come upon the two of them kissing just now, he must have felt his worst fears had come true.

Caroline buried her face in her hands. She wanted desperately to go after her son, to take him by the shoulders and force him to listen while she swore that she would never abandon him, that from now on it was just going to be the two of them so that Ethan never had to worry about losing someone he loved again.

But maternal intuition also cautioned her that Ethan was too upset to listen right now. Better to do what he'd angrily demanded and leave him alone for a while. Give him a chance to calm down before she went upstairs and tried to reassure him.

Which would also give Caroline a chance to figure out how she was going to explain what Ethan had seen. How she was going to make him understand that just because she and Noah had kissed each other, it didn't mean...well, didn't mean what? That they cared for each other? That they were ever going to see each other again?

Caroline dropped her head to the table and let the tears come. How could she expect Ethan to understand, when she didn't even understand it herself?

An hour had passed since Ethan had fled from the kitchen. It was one of the slowest hours of Caroline's life. She couldn't bear the thought of her little boy closeted in his room upstairs, terrified of sharing her with someone else. Resenting Noah. Resenting her, too, probably.

She *had* to convince Ethan he never had to worry about losing her. About sharing her with anyone else.

Caroline prowled restlessly around Noah's living room, absently adjusting the furniture by moving a lamp a bit to the right, nudging a chair an inch to the left. This house actually had quite a bit of potential, if Noah ever bothered to hire a decorator. A ghost of a smile brushed her lips. Somehow she couldn't imagine that ever happening.

When she glanced at her watch again, less than two minutes had passed since the last time she'd checked. Had she waited long enough for Ethan to calm down?

Noah would be arriving at the jail to interview Buckman soon. Would the man confess to killing Jeff? Would that mean she and Ethan could fly back to Baltimore today after all?

Lots of questions, but answers were in short supply. Caroline sighed. Perhaps subconsciously she was putting off talking to Ethan because she still hadn't figured out what to say to him. She wasn't about to lie to her son by pretending that Noah meant nothing to her.

But she was hardly about to admit the true extent of her feelings, either.

She folded her arms and drummed her fingers. "For heaven's sake, quit being such a chicken," she scolded herself. "You'll find the right words somehow."

Encouraged by that brief pep talk, she headed determinedly upstairs. Ethan might be too young to understand all the complicated subtleties of adult relationships. But he would certainly understand a big, loving hug from his mother.

Caroline brought her ear close to the door of his room and listened. Silence.

She took a deep breath and knocked.

No reply.

"Ethan?" She knocked again.

Still no sound from the other side of the door.

A touch of foreboding nudged the base of her spine. It probably meant nothing. But she went ahead and opened the door. "Sweetheart?"

One corner of Ethan's pillowcase fluttered in the breeze coming through the open window above his unmade bed. The sense of foreboding grew stronger. Caroline peered behind the door, then hurried across the room to check the closet.

Empty.

So was the whole room.

Ethan was gone.

As soon as the Marshall County deputy escorted the prisoner into the interrogation room, Noah knew they had the right guy. Not that Buckman turned out to be a dead ringer for the police sketch, although Ethan had done a good job of describing the unkempt hair, the wild beard, the prominent scar zigzagging through one bushy eyebrow.

What made Noah so sure was the mixture of guilt and fear that skittered furtively across Buckman's face like a wild animal the second he and Noah made eye contact. Clearly Buckman recognized him from Eagle River, though Noah could swear he'd never laid eyes on the man before.

"Have a seat." Noah gestured at one of the molded plastic chairs arranged around the scarred table. He nodded to the deputy, who left them alone, closing the door behind him.

Buckman scraped back a chair and slumped into it. He wasn't wearing handcuffs. "They advise you of your rights?" Noah asked him. "Tell you you're entitled to a lawyer?"

Buckman nodded once and scratched his nose. "Got no use for lawyers," he mumbled. "Don't like 'em."

"Okay. How about some coffee?" Noah hoisted his own cardboard cup of the stuff. "Though in all good conscience, I can't recommend it."

Buckman blew a disdainful sound through his cracked lips. "How 'bout a *real* drink?" he asked, though there wasn't much hope in the question.

Noah gave him a tight smile. "Sorry." He flipped around

a chair and straddled it backwards. Time to get down to business. "What'd you think of Eagle River?" he asked conversationally. "Nice town, isn't it?"

Buckman had deep-set eyes that enhanced the skeletal effect of his sunken cheeks. "Guess so." His eyes shifted warily. The Marshall County jail had given him a clean orange jumpsuit and a bath, but Noah could still smell an odor of fear coming off him.

"You left in kind of a hurry, from what I hear."

Buckman shrugged. "No hurry. Just time to move on." He started tapping his thumbs together. Noah observed his nails were well-chewed.

"Huh." He reached into his jacket pocket and produced a blowup of Jeff Tate's driver's-license photo. "You ever bump into this fellow while you were in Eagle River?"

Buckman stared at the picture Noah had laid between them on the table. "Nah." Flecks of sweat dotted his brow. They might as well have spelled out "I'm lying."

"Come on, now, Pete," Noah said, studying the man before him. Peter Alvin Buckman, born fifty-six years ago in Lima, Ohio, according to the information Marshall County sheriff's department had dug up on him so far. Former factory worker, current alcoholic. A longtime transient who'd left a cross-country trail of petty convictions behind him.

"Take another look." Noah pushed Jeff's picture a little closer. "I got a witness who saw you arguing with this guy a couple weeks ago."

Buckman shied away from the photo as if it were a coiled-up rattler about to strike. "I...can't see so good, close up."

"His name is Jeff Tucker. Also known as Jeff Tate. Runs the gas station at the east end of Main Street in Eagle River. Ring any bells?"

Loud and clear, judging by Buckman's sickly, cornered expression. "I—dunno." He gave an elaborate shrug of one shoulder. "Maybe I seen him."

"I think you did more than just *see* him, didn't you, Pete?" Noah wagged an admonishing finger. "I think you talked to him. Argued with him. Lost your temper.'' He leaned forward over the back of his chair. ''What'd you two argue about, Pete?''

Buckman shoved out his chin. ''We didn't argue.''

''Something about money, wasn't it?'' Noah tapped Jeff's photograph. ''You were trying to shake him down, only he wouldn't go for it, right?''

Buckman shook his head stubbornly.

Noah sprang from his chair and knocked it aside. Time to crank up the pressure. ''Weren't you down at the Mineshaft Saloon, bragging about the big money you were about to score?''

Buckman hesitated, then once more turned his shaggy head from side to side.

''Yessir, I'll bet you had lots of plans for that money.'' Noah rubbed his jaw thoughtfully. ''And when Tucker finally claimed he couldn't come up with it, you got pretty mad, didn't you?''

''You're crazy, man,'' Buckman muttered.

''You got mad, lost your temper, so you grabbed something and took a swing at him, right?'' Noah slapped a palm flat on the table.

Buckman continued to scowl at him.

Noah dropped the volume of his voice. Coaxing, now. Cajoling. ''Probably didn't mean to hit him that hard, did you?'' He winked. ''Come on, Pete. Tell me how it happened. A judge'll go easier on you if you didn't actually mean to kill Tucker.''

Buckman's jaw clunked open, revealing a junkyard of rotting teeth. ''*Kill* him?'' he squawked. ''You think I *killed* the guy? *That's* what this is all about?''

Noah made a give-it-up motion with his hand. ''Come on, tell me how it went down. If you cooperate, I'll make sure the district attorney knows about it so he can put in a good word for you when it comes time for sentencing.''

Buckman lurched to his feet. His chair fell over backward. The deputy hovering outside the interrogation room peered

suspiciously through the window near the top of the door.
"Look, I didn't kill nobody!" Buckman exclaimed.

"Yeah? Well, there's plenty of guys on Death Row singing
that same song." Noah checked his watch as if he was late
for an appointment. "I'll be able to prove you killed Jeff
Tucker sooner or later. But if you save me time by telling me
right now what happened, I'll return the favor and ask the D.A.
to cut you some slack."

Buckman clutched his hands to the sides of his head as if
a terrible migraine had seized him. "No, no, no," he moaned.
"I ain't takin' the rap for this. No way."

Noah tucked the photo and his notepad into his jacket
pocket as if preparing to leave. "Last chance to take me up
on my offer. Tell the truth, and I'll tell the D.A. how coop-
erative you were."

Buckman howled at the ceiling. The deputy's scowl appeared in the window again. Noah sent him a quick everything's-under-control signal.

"Look, I didn't kill the guy, all right?" Buckman was shaking as if he was coming down off a week-long binge. "I just
talked to him. 'Cause of the kid's picture, you know?"

"No, I don't know." Noah settled himself on the edge of
the table, taking care to conceal his excitement. "Explain it to
me."

Buckman paced back and forth in agitation. "I seen that
kid's picture on one of them...whaddaya call 'em? Fliers. It
said he'd been kidnapped by his daddy. Only I recognized
him, see? It was the kid at the gas station, and that was his
daddy, the guy who ran the place, see?"

Ethan, Noah thought. One of Caroline's desperate fliers had
somehow found its way into Buckman's hands. "Yeah, I see,"
he said. So that's how the drifter had discovered Jeff's secret.

Buckman didn't require much encouragement at this point.
The words tumbled out of him in an eager avalanche. "So I
thought, hey, how do I know I'll ever get this reward the flier
was talkin' about? Then I figured it might be worth somethin'
to the kid's daddy if I kept quiet. Bird in the hand and all that,

see? So I went and saw the guy at the gas station and told him I thought we should make a deal.''

Blackmail. That must have been the argument Ethan had witnessed between his father and Buckman.

"How much money did this deal involve?" Noah asked, pulling out his notepad again.

Buckman jammed a hand through his matted hair, looking as if he was sticking a pitchfork into a haystack. "Uh, I guess it was like…twenty grand," he muttered.

Twenty thousand dollars. The exact amount of the loan Jeff had applied for, according to what Quincy Medford, the bank manager, had told Noah.

"How did Tucker react to your proposal?" Noah asked, though it wasn't hard to imagine.

Buckman squirmed. "Started yelling. Said he didn't have that kind of money. I asked him, ain't your kid worth it? He got all red in the face." Incredibly, a note of self-righteousness crept into Buckman's tone. "I told him I'd give him till Thursday to come up with the dough, or else I was gonna consider it my civic duty to report him to the cops."

Thursday was the day Jeff had been killed. Buckman certainly wasn't helping his case any by admitting his blackmail deadline coincided with the day of the murder. Why mention that incriminating detail if he planned to deny killing his blackmail victim? Unless…

Noah frowned.

Buckman interpreted his look as skepticism. "I swear, that was the last time I ever saw the guy!" he cried. "I was gonna get my money from him Thursday afternoon, but when I got to the gas station that yellow police tape was hanging all over the place. Cop cars and ambulances everywhere!" Buckman clamped his hands to his head as if to crush the distressing memory. "Somebody in the crowd told me the place got robbed and the guy that ran it got hit over the head. Man, I took off! I didn't want no trouble!"

He held out his fists to Noah, not threatening but pleading. "Look, you gotta believe me! I didn't kill the guy!"

Through his years in law enforcement, Noah had developed a sort of internal lie detector that told him when people were telling the truth. It wasn't always reliable, any more than a real lie detector was. But he'd learned to listen to it, even when the facts of a case seemed to contradict what the person was claiming.

Much to Noah's surprise, his needle of instinct about Buckman's story was tilting toward the Truth side of the scale. Maybe because Buckman had been so forthcoming with details right away. Most suspects were smart enough not to be too specific with the facts till they'd had a chance to carefully tailor their version of events, because the details were what would trip you up every time.

Now that Noah was face-to-face with the real Buckman instead of a sinister, two-dimensional sketch, he found himself having to revise some of his preconceived impressions about the man. Frankly, Buckman struck him as pathetic rather than violent. A loser, not a dangerous killer.

Although Noah badly wanted to believe he'd found his man, something about Buckman's story rang true.

Which meant Noah still had a lot of work ahead of him. In the end, odds were that Buckman would turn out to be the killer after all. Either he was simply a more convincing actor than Noah usually came across, or he'd been lucky enough to stumble onto just the right blend of truth and lie to raise doubt in Noah's mind.

For now, though, this case was a long way from closed.

Noah put away his notepad again and signaled to the deputy that he was ready to leave. He needed to make arrangements to have Buckman transported back to Eagle River so Ethan could identify him. Noah still hoped that seeing Buckman in person again might jog Ethan's memory. Without an eyewitness or any physical evidence tying Buckman to the actual murder, getting a conviction was going to be difficult, if not impossible.

"I didn't do it," Buckman said again.

The deputy opened the door. "Let's go," he told Buckman,

jingling his keys. With one last despairing look at Noah, Buckman turned to shuffle back to his cell.

As he passed the deputy, the deputy said to Noah, ''You
got a message out at the front desk.''

Preoccupied by his uneasiness over Buckman's guilt, Noah
nearly forgot to stop for his message on his way out of the
building.

''Someone named Caroline Tate called for you.'' One of
the secretaries flagged him down with a piece of paper. ''She
said to tell you Ethan's missing.''

Chapter 13

"Don't you worry, ma'am. We'll find him." Grady Reeves gave Caroline's shoulder a patronizing pat that would have annoyed her under different circumstances. But she was too consumed with fear to resent the sheriff's condescending manner.

At least he was taking this search seriously. When Caroline had first found Ethan missing from his room and established that he was nowhere in the house, she'd rushed outside to look for him herself. But there were simply too many directions a small boy could have run in this wooded, mountainous terrain. After calling his name till her voice was hoarse, and nearly getting lost herself, Caroline had been forced to return to the house and call for help.

When the Marshall County sheriff's office had informed her Noah was interviewing a prisoner and couldn't be interrupted, Caroline had left him a quick message and then promptly called the sheriff of Tamarack County. Noah's boss, Grady Reeves, was familiar with the Tate case and seemed to appreciate the urgency that had vibrated in Caroline's voice along the phone wires.

Sheriff Reeves had driven over from Carleton himself to take charge of the search, having assembled a rescue team in what seemed amazingly short time, even from Caroline's panic-stricken perspective.

The sheriff had just finished dispatching the mixed group of civilian volunteers and law-enforcement personnel in all directions. Now he himself was preparing to join the search for Ethan. Caroline had to give the man credit. Judging from his appearance, tromping up and down the rough backcountry wasn't part of his daily routine.

"You just sit tight in case your boy happens to call," Reeves told her. "He might stumble out of the woods some-place and find himself a telephone, you never know." Another paternalistic pat. Caroline ignored it. All she cared about was getting Ethan back safe and sound.

She followed Reeves out to the front porch. "Are you sure I wouldn't be more use joining the search?" she asked for the third or fourth time. It chafed against her every instinct to wait here and do nothing, while Ethan was lost out there in the woods someplace. To have found her stolen child against such impossible odds, only to lose him again in such a cruel twist of fate...

A blade of anguish knifed through her heart.

"Miz Tate, you don't know these mountains like the rest of us do." The sheriff hoisted his belt so that all the gear attached to it jingled. "Can't have *you* gettin' lost, too, now, can we?" He winked. "Besides, that boy needs to hear his mama's voice on the phone if he calls." The belt sagged again under the bulky weight of the sheriff's belly.

He was right, of course. But Caroline didn't know how she was going to stand the waiting.

She watched the sheriff march off into the trees. Before the forest swallowed him up, Caroline could see he was already huffing and puffing. It would have made more sense, probably, for *him* to have stayed here by the phone.

It had felt so odd when the searchers had arrived, to be surrounded by people again. For days and days Noah and Ethan had been Caroline's only human contact. Now she was alone again. Truly alone.

She clutched one of the posts that supported the roof of the porch. It would have to support her, too, if fear kept turning her knees weak like this. The front door was open so she could hear the phone if it rang. But Caroline intended to wait outside so she would see Ethan the moment he came out of the woods.

If he came out of the woods.

Oh, dear God, don't let anything happen to him! Caroline squeezed her eyes shut and bit back a moan of anguish. If only she hadn't been careless enough to kiss Noah in the kitchen this morning. If only she hadn't let herself become so distracted by her feelings for him that she'd forgotten Ethan might see them.

If only she hadn't become involved with Noah in the first place. The pain Caroline had felt anticipating their final parting was a pinprick compared to the raw, desolate agony that surged through her when she imagined something happening to Ethan.

That sensible voice inside her head had warned Caroline from the beginning that letting a man into her life was a huge mistake. If only she'd listened to her brain instead of her heart.

When Caroline opened her eyes, a figure was walking slowly up the driveway. Wild hope leaped inside her, then collapsed. It wasn't Ethan.

It was a man with a dog. Both of them looked rather mangy. The dog had long legs, long ears and probably a long list of breeds in his ancestry. The man wore patched-up blue jeans, a dirty checkered shirt and a faded bandanna tied around his neck. He had a bunch of tools hanging from his belt—a small rusty spade, a pickax, a metal drinking cup. The jangling sound he made when he walked reminded Caroline of Sheriff Reeves and his belt.

This guy looked like a gold miner who'd been wandering around lost in these mountains for the better part of a century.

As he approached the porch, Caroline could see that beneath his Rip van Winkle hair, his grizzled beard and weathered complexion he was probably only in his mid-fifties.

He stopped about ten feet away. The dog plopped down beside him and began to scratch fleas. "Heard in town your boy's missing," her visitor said without preamble. His voice was rusty, as if he didn't use it much.

Caroline swallowed a sob. "Yes."

The man nudged the dog with his foot. The dog yawned. "Ol' Blue here's got a lotta hound in him. He's a good tracker."

"Is he?"

The man scratched his beard. Possibly *he* had fleas, too. "If you got some piece of your boy's clothes, like a shirt, maybe, Ol' Blue here can pick up his scent."

It took a few seconds to dawn on Caroline what he was saying. "You mean your dog might be able to follow my son's trail?"

"Yes'm."

She tried to shove down the sudden spurt of hope inside her. Was there really a chance this flea-bitten, lazy-looking mutt could turn out to be Ethan's rescuer? The sheriff *had* mentioned bringing in bloodhounds if Ethan didn't turn up soon. Anyway, what did she have to lose by letting him try?

"Stay right here," she told the man, fearful he might up and disappear now that she'd let herself hope that he and his dog might really be able to find Ethan. "I'll go get some of my son's clothing."

She flew upstairs and grabbed Ethan's pajamas from the floor by the bed. She was breathing hard by the time she got back outside. "Here." She nearly stumbled in her haste to descend the front steps. She halted a prudent distance away and stretched out her arm. The dog hardly seemed vicious, though. Biting her would probably require too much effort.

The man took the bundle of pajamas and held it down in front of the animal's nose. The dog continued to act bored at first, then his tail began to wag back and forth like a wind-shield wiper.

"That's a boy. You smell him now? You got the scent?"

The dog barked in reply to his master's encouragement. Then he scrambled to his feet and started to run in circles, sniffing the driveway and whining.

Caroline cautiously allowed herself to believe the mutt might actually know what he was doing.

The dog trotted off toward the woods, nose to the ground, tail waving madly. There was a sense of purpose to his movements now.

"I believe he's sniffed out the trail!" the man chortled. "Hot damn." He seemed so pleased, Caroline felt an instant warmth toward him. "All right, ma'am, we'll do our best to find your boy." Still clutching Ethan's pajamas, he started after the dog.

"Wait!" Caroline called. "I'm coming with you."

The man halted with a startled hunch of his shoulders as if he'd been shot in the back. Warily he wheeled around. "No need for that, ma'am." He seemed alarmed by the prospect of her company. Probably because he was some kind of crazy hermit. "You just stay put and me and Ol' Blue, we'll find your boy."

"No." Caroline had spoken on impulse, but now that the idea had entered her head it was stuck there. There appeared to be every chance the dog would lead them straight to Ethan. Except that Ethan might be scared or hurt. How would he react to the sight of this big galumphing dog and wild-haired stranger bearing down on him?

Caroline was frantic to be reunited with Ethan as soon as possible. Every single extra moment of delay was intolerable. On the remote chance that Ethan did call from someplace, even if she wasn't here to answer, at least it would mean he was all right.

But Caroline didn't truly believe Ethan would call. She'd spent too many years waiting by the telephone, praying for the sound of her precious little boy's voice every time she snatched up the receiver. She'd been disappointed too many times to keep waiting here at Noah's house while her child was out there somewhere, lost.

She had to get to him right away.

"I'm coming with you," she told the stranger again.

He shook his head. "Best if you wait here," he said ominously. "Them woods is rough." His bleary eyes brightened as if he'd just had an inspiration. "Me and Ol' Blue can go a lot faster without you tagging along. Find your boy quicker."

"I can keep up." Caroline hustled toward him as if to prove her claim, then realized she ought to leave a note for anyone who came back to the house expecting to find her here. "Wait. I'll be right back."

"You shouldn't come with us!" the man hollered after her. "Me and Ol' Blue do best by ourselves!"

She was going to have to scribble that note fast, or else man and dog were going to disappear by the time she got back. As she crossed the front porch Caroline was already composing the note in her head. Man brought dog. Dog picked up Ethan's scent. I went with—

"Excuse me," she called. Her guide was already sneaking off after the dog, who was yipping around in impatient circles at the edge of the woods.

The man's less-than-perfect posture slumped even further when he turned around.

"What's your name?" Caroline asked.

He moved his lips as if he'd just tasted something bad. "Rollie," he finally answered grudgingly.

Noah slammed down the phone at the Marshall County sheriff's department with a sinking feeling in his gut. Caroline hadn't picked up the phone at home, even after the answering machine had come on and Noah had spoken into it for several minutes. She must be out looking for Ethan.

He dialed his office. "Ruby? You get any report of a missing kid?"

"You mean that little Tate boy? Sure! Half the town's out

looking for him right now. His mother says he crawled out the bedroom window and ran away." Her tone took on a tart edge. "You might have mentioned you were hiding them out at your place. I *can* keep a secret, you know."

"Has Grady been notified about the boy?"

"Heavens, from what I hear he's out there leading the search himself."

"Good." Grady understood the situation, the possibility that Jeff Tate's killer might harm Ethan if he got the chance. Of course, the killer was probably behind bars right now, lodged in the very same jail where Noah was standing.

But Noah's newfound doubts about Buckman's guilt took on a different importance in light of Ethan's disappearance. If Buckman wasn't the killer, and the killer was still in Eagle River...well, Ruby had just told Noah half the town was out looking for Ethan. If the killer happened to be one of the searchers...

Noah assured himself it was highly unlikely the killer would be the one to find Ethan. Highly unlikely he would come across Ethan when no one else was around, in remote, dangerous terrain where it would be so easy to make murder look like an accident...

But then, a number of highly unlikely events had already come to pass during the course of this case.

Noah shuddered. The vision of Ethan coming to harm was like a swift sucker punch to his gut. Ethan was a sweet, brave, terrific kid, who'd already suffered more trauma than most people endure in a lifetime. Noah hadn't realized until just this second how fond he'd grown of the boy. The idea of him lost in the woods or trapped at the mercy of a killer brought back with sickening force the terrible memories of Noah's own tragic loss.

And Caroline. Noah could hardly stand to contemplate what it would do to her if anything happened to her son.

"I'll check in with you later," he told Ruby, hanging up abruptly.

He was about an hour's drive from Eagle River. Less than that if he pushed it.

Which he did.

Caroline leaned against a tree, pausing to catch her breath and wipe the sweat from her eyes with the back of her hand. The June sun was high overhead, and even the filtering screen of pine and fir didn't provide much protection from its brilliant, brutal rays.

She suspected this character Rollie was deliberately setting a punishing pace so that she would turn around and go back.

Not a chance.

He and his dog had nearly disappeared over the top of the next rise just in the short time Caroline had stopped to rest. She pushed away from the rough bark with a groan and forced herself to pick up the pace, to hurry and catch up with them. If that dog was indeed leading her to Ethan, she wasn't going to let him out of her sight.

How long had they been combing these woods, anyway? It seemed like hours. And they hadn't encountered one other searcher the whole time—an indication of how vast and remote this area was. Caroline's sense of direction had become confused by the meandering course they'd followed. She was completely disoriented. It seemed to her they'd been traveling in circles. If the dog actually was tracking Ethan's scent, then clearly Ethan, too, had become lost and confused in these mountains.

In Caroline's frantic state of agitation it hadn't occurred to her to change her shoes before setting out, so now she found herself trudging through the rugged, rocky terrain in her leather pumps. She winced when one high heel came down in a hole, twisting her ankle. Wearily she glanced down to inspect the damage even as she kept moving. Her nylons had long ago been shredded by the greedy, clutching talons of branches, her dress was torn in several places.

None of it mattered. Not the side-stitching exhaustion, not the pain shooting up from her ankle, not her ruined wardrobe.

The one unshakable image that kept Caroline moving forward despite the sweltering heat and her aching, rubbery muscles was the face of her son.

She could conjure up in perfect detail every single aspect of Ethan's appearance. That tousled blond hair with the cowlick that just wouldn't stay tamed...those vulnerable brown eyes, gazing up at her with such need...that adorable sprinkling of freckles across his sweet nose...

Oh, God. Caroline crushed a shaky hand to her mouth. She bit down on one knuckle to hold back a sob. She couldn't lose her darling boy again. She just couldn't. Her heart would shatter into a million pieces and she would simply drop dead of sorrow. Panic roared up inside her like a dark, dangerous beast, blotting out her vision, filling every empty space inside her until she felt as if she couldn't breathe.

The sound of a dog barking brought her out of it. When her vision cleared she saw there was a fallen tree blocking her path. Was that a voice she'd heard up ahead, too? She clumsily hurdled the log, oblivious to the sharp twigs jabbing her flesh and tearing her clothes. She stumbled when she hit the ground on the other side. Branches whipped her hair as she ran through the woods.

The sunlight hit her in the face when she emerged into a rocky clearing. The far edge appeared to drop away in a sharp slope, for she could see nothing beyond it. She heard the dog bark again.

There! Shading her eyes with her hand, she spotted Rollie and the dog off to one side of the clearing. Both had their backs to her. The dog's tail was wagging like an out-of-control metronome. Rollie was bent over something on the ground.

Caroline shouted as she started to run. An incoherent greeting that caught Rollie's attention, made him stand up and turn around.

Breath seared in and out of Caroline's strained lungs as she raced across the clearing. Almost reluctantly, it seemed, Rollie moved aside so she could see what the dog had found.

Ethan!

Caroline's heart soared toward the sky. He was alive! As she ran, panting, narrowing the distance between them, she saw he looked pale and scared. There was a scratch across his forehead. But whatever other injuries he might have were plainly not severe. She lifted her hand and called out to him, but his name got all tangled up with the sobs in her throat.

The dog ran out to meet her, barking, bounding along beside her as she flew across the last few yards to her son. He was huddled in the twisted shade of a gnarled, dead tree trunk that Caroline now saw was perched only a few feet from the edge of a steep drop-off. Thank God Ethan hadn't stumbled over the cliff!

His dark, frightened eyes hurtled back and forth between her and Rollie. Caroline flung herself to the ground and threw her arms around him. *Thank you thank you thank you* she chanted silently, eyes squeezed shut as an enormous balloon of joy and relief expanded inside her. Once again she could barely breathe, but for a much happier reason this time.

She ran her hands over her son's small, thin body, checking for injuries, savoring the warmth and smell of his skin, rejoicing in the impossibly precious beating of his heart. She framed his face between her hands and covered his cheeks with kisses. Then she hugged him again. "Ethan, honey, I was so worried," she managed to choke into his hair. Little bits of leaf and twig clung to the blond strands. His clothes were even filthier than hers, and through a brand-new hole in his jeans she could see a scrape on his knee that made her wince with sympathy.

"Are you all right?" She pushed the hair out of his eyes to examine the scratch on his forehead more closely.

"M-mom..."

Nothing serious, thank goodness. The minor gash wouldn't even need stitches, just a thorough cleaning followed by a splash of antiseptic.

"Mom," he whispered.

She peered deep into his eyes, scanning for any sign of concussion. Not that she knew what signs to look for, but she was reassured by the absence of anything abnormal. His cheeks were streaked with tears and he must have rubbed his eyes with his dirty fists, leaving muddy rings that made him look like a raccoon.

He tugged on Caroline's sleeve. *"Mom,"* he whispered more urgently.

For the first time, Caroline realized he was shaking as if he was cold. Yet even in the shade it must be over eighty degrees. "Ethan, what is it?" Could he possibly have a fever? She curved her hand gingerly over his forehead, mindful of the scratch there.

Below her hand, his eyes kept jerking back and forth as if he were watching something behind her. Now she noticed his breathing seemed unnaturally rapid. Concern began to creep over the borders of her relief.

The dog nudged his muzzle forward to sniff at her wrist. Caroline crinkled her nose. The dog needed a bath. "Ethan, do you feel okay, sweetie?" His symptoms seemed almost like shock.

She heard a twig snap behind her. A footstep, as if Rollie had moved closer.

"Mom, that's the guy!" Ethan's fingers dug sharply into her arm.

"What guy?" Caroline asked, lowering her voice to match his.

A shadow edged across them.

"I saw him. I remember now. That ax thing on his belt—" Ethan's teeth were chattering. He stared past Caroline's shoulder, huge, scared eyes filling his face. His fingers clutched her arm even tighter. When he spoke, his voice quavered with terror. "That's the guy that killed Dad."

Noah frowned at the note Caroline had left in the center of the kitchen table, weighted down with a salt shaker. Impossible to tell how long ago she'd written it. Two minutes? An hour?

He'd come barreling into the house only to find it empty,

although the driveway was lined with vehicles belonging to the searchers. He'd recognized Grady's cruiser immediately, but no sign of the sheriff himself. Apparently, as Ruby had said, Grady was out there leading the rescue party.

He must have left Caroline here by herself, to wait by the phone in case Ethan called. Standard procedure. It never helped a search to have frantic relatives charging around out there in a panic, obliterating tracks and maybe getting lost themselves.

Noah read Caroline's note again, though by now he had it memorized. Rollie Fletcher had brought by that mongrel hound dog of his. Maybe the dog had picked up Ethan's trail, or maybe something else that would interest a dog. Like the scent of a rabbit. But Caroline must have been convinced the dog could lead her to Ethan. And after that, Noah knew there was no power on earth that could have kept Caroline here cooling her heels by the telephone.

Noah scratched his neck, but a little itch of disquiet persisted. He'd known Rollie a good many years, but he'd never before known him to volunteer to do anyone a good deed. Rollie's obsessive goal of striking it rich consumed his every waking moment, as far as Noah could tell. The eccentric miner wasn't about to waste time helping someone else when he could be digging through some new chunk of dirt for gold.

Yet for some reason he'd brought his dog all the way out here to help search for a missing boy he didn't even know....

Noah's instincts were dragging him in a direction he didn't like one bit.

He reread the last part of the note Caroline had obviously scrawled in great haste.

Ethan, if you come back and read this note, please PLEASE stay right here in the house and wait for me, honey. I'll be back.

But she wasn't back yet.
Noah set the note down on the table and moved the salt

shaker on top of it. Then he headed for the door.

Rollie's name had come up somewhere else on the fringes of this case, hadn't it? Noah racked his brains while he inspected the gravel in his driveway. Something about booze...

Oh, yeah, that was it. Noah had been talking to Ozzie Baines in the Mineshaft Saloon. Asking him about Peter Buckman, though Noah hadn't actually known Buckman's name at that point.

Last time he come in here was the day Rollie Fletcher was showin' off that gold nugget he found.

So the last time Buckman had been seen in Ozzie's bar was the day Rollie had come into Eagle River with his ill-kept secret. After years of struggling to strike it rich, Rollie hadn't been able to resist bragging about the sizable nugget he claimed to have found. Noah had heard the gossip, just like everyone else in town.

He hunkered down to peer more closely at the chaotic collage of footprints in his driveway. The searchers would have assembled here before heading out in different directions, so it was tough for Noah to find what he was looking for.

His thoughts reeled backward to some of the other people he'd talked to during his investigation. Ellie Conover, the minister's daughter who worked at the local food bank. The last time she'd seen Buckman was the day Jeff Tate had been killed. That tallied with what Buckman himself had sworn to Noah, that he'd hightailed it out of town right after Jeff had been attacked.

Had Buckman also paid a visit to Ozzie's saloon that day? If so, that meant Jeff had been murdered the same day rumors had been flying around town about Rollie's gold nugget. What was the connection here? Or maybe there wasn't one. Maybe Rollie's good fortune had transformed him somehow, turned him into a Good Samaritan.

Except Noah was too cynical to believe people could change that much. Not that fast, anyway.

Aha! That was definitely a trail of paw prints emerging from the tangle of scuffle marks in the driveway.

Moving as quickly as he could, Noah started to follow it.

Caroline heard the rush of distant water coming from somewhere behind and below her. Wheels spun rapidly in her brain, but so far they hadn't shown her an escape route from this nightmare. What she *had* figured out was that a river must run through the bottom of the gorge that opened up a few feet behind her and Ethan. A very deep gorge, judging by the faraway sound of the current.

She was scared. Scared sick. More scared than she'd ever been in her life. But she had to keep her wits about her if she was going to save her son's life.

She didn't doubt for an instant his astonishing claim that this man named Rollie had killed Jeff. The terror in Ethan's voice had been too real.

She swung around, doing her best to shield him behind her. From her position on the ground, she looked up to see Rollie towering over them.

"I *told* you not to come with me," he whined.

Caroline swallowed, doing her best to mask her fear with a friendly, trustworthy expression. "We won't tell," she said, barely recognizing the strained sound of her own voice. "I swear we won't. You can easily get away. Just leave us here, and it'll be hours before anyone finds us. Plenty of time for you to get far away from Eagle River."

She felt Ethan quaking behind her.

Rollie shook his head mournfully. "I can't leave, see. All this time I been looking for the big bonanza, and now I finally found it."

"I—don't understand." The dog nuzzled Caroline's hand as if seeking attention. Was there any possible chance she could win over his loyalty in the next thirty seconds? She forced herself to pat his bony head.

Rollie stomped his boot heel as if exasperated by her denseness. "Gold," he said. "Here." He dug into his pocket, min-

ing around with a concentrated look on his seamed face until
he located his treasure. "See?" He produced a dirty rock on
his palm, extending it just so far, as if he feared Caroline might
lunge for it.

She barely glanced at it. "Well, that's wonderful," she said
with as much enthusiasm as she could muster. "You can use
your gold to start a new life some place far away where no
one will ever find you."

Rollie gave an impatient jerk of his head as he carefully
restored his precious find to his pocket. "Nope. I'm stayin'
right here. There's more where this came from, I can feel it
in my bones. I ain't running away from it." He snorted as if
the very idea were preposterous. "I been tryin' to strike it rich
my whole life, and now I done it finally." He stuck out his
lower lip. "I ain't goin' nowhere."

Caroline's gaze followed his hand as it brushed against his
pickax. A fresh thrust of horror speared through her. Could
that be what he had used—was that the weapon that had
killed—

Rollie moved a step closer. The dog slapped his tail against
the ground. "Okay, I understand why you'd want to stick
around," Caroline said quickly. "But it's still not a problem.
Ethan and I won't tell anyone about this. I promise." Absurdly, she crisscrossed a finger over her heart.

Rollie plucked at his beard, looking as if he wanted to believe her. Caroline summoned all her persuasive skills. If ever
she'd needed them, it was now. "Look, I'm a woman of my
word. I swear we won't tell the police anything. All I care
about is taking my son and going home." Behind her back,
she squeezed Ethan's hand reassuringly. "We live way across
the country, in Baltimore. Three thousand miles away. We'll
never cause you any trouble, I swear it."

She could almost hear the creaky gears in Rollie's brain
adjusting to this, slowly rotating while they weighed his options. He didn't really want to kill them, Caroline was sure of
it.

She held her breath. Even the dog seemed to tense beneath her hand.

Rollie grabbed fistfuls of his hair and tugged. "Naw," he said. "I just can't take the chance." He spread his hands as if pleading with Caroline to understand the reasonableness of his position.

She tried to draw air past the obstruction in her chest. Now her only chance was to keep him talking. With all the searchers combing these woods, surely *someone* might find them in time.

Of course, she hadn't seen hide nor hair of another searcher since leaving Noah's house.

Noah. If the strength of her need to see him could have influenced the workings of the universe, Caroline's thoughts would have plucked him from wherever he was right now and magically set him down right in front of her.

Would she ever see him again?

She choked back a sob of despair. Crying would accomplish nothing.

"Can you at least tell me why you killed Jeff?" she asked Rollie. She hated for Ethan to hear this, but it was the only subject she could think of that might distract Rollie from consigning them to the same fate.

Rollie's face turned red. "It was his own fault!"

"What did he do?" Caroline asked, trying to sound sympathetic.

"He stole my gold nugget, that's what." Rollie slapped his pocket as if to reassure himself the valuable object was still there. "He followed me back to my camp and spied on me till he saw where I hid the nugget. Then when I left for a while to go work my mining claim, he sneaked in and stole it!"

Jeff. Desperate for money to pay a blackmailer, after all his other efforts to come up with it had failed.

"But I forgot somethin' and had to go back, so I saw him running off through the woods," Rollie said smugly. "When I checked on my gold and found out it was missing, I knew who'd took it!'' He tapped his skull, obviously proud of his mental powers. "So I went to the gas station to get it back, and he had the nerve to tell me he didn't take it.'' Indignation crept into Rollie's tone. "I told him to hand it over, but he wouldn't. He made me real mad. He just stood there, telling me a bold-faced lie, when I knew he had my nugget stashed away somewheres.'' Rollie hoisted one shoulder. "So I hit him. I had to. How else was I gonna get my gold back?''

Ethan whimpered, a small animal sound that clawed at Caroline's heart. Ethan must have seen Rollie strike the fatal blow. How on earth had he escaped with his life?

Now Rollie planned to correct his oversight. Except he was going to have to kill Caroline first.

Clearly he was still bothered by the injustice of it all. "In my book, turnabout's fair play. That's why I took the money out of his wallet, after I found which pocket he was hiding my nugget in. He needed to be punished for what he done, didn't he?''

Apparently death hadn't been punishment enough to satisfy Rollie's warped sense of fairness.

Ethan was gripping her so tightly Caroline couldn't feel her fingers anymore. "But first you made Jeff open the safe, didn't you?'' She knew it might be dangerous to provoke Rollie, but she was desperate to prolong the conversation. "You robbed the gas station, too.''

"Did not!'' His indignation appeared genuine.

"Then what happened to the money that was stolen from the safe and cash register?'' Frankly, Caroline didn't care. But she was running out of conversation material. Running out of time.

Rollie flailed his arms through the air. "How the hell should I know? Oops.'' He fidgeted with his beard. "Sorry,'' he mumbled. "Shouldn't talk that way in front of a young'un.''

The irony that he was planning to kill the young'un shortly seemed to escape him.

"Come here, Blue.'' He slapped his thigh.

The dog clambered to his feet and padded over to his master. Caroline actually missed him, fragrant smell and all. Having the dog between her and Rollie had given her a steadying, though false, sense of security.

Rollie fisted and unfisted his hands. "I'm sure sorry about this," he said.

Caroline scrambled to her feet, helping Ethan up but making sure he stayed behind her. Whatever fate held in store, she wasn't going to take it sitting down.

"I warned you not to come. Now I gotta get rid of *both* of you." Rollie's injured expression implied she ought to apologize for causing him extra work.

"Don't do this," Caroline said, trying to keep her voice level. Her gaze kept jumping to the pickax dangling close to his hand. Except he didn't even need it, did he? A couple of well-placed shoves, and—

"Everyone'll think it was an accident," he said in a consoling voice. "I'll tell 'em how we found the boy hanging off the edge of the cliff, and we tried to rescue him, and somehow you fell over, too."

The rush of the river far below seemed to grow louder. Caroline tensed her muscles, making every effort not to move. Rollie stepped toward them. "I wish you hadn't made me do this," he said. Regret tugged down the corners of where his mouth was hidden in a thicket of whiskers.

Ethan, I love you. Caroline didn't dare say it out loud. *Noah…if only you could have known that I love you, too.*

Behind Rollie, the dog pricked up his ears, emitting a puzzled whine.

Rollie came closer…closer….

Caroline squeezed her son's hand one last time before she let go.

Now!

She launched herself at Rollie with every ounce of strength and determination and fury she possessed. The dog erupted in a frenzy of barking. "Ethan!" she screamed as both she and Rollie toppled toward the ground. "Run!"

Chapter 14

Noah started down the ridge, nearly skidding in his haste, driven by an urgency he didn't exactly understand. The whole time he'd been following the tracks through the woods, the weight of dread on the back of his neck had increased its pressure till it had become almost a living presence, whispering in his ear, spurring him onward faster, faster....

Fortunately, he had not only the dog's trail to follow but also the prints left by Rollie's work boots and Caroline's high heels. Noah had groaned when he'd realized what she was wearing on her feet. He could just imagine the agony her arches must be causing her by now. But that was the kind of woman she was, dashing off to the rescue without one whit of concern for her own comfort.

It was one of the reasons Noah had such powerful feelings for her. Why he could have loved her, under different circumstances. Maybe in a different life.

Oh, God, if anything happens to her or Ethan...

Dread turned to fear, pressing down on him like an anvil, crushing the air from his chest. Although sunlight streamed down through the trees, a tunnel of darkness descended over Noah. He saw the headlights swerving toward him, racing toward that sickening crash of glass and steel, toward disaster. Annihilation.

At the last second he broke away from the headlights and fought his way out of the darkness. He couldn't save Beth and Molly. But Ethan and Caroline needed him now.

He continued through the woods at an even more punishing pace than before, sweat stinging his eyes, exertion searing his lungs. His jacket hung over his shoulder from the hook of his finger. The trail wandered around quite a bit, forcing him to take unnecessary detours. If only he were in a helicopter—

A faint cry reached Noah's ears. He braked to a halt, alert, straining to hear. Had he only imagined it, or—

No, there it was again. He changed direction and jogged through the trees, dodging rocks and clumps of brush like a wide receiver heading for the goal line.

"Help!"

The voice was louder now, but still unrecognizable. It could have been a woman's. Or a child's.

Noah shouted, "Where are you?"

No answer. He tossed his jacket aside and kept running.

"Here!"

Noah adjusted his course. He caught a flash of movement up ahead through the woods. The glint of blond hair?

"Help! Help!"

"Ethan?" he yelled.

A small figure burst through the trees, speeding toward Noah as if a pack of wolves were snapping at his heels. He flung himself into Noah's arms. "Mom!" he gasped. "He's got my mom!"

Noah didn't waste time asking who. He crouched down so they were at eye level and grasped Ethan by the shoulders. "Show me where they are."

Ethan was positively vibrating with fear. Other than a few scratches, he seemed unharmed. It was the raw terror in his eyes that worried Noah the most.

He grabbed Noah's hand and pulled. "This way." The poor kid was panting so hard he could barely talk. But it didn't slow him down. He led the way back through the woods at high speed, his hand firmly latched to Noah's.

They burst out of the trees. On the far side of the clearing, where the terrain dropped in a steep cliff down to the river, two figures were struggling. A barking dog ran back and forth in front of them.

Noah pried Ethan's hand from his and took off. Automatically, he reached for the gun at his side, but immediately realized it would be useless. He couldn't get a clear shot at Rollie, not when he and Caroline were locked together in a deadly embrace.

Rage and adrenaline and something else Noah didn't have time to identify propelled him across the clearing like a champion sprinter. The two figures on the ground rolled dangerously close to the edge of the cliff, each one clearly trying to wrestle the other over the side. Caroline was putting up a heroic fight, but she was no match for Rollie.

Noah was about ten yards away when Rollie's hands went around Caroline's neck. Once she lost consciousness, it would be a simple matter to push her off the cliff.

Noah leaped at her attacker. It felt as if all the pain and anger and helpless fear he'd ever known collided inside him, creating a huge combustion of superhuman strength. He could feel power surging through his hands, sparks flying off his skin as he grabbed Rollie in a chokehold.

Noah fought to pull him off Caroline, but the miner, too, possessed surprising strength. A howl of frustrated outrage erupted from Rollie's throat so that he sounded uncannily like his dog. Even though it would do Rollie no good now to kill Caroline, he was clearly bent on achieving that goal anyway, as if his obsession had driven him to the point of no return.

"Mom!" Ethan screamed from somewhere close by.

Nothing Noah did could dislodge the miner's fingers from Caroline's neck. Then all at once Ethan entered the fray, punching and kicking his mother's attacker in a whirlwind of small fists and feet. "Let her go!" he yelled.

But Rollie hung on with the strength of a madman. Caroline's eyes grew crazed with terror as he attempted to choke the life out of her. Noah would have to shoot him. "Ethan, get back!" he shouted. "Now!"

The instant the boy obeyed, Noah unholstered his gun and brought it to Rollie's head. He had a split second to consider what this would do to Caroline and Ethan, watching up close while a man got his brains blown out.

He flipped his weapon around and cracked a solid blow against Rollie's skull with the butt of his gun.

Rollie froze like a statue, then slowly keeled over and collapsed on top of Caroline.

Noah dragged him off. The dog quit barking to nudge his nose at his master's limp body and whimper in bewilderment. Ethan flung himself to the ground next to his mother. "Mom, Mom," he sobbed, burying his face in her neck.

Still struggling for air, Caroline managed to lift her arms around him. The look she gave Noah when he knelt down beside them made something shift inside his chest.

"You saved us," she said in a voice that rasped with effort. The vicious red marks around her neck were already fading, though Noah knew they would leave bruises. Her eyes shone up at him like a healing benediction. "Thank you."

Relief and exhilaration poured through Noah, along with a few other emotions he was too exhausted to analyze. He wanted to haul mother and son into his arms and never let go. Instead, he grazed the pads of his fingers across Caroline's cheek, savoring the warm velvet of her skin, the delicate perfection of her face. "Just doing my job," he said.

She smiled back up at him. "I—" her lips trembled "—sure am glad to see you." She closed her eyes and pressed a kiss against her son's forehead.

For some reason, Noah thought she'd been about to say something else.

* * *

Less than two hours after they had limped out of the woods, Noah marching Rollie ahead of them at gunpoint, the doctor pronounced Ethan and Caroline fit to go home. "Purely superficial damage," he assured Caroline, referring to Ethan's assortment of bumps and scratches. "As for you, you'll probably have a sore throat for a day or two. And take it easy on that ankle the next few days." He winked at Ethan. "I'll bet this young man will be happy to pitch in and help his mom out for a while."

Ethan just kept staring at the white-tiled floor. Caroline sent the doctor a helpless, apologetic smile as she curved an arm around her son's drooping shoulders and gave him a hug. Ethan had barely spoken two words since their rescue.

When they emerged from the examining room, Noah was pacing back and forth right outside the door. His handsome face lit up when he saw them. Caroline's heart did a flip-flop as he came toward them. "Darned nurses," he grumbled. "They made me wait out here in the hallway."

"I thought you'd still be down at the jail, questioning Rollie," she murmured, averting her face when Noah brought his head down to kiss her.

He pulled back at the last second, clearly puzzled by her cool reaction. "I...didn't have to ask that many questions, as it turned out." Though he tried to conceal it, Caroline saw a glimmer of hurt in his eyes. "Rollie was only too eager to explain how Jeff had stolen his gold and how he was within his rights to take it back. His lawyer couldn't shut him up."

Caroline wanted more than anything on earth to throw her arms around Noah's neck, to kiss him till they were both breathless, to tell him everything that was in her heart. But she couldn't, because of Ethan. Because seeing Noah kiss her was what had made Ethan run away, and nearly cost them both their lives.

Caroline shuddered. As they moved down the hospital corridor she tightened her hold around her son's shoulders. Her heart was being torn in opposite directions, between the two people she loved most in the world. But she and Noah had no future together. Ethan was her future. He was her whole life.

"There *is* one more person I need to talk to, though." Noah paused with his hand on the exit door. He said gently to Ethan, "Your mom tells me you can remember now what happened the day your dad died."

Ethan scuffed his shoe on the floor. "Yeah."

"When we get home, you think you can tell me about it?"

"Okay," he said in a tiny voice.

"Good." Noah let his hand rest briefly on top of Ethan's head. A strange, yearning expression crossed his face, too complicated for Caroline to decipher.

She was sure it couldn't really be what it looked like.

"It always bothered me, that both the safe and cash register had been closed back up after the money was stolen," Noah said. "It just didn't seem like something a typical robber would take the trouble to do." He lowered his voice so that Ethan wouldn't hear them from the kitchen, where he was nibbling apathetically at the sandwich Caroline had insisted he eat. No need for the boy to be reminded once again of his father's less-than-noble behavior. "But it was Jeff himself who took the gas-station money, after all his other efforts to get the blackmail payment had failed."

"And he still didn't have anywhere close to the twenty thousand dollars Buckman was demanding." Caroline sat at the far end of the sofa, barefoot, legs tucked beneath her. She shook her head and sighed. "Then Jeff must have heard about Rollie's gold nugget and decided he needed to steal that, too."

"Rollie's big find was the talk of the town the day Jeff was killed. By that point Jeff was desperate enough that it must have seemed like his only solution." Noah hated that Caroline was sitting so far away. But ever since they'd arrived back at his house, she'd made a not-so-subtle effort to keep her distance from him.

She fiddled with the zipper of a sofa cushion, absently sliding it back and forth. "So the money from the safe and cash register was in Jeff's wallet when Rollie attacked him and then went through his pockets.''

"Zack Hastings, my deputy, found a wad of bills squirreled away at Rollie's campsite when he went out there this afternoon." Noah casually extended his arm along the back of the couch. It didn't reach her. "The amount of cash Zack found is about what was missing from the gas station. Rollie apparently hadn't gotten around to spending any of it yet."

"What will happen to him now?"

"He'll stand trial for Jeff's murder and for attempting to kill you and Ethan, unless the lawyers work out a plea bargain." A chill shivered down Noah's spine like the touch of cold steel. He couldn't believe how close he'd come to losing Caroline.

Except he was going to lose her, anyway, wasn't he? Both her and Ethan.

"And Buckman?"

"He's going to be getting free room and board for a while, courtesy of the county jail. He'll be an important witness at Rollie's trial, assuming there is one." Noah scratched his jaw. "In light of Buckman's nomadic life-style and habit of disappearing, Grady and I agreed we'd better keep him under lock and key until after he testifies."

Caroline sent an anxious glance toward the kitchen. "Ethan will have to testify too, won't he?"

"Yeah. I'm afraid you'll have to bring him back here for the trial. Unless Rollie plea-bargains, of course. In which case you, uh, won't need to come back."

"I see." Caroline had changed into a blouse with a high collar that partially hid her bruises. But Noah would never forget the sight of Rollie's fingers around her neck as long as he lived.

"Caroline," he said.

She glanced up quickly, as if startled by something in his voice. "Yes?"

"Why are we sitting so far away from each other?"

She caught her breath. Tears misted her eyes. "Oh, Noah." She pressed her hand to her mouth.

Noah wasn't even aware of moving, but all at once his arms were around her and she was hugging him back as if she meant it. "Ah, Caro," he muttered, "you don't know how much I've wanted to do this all day. Ever since—"

He closed his eyes, unable to complete the image of her brush with death. He held her even tighter, as if wrestling her back from the edge of the cliff.

Her head came down on his shoulder, fitting perfectly into the curve of his neck. He wove his fingers through the long, smooth hair spilling over his hands, inhaling deeply of her sweet, sexy perfume. An odd bubble of emotion expanded inside his chest, pressing outward against his ribs, squeezing his heart, making it hard to breathe. He was suddenly afraid of what might happen if that bubble were to burst.

Caroline lifted her head. Her exquisite features were alive with a tender, wistful longing that Noah couldn't bear to face right now. He lowered his mouth and kissed her.

He sensed guardedness in the way she held her head, in the taut arch of muscles in her back, in the grip of her fists in his shirt. There was a hesitant, leashed quality to her kiss for which Noah supposed he should be grateful. No telling what reckless move he might make, what rash words might come out of his mouth if Caroline gave herself up to this kiss with the sensual, no-holds-barred passion that drove all rational thought from his brain.

"Caroline, what's wrong?" he murmured into the tiny space between their lips.

Her fists crumpled his shirt. With apparent reluctance she pushed against his chest, widening the wedge of airspace between them. Though she lowered her lashes, Noah didn't miss the quick sideways glance she sent toward the kitchen.

"It's...Ethan." When she met Noah's gaze, her eyes were unhappy with conflict. "The reason he ran away..." She cleared her throat, brushed a strand of hair from her face, looked everywhere but at Noah. "Ethan saw us kissing this

morning. In the kitchen. He got very upset about it and—and
that's why he ran away.''

''Damn.'' Noah's stomach reeled with a queasy, guilty sensation. So it had been his fault that Ethan had run away. That
the killer had caught up with him. That Caroline and Ethan
had both nearly lost their lives.

He bounded to his feet. ''Caroline, I'm so sorry. I had no
idea—''

Now she was on her feet, too. ''Noah, you're not to blame.
I was equally responsible, remember? Neither one of us knew
Ethan was there.''

Noah plowed a hand through his hair. ''Caro, you both
could have been killed!''

She dismissed the danger with a cavalier wave. ''In the end
it all worked out for the best, didn't it?'' She laughed ruefully.
''Not that I exactly enjoyed being nearly shoved off a cliff,
but if Ethan hadn't run away, then we might never have found
out Rollie was the killer.''

Noah gritted his teeth. ''It wasn't worth it,'' he said.
''Never, ever in a million years would I risk harming one
single hair on either your or Ethan's head just to solve a case.''

Caroline stepped close to him. Her eyes were shining when
she placed her hand against his cheek. ''Don't you think I
know that?'' she said quietly.

Noah seized her wrist and burned a kiss into her palm. It
was the most efficient way he could come up with to block
the flow of his words before he revealed more than he intended.

They might have stood there like that for a long time, except
for the approaching sound of Ethan's footsteps.

Caroline took a step back. She smoothed her hair, straightened her blouse, did her best to store her feelings back where
they belonged. She had a bright smile ready for Ethan when
he appeared in the doorway. ''Come in, sweetheart.'' She held
out her hand. ''Noah needs to ask you some questions, if that's
okay with you.''

Ethan laid his hand limply in hers. Caroline drew him over

to the sofa, wishing she could pinpoint the exact source of his melancholy. Was it their recent terrifying brush with death? Or Ethan's newly returned memory of whatever he'd seen when Jeff was killed?

Maybe he was still upset about seeing her kiss Noah this morning. Or else it was a combination of everything. This day had certainly held its share of traumatic events to choose from.

Noah sat down on the other side of Ethan. "What was it that helped you remember what you saw the day your dad died?" he asked gently.

Safe in the shelter of Caroline's arm, Ethan shivered. "When I saw that ax on his belt."

"You mean Rollie's pickax?"

Ethan nodded. "He found me in the woods. First his dog came, and then him. I saw the...pickax, and I reco'nized it."

"You'd seen it somewhere before?"

"Uh-huh."

"When?"

Ethan's voice wobbled. "When my dad was killed. That man...Rollie...I saw him hit my dad with it."

Caroline hugged her son close for a moment. She wanted to weep for him. To storm around the room and smash things and rail against the unfairness of it all.

Across the top of Ethan's head, Noah sent her a look of understanding. But he needed the answers to his questions, no matter how painful. "Where were you when you saw Rollie hit your dad?"

"I was..." Ethan kicked his feet against the couch and stared down into his lap. "Hiding," he finished miserably.

"Hiding? Where?"

"Behind the desk," he mumbled. "In the office at the gas station."

"Why were you hiding?"

Ethan started trembling like a leaf. "'Cause I'm a big chicken, that's why!" he burst out.

Caroline stared at him. "Honey, what are you—"

Noah silenced her with a look. He sounded a lot calmer

than Caroline when he spoke. Soothing. "Why do you say you're chicken?"

A tear trickled down Ethan's freckles. "I heard all this yelling when I got near the office, so I peeked in and saw Rollie shaking his fists at my dad." He sniffed. "They didn't see me, 'cause I was standing over by the door. Then Rollie—he took his pickax off his belt an' hit my dad with it!"

Tears were streaming down Ethan's face now. Caroline went numb with shock and sorrow. "I shoulda run and helped him, but I—I got scared!" Ethan wailed. He was quaking with sobs. "So I hid under the desk. And I saw Rollie goin' through my dad's pockets, stealing his money. But I was too chicken to do anything. I just stayed there under the desk like a big dumb scaredy-cat instead of helping my dad, and that's why he's dead!"

Ethan collapsed against Caroline, burying his face in her blouse and crying as though his heart would break. Hot tears slid down Caroline's cheeks. When she looked across at Noah, she saw her own horrified dismay reflected in his eyes.

By the time Ethan's sobs had subsided, Caroline's throat had unclenched enough to speak. "Honey, it wasn't your fault, what happened to your dad."

"Yeah, it was!" Ethan's hoarse words were muffled against her. "I was too scared, just like a *baby,* and that's how come my dad didn't make it."

"Ethan." Noah spoke sternly. "Look at me, son. I want to tell you something."

Ethan slowly turned around. His face was blotched with tears. Noah put a reassuring hand on his knee. "I want you to listen very carefully," he said. "'Cause I know a lot about people getting killed and whose fault it is, okay?"

Ethan bowed his head. A dejected nod.

"The truth is, there wasn't anything you could have done to help your dad. I know that for a fact, because that's what the doctor told me." Noah's voice was steady, sympathetic, filled with conviction. "Once Rollie hit him, it was too late. There was nothing you could have done to save him. You did the smartest thing you could have. You made sure Rollie didn't see you. Because if he had, then he would have come after you, too, just like he did today.''

Noah lifted Ethan's chin, coaxing him to look up and see the truth in his eyes. ''You did exactly what your dad would have told you to do, son. He would have wanted you to be safe. To stay alive, even though it was too late for him.''

''But my dad *needed* me.'' Ethan wiped his nose on his sleeve. ''An' I was too scared. I let him down.''

''You think you're a coward, is that it?''

Ethan nodded unhappily.

''Well, you're flat-out wrong.'' Noah gave him a gentle shake. ''I saw what you did today. How you saved your mom's life. A coward wouldn't have run through the woods so fast to get help. A coward wouldn't have jumped on Rollie and tried to pull him off your mom.''

Ethan rubbed his red-rimmed eyes.

''Look, I don't believe in sugarcoating the truth,'' Noah said. ''I'm being straight with you. Man-to-man, understand?''

Ethan hiccuped. ''I guess so.''

Noah shook his head with regret. ''It's a tough thing to accept, but sometimes there just isn't anything we can do to save people we love. We would if we could. But it just isn't possible.'' He squeezed Ethan's arm. ''So don't you feel bad about not being able to help your dad. You couldn't. That's just the way things worked out, and it didn't have anything to do with you. Your dad would have been proud if he'd seen you today, the way you saved your mom's life.''

Ethan blinked. ''He would?''

''I guarantee it.'' Noah ruffled Ethan's hair. ''Because I'd be mighty proud to have a son like you myself.''

Ethan looked to Caroline for confirmation. ''It's true, honey.'' She smiled down at him. ''Your dad would have been proud of you.''

Was it also true that Noah would be proud to call her son his? she wondered.

The phone rang in the other room. Noah stood up. "I'll get it."

Caroline hugged Ethan. "I'm awfully proud of you, too," she whispered into his hair.

A moment later Noah was back. "The call's for you." His face stayed perfectly neutral. "It's the airline. Calling to confirm your rescheduled reservations for tomorrow."

"Oh." A pang shot through Caroline as she eased herself up from Ethan. Once again she faced the soul-shattering prospect of saying goodbye to Noah tomorrow. Except this time it would be for real. Forever. "I'll be right back."

As she left the room she carefully avoided Noah's eyes. Almost as if she were embarrassed. A gaping cavern had opened inside Noah's chest when he'd heard the reason for the phone call. The emptiness reverberated with all the lonely echoes of the days to come. He couldn't believe how much he'd gotten used to having them around.

Ethan looked like he could use some cheering up himself. When Noah sat down on the couch again, Ethan tilted his head to peer up at him. "Are you and my mom getting married?" he asked.

Noah coughed. "Well...we, uh, haven't discussed it," he answered evasively. "What makes you ask?"

Ethan poked at a sofa cushion. "I saw you kissing her, that's all." He shrugged. "I thought when grown-ups did that, it meant they were gonna get married."

If only it were that simple. Noah chose his words carefully. "Your mom's a very special person, Ethan. The reason I kissed her was to show her that I...like her. A lot."

"You do?"

"Yep." He tugged a lock of Ethan's hair. "Matter of fact, I like *you* a lot, too."

Ethan's startled eyes widened. "You're not gonna kiss *me*, are you?"

Noah chuckled. "How about a handshake instead?"

Ethan sagged with relief. "Okay."

Noah stuck out his hand. "Friends?"

Ethan studied him. No rash decisions here. "Friends," he said finally. They shook on it. Noah felt a warm, sad tug of affection.

"I wish me and my mom didn't have to go back to Baltimore tomorrow."

So do I, Noah thought.

All at once Ethan leaned into him. Noah's arm went around the boy. "I'll miss you," he said into the front of Noah's shirt.

Overcome with emotion, Noah couldn't answer.

"This is the final boarding call for Flight 892 to Baltimore."

Caroline's heart made a crash landing. The moment she'd been dreading for so long had finally arrived. The hustle and bustle of the airport terminal, the whine of jet engines, the roar of a plane taking off in the distance were certainly a fitting backdrop for the emotional chaos inside her.

Rollie Fletcher had pleaded guilty to manslaughter charges that morning. There would be no trial for her and Ethan to come back for. This was the last time she would ever lay eyes on Noah.

Somehow Caroline pinned a semblance of a smile to her lips. "Well, I guess this is goodbye."

Oh, my love...

Noah turned to Ethan and stuck out his hand. "So long, Slugger. Thanks for all your help."

"Bye, Sergeant." Ethan solemnly shook hands.

"Sweetheart, would you wait for me right over there?"

"Okay, Mom." Ethan's posture slumped as if he were toting all their luggage back to Baltimore on his shoulders. He obviously wasn't any happier about leaving than Caroline was.

As soon as they were alone, she said quickly to Noah, "I need to ask you something."

He arched his brows. "What?"

She took a deep breath. "Did you mean what you said to Ethan yesterday? About how he shouldn't blame himself for Jeff's death?"

Noah looked surprised. "Of course I meant it."

Caroline dropped her carry-on bag, grabbed the lapels of his sport coat and pulled herself toward him. The kiss she gave him was brief and bittersweet. "You told Ethan that sometimes there's nothing we can do to save the people we love, no matter how much we want to." She blinked rapidly, her eyes sparkling with tears. "Maybe you should listen to your own words, Noah Garrett."

She turned and walked rapidly away from him.

Noah did think about his own words. During the entire long, lonely drive back to Eagle River.

He knew what she was trying to do. Trying to absolve him of guilt for Beth and Molly's deaths. No, that wasn't exactly accurate. Caroline had never believed he was to blame for the tragic accident that had stolen those two precious lives. She wanted Noah to forgive himself.

That night he sat in his office, feet propped on his desk, the house eerily silent. Empty. Just like his heart.

He opened one of the desk drawers. Pulled stuff forward until he got to the back of the drawer. When he found what he was looking for, he set it on top of his desk. Right beside his answering machine, where he would see it every time he reached for the telephone.

He studied Beth and Molly's picture for a long, long time. Searching for forgiveness.

Chapter 15

"This is Caroline Tate at Souper Naturals. I understand there's some problem with the new design for our Savory Split Pea soup mix?"

Caroline was working from home today, as she had for most of the two weeks since she and Ethan had returned to Baltimore. During the last three years, Caroline had devoted more and more time to her business as a way of distracting herself from the nightmare of Ethan's disappearance. In the process, Souper Naturals had become even more profitable, allowing Caroline to channel more money into the search for her son.

Now, with Ethan blessedly home at last, Caroline was considering promoting her assistant and putting her in charge of the day-to-day operations of the company. That would allow Caroline to spend more time with Ethan. The business had run fairly smoothly during her recent absence. She'd returned from Eagle River to find her assistant had handled things quite capably while Caroline was away.

Eagle River. Inevitably those two words opened up the suitcase of painful memories Caroline had brought home on the plane with her. Memories of Noah. Of that brief interlude the three of them had lived together almost like a real family. Memories of how she'd loved him.

Correction. How she *still* loved him, despite her best efforts to forget him.

Even amidst all the hectic activity of returning to Baltimore, catching up on work, helping Ethan get resettled in his "new" home, Caroline didn't go more than a few minutes at a time without thinking of Noah. Seeing his eyes. Hearing his voice. Feeling his mouth and hands doing indescribable things to her body.

The memories beckoned her, taunted her, broke her heart. They seduced her away from whatever she was doing…

Like now. "Hello? Yes, I'm still here. Sorry." As rapidly as possible, Caroline concluded her phone call with the graphic-design firm that created the packaging for her soup mixes.

"Probably thought I was a complete flake, drifting off like that in the middle of a business discussion," she muttered after she hung up the phone.

Outside she heard a car door slam. That must be Ethan. Caroline had reintroduced him to the neighborhood boy who'd been his favorite playmate when they were younger, and the two had become fast friends again. The other boy's mother had taken them in-line skating today, promising to have Ethan home before dinner. It sounded as if she'd just dropped him off out front.

Footsteps. Caroline frowned. She would know Ethan's footsteps anywhere, and those weren't his. Three years of listening for them only to be disappointed was a hard habit to break. She had to remind herself that even though it wasn't Ethan coming up the front sidewalk right now, her son would be home shortly.

When the doorbell chimed Caroline was halfway across the living room. She checked the peephole before opening the door.

Shock nailed her to the floor. Noah! A hundred chaotic

thoughts crowded her mind, among them that she should pretend she wasn't home. They'd already said goodbye once. Caroline didn't think she could bear to do it again.

But he must have had a powerful reason to come all this way. If she didn't face him now, he would be back.

She took a deep breath and opened the door.

"Hello, Caroline."

Well, two weeks' separation hadn't dimmed the effect of his crooked, devastating smile on her one bit. Heat flowed through her bloodstream like warm syrup.

"I'm…surprised to see you," she said. The understatement of the year. "Please, come in."

She was regretting her polite invitation even as he stepped past her into the living room. Now she would have memories of him here, too. From now on she would think, that's the carpet he walked across. The chair where he sat. The glass he touched.

Maybe she should just sell the house and move.

As it turned out, Noah didn't sit down. He made a casual survey of her living room, with its simple, modern furniture and light, airy setting. "Nice place you have here."

"Thank you."

Noah was out of uniform, so to speak. No coat or tie. In deference to the Baltimore heat and humidity he wore a short-sleeved blue shirt and tan chino trousers. The dark hair visible in the open V of his collar brought back such a rush of erotic memories that Caroline blushed.

"How's Ethan?"

"Fine, thanks." She fanned her face with her hand, hoping Noah would think it was the weather. "He and a friend went in-line skating. He should be home soon. I—know he'll be happy to see you." There was a hint of a question mark in that statement, a cue for Noah to tell her how long he planned to stay.

"Think so? That he'll be glad to see me?" Noah fixed his gaze on her intently, as if he attached great importance to her answer.

"Of course!" Caroline produced a faint smile. "He talks about you all the time. How you caught the man who killed his dad, and saved both our lives."

A broad grin broke across Noah's face. "Really?"

Caroline stared. She'd never, ever seen Noah smile like that before.

Now that her initial shock had worn off and she studied him more closely, she noticed another change in him. That tense guardedness was gone, as if he'd ripped up those No Trespassing signs and thrown them away. Instead, she saw a kind of peace in his eyes.

"Noah, what are you doing here?" she asked bluntly.

Now he looked tense. Well, not tense, exactly. More like nervous.

He took both her hands in his. Caroline tried not to react visibly, but this unexpected physical link between them nearly took her breath away. It was so good to touch his skin again, to feel the warmth of his flesh, the reassuring beat of his pulse....

"You know I'm not a man to act impulsively," Noah began. "It's taken me two whole weeks to get things sorted out in my head."

"What things?" she asked softly.

"The things you said." He squeezed her hands. "About how I should listen to my own words."

"You mean about not blaming yourself for Beth and Molly's deaths?" Whenever Caroline had mentioned their names before, Noah had retreated inside himself, withdrawing into a bleak world only he could see.

This time he simply nodded. "The more I thought about it, the more I thought about *them,* the more I realized you were right. They would have wanted me to move on with my life, to find happiness again."

"Oh, Noah, I'm so glad for you." And she was. If only..

"Beth and Molly will always be a part of me. One of the best parts. But torturing myself with guilt won't bring them back. I had to face that fact, along with the fact that there was nothing I could have done to save them.''

Caroline's eyes misted. "And you *have* faced it. I can tell.''

"Thanks to you.''

She swallowed a lump in her throat. "Don't thank me. You did all the hard work yourself.''

Noah shook his head. "Only because you made me face the truth. You made me *want* to face the truth, for the first time in four years. And once I did, I was able to face the truth about my feelings, too. My feelings for you. And Ethan.''

Caroline's heart began to pound faster. What was he saying?

"Every time I remember nearly losing you that day by the cliff—'' Beneath his tan Noah turned pale for a moment. He slid his hands up Caroline's arms, coaxing her closer.

She surrendered reluctantly, afraid of what he was going to say. Afraid of what she would answer.

Noah wove his hands through her hair and tilted her face up to his. "I love you, Caro,'' he said hoarsely. "And I'm crazy about that terrific kid of yours, too. I want the three of us to be a family.''

Oh, Noah, so do I...

"Will you marry me, Caro?''

Her gaze explored his handsome, beloved face—the face she'd thought she would never see again. The face of the man she longed desperately to spend the rest of her life with.

"I can't,'' she replied softly. Saying those two words was one of the hardest things Caroline had ever done.

Watching the crush of disappointment, the hurt, the rejection in Noah's eyes was another.

She should have known, though, that he wouldn't give up without a fight. "Is it because of Ethan?'' he asked. "Because you don't think I'd be a good father to him?''

"You'd make a wonderful father!'' Caroline exclaimed. "I've always thought so.''

Noah feathered his thumbs across her cheekbones. "Then...is it because you don't...return my feelings?''

Despite the anguish clawing at her heart, Caroline laughed "You mean, do I love you?"

His mouth tensed. "Yes."

She brought her hands to his face. "Read my lips, Noal Garrett. I...love...you."

He did more to her lips than read them. The kiss he gave her was exuberant and erotic, full of tenderness and rejoicing It sent a delicious current tingling down her spine and raised her skin temperature by several degrees.

But Caroline didn't feel much like celebrating.

When Noah broke their kiss, she wriggled out of his embrace and put a nice, safe distance of several feet between them. Unfortunately, even a distance of several light-year wouldn't have kept her safe from the treacherous pull of her yearning for him.

"I said I love you. I didn't say I'd marry you." Caroline combed her fingers through her hair, trying to restore order If only it were as easy to restore order to the jumble of conflicting emotions inside her.

He loves me! her heart sang out.

His feelings don't matter and neither do yours, warned her brain. *Remember what happened the* last *time you followed your feelings for a man.*

Noah focused on her with an intense concentration Caroline found unsettling. As if he thought that if he studied her long enough, he could figure out the correct sequence of buttons to push. "So you love me, and I love you, but you won't marry me," he summed up slowly, as if trying to puzzle out an algebra equation.

"I told you before that I couldn't marry anyone again. I can't trust my own instincts where men are—"

The sound of racing footsteps cut her off. She turned toward the front door just as Ethan burst through it, a pair of in-line skates slung over his shoulder. "Hi, Mom! I'm home. Hey!" A big grin split his freckled face when he caught sight of Noah. "Hi, Sergeant Garrett!"

When Ethan came bounding across the living room, Noah

could hardly believe this was the same withdrawn, unhappy boy he'd lived with for over a week. There was an eagerness in his movements, a liveliness in his eyes that Noah had never seen before. Despite the traumatic events in Eagle River, it was clear that Ethan was going to be all right.

"Hey, Slugger!" Noah reached out to shake hands, but Ethan slapped a high-five against his palm instead. "How've you been?"

"Great! Me and my friend Kyle just went skating, and now Kyle's mom wants to know if I can come over to their house for dinner. They're waiting outside in the car." He looked at Caroline. "Can I, Mom? Please?"

Caroline bit her lip as if reluctant to say yes. Noah wondered whether it was because she still wanted Ethan all to herself as often as possible, or because Ethan's continued presence would prevent her and Noah from resuming their conversation about marriage.

Noah hadn't exactly been stunned when Caroline had turned him down. He knew she had reasons of her own to steer clear of marriage. But he didn't intend to leave until he'd taken his best shot at changing her mind.

"All right," she said with a smile. But she was responding to Ethan, not to him. "Remember to thank Mrs. Thomson for dinner, okay?"

"Sure, Mom!" Ethan dropped his in-line skates and dashed toward the door.

"Just a minute, young man." Ethan wheeled guiltily around. Caroline pointed at the skates without saying a word.

Ethan sheepishly hunched his shoulders and sauntered over to pick them up. "Guess I'll go put these back in my room first."

"Good idea." Caroline gave him an affectionate swat on the backside as he passed her on his way out of the living room.

"He's a great kid," Noah observed when they were alone.

"The greatest." Love lit up her eyes, softened her mouth.

Now Noah knew what it felt like to have Caroline look at him
that way. But it wasn't enough.

"Just think, you never would have had Ethan if you hadn'
made the big mistake of marrying Jeff Tate," Noah remarked
casually. The stare Caroline gave him in return, though, wa
far from casual. "Maybe it wasn't such a big mistake, afte
all."

Her beautiful green eyes were enormous, shocked. "I—'
She swallowed.

Just then Ethan jogged back through the room. "Bye, Mom
Bye, Sergeant." His steps slowed. Wariness crept into hi
voice. "Hey, uh, how come you're here in Baltimore?"

"Personal business." Noah shoved his hands into his pock
ets. "Nothing to do with your dad's death."

"That guy Rollie's still in jail?"

"Oh, he'll be there for quite a while, I can assure you."

"Yeah?" Ethan looked relieved. "Well...good." He gav
a self-conscious wave. "Bye again."

"So long, Slugger. Hope I see you again soon."

"Yeah, me, too!" He opened the front door. "Bye, Mom,'
he called as it slammed shut behind him.

Silence settled over the room like the aftermath of a whirl
wind. Noah finally broke it by saying, "Was it worth it?"

Caroline rubbed her temples, looking dazed.

"Was it worth marrying Jeff Tate? Suffering all the heart
ache he put you through? Was it worth it, to have Ethan?"

Caroline dropped her hands. Her jaw fell open. "Of *course*
it was!"

"Then it wasn't really a mistake on your part, was it?'
Noah spoke logically, but there was passion behind his words
"Maybe Jeff didn't turn out to be the person you thought he
was. Maybe your marriage didn't have the happy ending you'
envisioned. But you would do it all over again if you had the
choice, wouldn't you?"

"Yes," she whispered.

"Because Ethan came out of it."

"Yes."

Noah grasped her shoulders. "Say that one more time, Caro. When I ask you to marry me."

"Noah, I—" Indecision shadowed her lovely face. Her eyes were turbulent with the emotions that were dragging her in all different directions.

Somewhere in those stormy depths, Noah saw his chance.

He smoothed the long, silky curtain of her hair. "Caroline, we both know that life doesn't come with any guarantees. I can't promise our marriage will work out exactly the way we envision it. Probably it won't, because life has a way of tossing in all sorts of twists and turns we can't anticipate."

He circled his arms around her waist and held her against him. Right where she belonged. "What I can promise is that I will spend the rest of my life doing everything in my power to make you and Ethan happy. To make all of us happy. Together."

He leaned his forehead against hers. He sensed how much Caroline wanted to believe him, even while she was shaking her head with doubt.

He had to convince her. "I know you think you can't trust your own judgment where men are concerned," he said, "because Jeff hurt you so badly. And now you're afraid to follow your heart again, because it led you astray once before. But your heart also led you to Ethan. And, by way of a very long and convoluted route, it also led you to me."

Noah cinched his hands behind her back, tightening his hold for emphasis. "So I think you can trust your heart. Listen to it, Caroline. Give me the answer it's telling you." He kissed her gently on the lips, transmitting every ounce of persuasion he could muster. "Will you marry me, Caro?"

Something flared in her eyes, a combination of hope and love and courage. As Noah watched, the flame grew stronger. "I guess if you can find the strength to let go of the past," she said slowly, "then so can I."

Noah's breath caught in his chest. "Does that mean—"

"It means *yes*, Noah Garrett!" Her eyes sparkled with mirth. "Do I have to spell it out for you?"

Joy soared inside him, an exhilaration he'd once thought he would never feel again. "Oh, I'm a very good speller," he promised her. "Let me see if I've got that right. *Y*..." He kissed her lightly on the mouth. *"E..."* He deepened the kiss, and felt something quicken inside him. *"S."* Then Noah simply let go and lost himself in her for a while.

A few moments later, while they were still breathless and dizzy, he asked, "Think the Baltimore cops have any openings for an experienced detective?"

Caroline drew back in surprise. "Well, I'm sure they do, but I was kind of looking forward to redecorating that house of yours."

"What's wrong with my house?"

Caroline giggled at the hurt indignation on his face. "It's a wonderful house," she assured him. "It just needs a woman's touch, that's all."

Noah brushed the tip of her nose with his. "So you'd really be willing to move back to Eagle River with me?"

"I've been toying with plans to expand Souper Naturals' distribution to the West Coast, anyway." Caroline smiled. "This way I can be on the spot to supervise the expansion personally. And I know Ethan will be glad to have his old school and his old friends back."

"Say it again."

Caroline tilted back her head, puzzled. "What? About Ethan's school?"

"No." He grinned. "The part about how you love me."

So Caroline said it again. And again. And again. Knowing she would never tire of repeating herself.

Knowing that this time, listening to her heart was the smartest move she'd ever made.

* * * * *

Take 2 bestselling love stories FREE

Plus get a FREE surprise gift!

Special Limited-Time Offer

Mail to Silhouette Reader Service™

3010 Walden Avenue
P.O. Box 1867
Buffalo, N.Y. 14240-1867

YES! Please send me 2 free Silhouette Intimate Moments® novels and my free surprise gift. Then send me 6 brand-new novels every month, which I will receive months before they appear in bookstores. Bill me at the low price of $3.57 each plus 25¢ delivery and applicable sales tax, if any.* That's the complete price, and a saving of over 10% off the cover prices—quite a bargain! I understand that accepting the books and gift places me under no obligation ever to buy any books. I can always return a shipment and cancel at any time. Even if I never buy another book from Silhouette, the 2 free books and the surprise gift are mine to keep forever.

245 SEN CH7Y

Name	(PLEASE PRINT)	
Address		Apt. No.
City	State	Zip

This offer is limited to one order per household and not valid to present Silhouette Intimate Moments® subscribers. *Terms and prices are subject to change without notice. Sales tax applicable in N.Y.

UIM-98 ©1990 Harlequin Enterprises Limited

***For a limited time, Harlequin and Silhouette
have an offer you just can't refuse.***

In November and December 1998:

BUY **ANY** TWO HARLEQUIN
OR SILHOUETTE BOOKS and
SAVE $10.00
off future purchases

OR BUY ANY THREE HARLEQUIN OR SILHOUETTE BOOKS
AND **SAVE $20.00** OFF FUTURE PURCHASES!

(each coupon is good for $1.00 off the purchase of two
Harlequin or Silhouette books)

••

JUST BUY 2 HARLEQUIN OR SILHOUETTE BOOKS, SEND US YOUR
NAME, ADDRESS AND 2 PROOFS OF PURCHASE (CASH REGISTER
RECEIPTS) AND HARLEQUIN WILL SEND YOU A COUPON BOOKLET
WORTH **$10.00 OFF** FUTURE PURCHASES OF HARLEQUIN OR
SILHOUETTE BOOKS IN 1999. SEND US 3 PROOFS OF PURCHASE AND
WE WILL SEND YOU 2 COUPON BOOKLETS WITH A TOTAL SAVING OF
$20.00. (ALLOW 4-6 WEEKS DELIVERY) OFFER EXPIRES
DECEMBER 31, 1998.

••

I accept your offer! Please send me a coupon booklet(s), to:

NAME: _____

ADDRESS: _____

CITY: _____ STATE/PROV.: _____ POSTAL/ZIP CODE: _____

Send your name and address, along with your cash register
receipts for proofs of purchase, to:

In the U.S.	In Canada
Harlequin Books	**Harlequin Books**
P.O. Box 9057	**P.O. Box 622**
Buffalo, NY	**Fort Erie, Ontario**
14269	**L2A 5X3**

PHQ4982

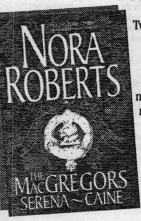
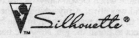

COMING NEXT MONTH

#895 CHRISTMAS LONE-STAR STYLE—Linda Turner
The Lone Star Social Club

Christmas was coming, and Phoebe Smith needed a place to stay with her orphaned niece and nephew—pronto! The solution? Handsome bachelor Mitch Ryan offered her a job—and a place to live—with him. Mitch found his sassy secretary pretty darn irresistible, but how could this confirmed cynic admit to his heart's deepest desire?

#896 IT CAME UPON A MIDNIGHT CLEAR—Suzanne Brockmann
Tall, Dark & Dangerous

"Crash" Hawken lived for danger, and not even the sweet temptation of beautiful Nell Burns had deterred him from his duty. But when a conspiracy posed a deadly threat, Nell offered the intense navy SEAL a safe haven for the holidays—and more. Now Crash wasn't just fighting for *his* life—but for that of the woman he cherished....

#897 HOME FOR CHRISTMAS—Patricia Potter
Families Are Forever

Legal eagle Julie Farrell would always be grateful to Ryan Murphy for rescuing her and her son. Now, in a twist of fate, the amnesiac police detective's life was on the line. As Julie fought to prove Ryan's innocence, she envisioned spending every night in his arms. But had she invited a murderer home for the holidays?

#898 FOR CHRISTMAS, FOREVER—Ruth Wind

Just as Claire Franklin was settling in for another uneventful holiday, a compelling secret agent brought passion—and danger—into her safe, secure life. She knew that Zane Hunter was bound to protect her from a killer, but then she found herself risking everything to be with him this Christmas—and forever!

#899 ONE SILENT NIGHT—Debra Cowan
Men in Blue

Although gorgeous Dallas Kittridge had lived to regret it, officer Sam Garrett couldn't forget about the night of love he'd shared with his best friend's widow. Now, as they worked together to track down a killer, Sam ached to hold Dallas close again. Would the magic of the holidays inspire Sam to bare his soul to the elusive beauty?

#900 A SEASON OF MIRACLES—Christine Michels
Try To Remember

It was a Christmas miracle when Devon Grayson discovered that her presumed-dead husband was alive! A mysterious plane crash had erased all of Geoff's memories, but Devon wasn't about to lose her beloved twice. Or allow his intended killers to finish the job. Now she had to convince Geoff that their love was worth fighting for....